THE NORMAN'S BRIDE

Terri Brisbin

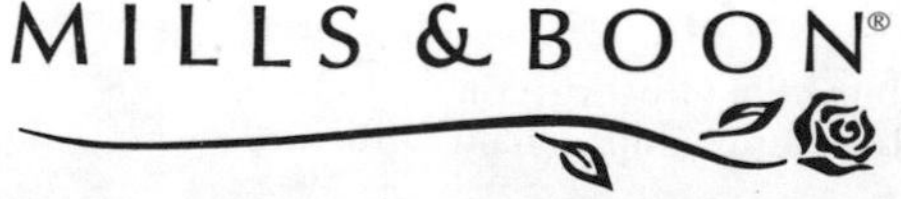

First published in Great Britain 2006
Large Print edition 2007
Harlequin Mills & Boon Limited,
Eton House, 18-24 Paradise Road, Richmond, Surrey TW9 1SR

ISBN-13: 978 0 263 19387 9
ISBN-10: 0 263 19387 X

Set in Times Roman 16¼ on 17¾ pt.
42-0307-73255

Printed and bound in Great Britain
by Antony Rowe Ltd, Chippenham, Wiltshire

Terri Brisbin is wife to one, mother of three, and dental hygienist to hundreds when not living the life of a glamorous romance author. She was born, raised and is still living in the southern New Jersey suburbs. Terri's love of history led her to write time-travel romances and historicals set in Scotland and England. Readers are invited to visit her website for more information at www.terribrisbin.com, or contact her at PO Box 41, Berlin, NJ 08009-0041, USA.

Recent novels by the same author:

LOVE AT FIRST STEP
(short story in *The Christmas Visit*)
THE DUMONT BRIDE

This book is dedicated in gratitude
to the real Harlequin Heroines in my life:

To Claire Delacroix and Sharon Schulze, the first Harlequin authors I met and who were generous with their time and knowledge in the face of my many, many questions;

To the Hussies, the group of wise and wonderful Harlequin Historical authors whose insight and support is endless and always appreciated;

To Melissa Endlich, my editor, whose support and enthusiasm for my work have been appreciated beyond words…

Prologue

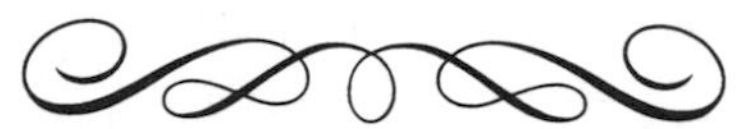

Silloth-on-Solway
England
1198 AD

"Will she live?"

He said the words in a whisper, not knowing why it meant so much to him, but recognizing that it did.

"She may," old Wenda, the village healer, replied. "Or she may not. 'Tis in my hands no longer."

William de Severin, now called Royce, stood by the blazing hearth in his small cottage and watched as Wenda finished sewing the unconscious woman's face. His gut gripped as though he were some untried boy rather than the tournament- and battle-tested warrior he was. He could not isolate the reason the sight of blood and some stitching bothered him so, and that disconcerted him even more. Hushing the whimpers of his hound, he moved closer to survey the extent of the woman's injuries.

Merde.

No wonder the old woman could not answer him. William had hoped that once the blood was cleared away, Wenda would declare her easily healed. 'Twas not so after all. He grimaced at the sight of the injuries this woman had sustained—a broken leg, stab wounds on arms and hands, defensive from the look of them and some very deep, and from her labored breathing, broken or badly bruised ribs. He shook his head and offered a silent prayer, for she was closer to death than he had first imagined.

"Should we move her to the keep or to your cottage?" William asked. The healer's doubts unnerved him. If Wenda did not think she would live, then how could he have hope?

"Nay, Royce. I fear she would not live through even the short journey there. Mayhap in a few days…" Wenda did not finish the words, but William heard them clearly—*if she lived.*

Wenda stood, her long gray braid falling over

her shoulder, and stretched her back, rubbing at its base probably to relieve the hours spent hunching over to repair the slashes, cuts, bruises and broken bones. She had accompanied him without question or hesitation when he roused her from her sleep. If she had thought that finding him, the loner, the outsider, at her door long after the moon's rising was strange, she said it not. She had simply gathered her supplies and followed him into the night.

He stood nearby, close enough to aid her but far enough to be out of her way during her work. Now she gathered the soiled cloths into a basket and stood.

"A fever will come," she said without looking at him. Passing her gaze over the woman once more, she shook her head. "Someone filled with anger did this. A terrible anger."

That someone wanted her dead was clear. The unconscious woman had cheated death this long, but William suspected it would be much longer before she could claim victory.

After giving him instructions, Wenda waved away his offer of a ride back to her cottage and left with the promise of an early return. William sat next to the pallet and leaned against the wall, settling down for the rest of the night. The only sound was the crackling of some peat on the hearth. As he dozed off, he strained to hear the shallow, rasping breaths the stranger took. Although sunrise was only a few hours away, it promised to be a long night.

Chapter One

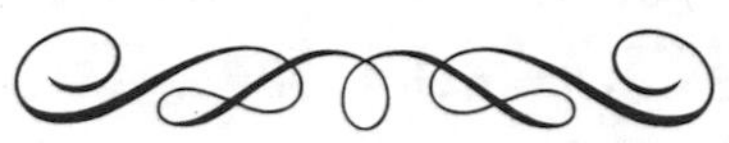

The wet, rough tongue sliding across his chin startled him, for he did not believe he would sleep at all when he closed his eyes. Pushing away the hound's face, William looked over at his guest. He feared that her lack of movement or sound meant she had lost the valiant battle she'd fought over this past fortnight. From his place next to the door, he could not tell if she breathed or not.

Rolling to his feet, he madc it to her side in a few steps. Touching the back of his hand to her less-bruised cheek, the coolness of her skin made him smile. The horrible life-draining fever had broken. A soft sigh confirmed that she had made it through the worst of her recovery. Watching the movement of the sheet as her chest rose and fell under it, William knew she faced many more days and weeks of pain before she could truly be declared healed. But, with the fever gone, she stood a good chance of making it through that recovery.

Worried that her thrashing movements through the night may have opened her deeper wounds, he gently checked to see if any of her wounds bled. He mumbled a quick thanks to heaven as he saw that all the stitches looked intact. Tucking the sheet higher over her shoulders, he left the cottage to handle his own morning needs and to bring back fresh water from the stream nearby. The hound nipped at his heels and followed him down the path.

After dipping his head in the icy water for a few minutes, William felt clearer minded and ready to face the day. The night had been a tough one; his mystery guest had become almost violent, thrashing and crying out for the first time since he'd found her. He did not know if this was a good sign or not, but he would share the information with Wenda when she arrived for her daily visit.

Twisting his dark hair to remove most of the water from it, William pulled it back and tied it with a leather cord. Even after three years he was still unused to having his hair so long. But, if it made him less obvious, he would continue with it. And the black beard he had forced himself to leave in place hid the gash on his neck. Better to be unremarkable in coloring or appearance than draw the wrong attention.

Completing his ablutions, he filled a bucket with clean water and returned to his home. He would wait until he tried to coax some of Wenda's broth into his guest before changing his tunic. If her strength was returning, it could be a messy affair.

Although he had lost most of his accent, he could not rid himself of the fastidiousness in grooming that had been the standard as he grew to manhood in Eleanor of Aquitaine's court. Though generations separated the French origins from most of the current border nobles, he had been but a few years removed from the people and places of his upbringing. 'Twould take more time than that to lose his habits.

No, he would not allow his thoughts to follow that path. There was no good in it, only regrets and recrimination. Nothing could change his past. Nothing.

Shaking his head at the wanderings of his mind and snapping his fingers behind him to gain the dog's attention, he carried the water into the small hut and prepared some broth for the unconscious woman. She had not moved at all since he'd left, so he warmed the clear soup and brought it closer to her. Then he carefully lifted her up and slid behind her. He cushioned her bruised body with his and cradled her head on his shoulder.

It took time to coax the warm liquid into her mouth without losing most of it on both of them. If he gauged it correctly, she had swallowed more this time than even last night. That had to be a good thing, didn't it? He would ask Wenda when she arrived. Bloody hell! He felt no more at ease in her care now than when he had found her bleeding to death near his door almost two weeks ago. Luckily Wenda had asked one of the village girls to stay here during the day and care for the stranger. Although he would most likely not give voice to his doubts, he would take all the help offered in this endeavor.

Men were not supposed to do this, he was certain of it. He was more comfortable fighting a dozen well-armed warriors than sitting at bedside tending this wounded woman. He hoped she would waken soon so that she could be moved to the keep or to Wenda's and he would be done playing nursemaid. Yet, even as the thoughts crossed his mind, he knew he lied to himself.

Something had called him to the little-used path where she lay dying in a pool of her own blood. Something had grabbed his soul in the night when she seemed to turn into his palm as he soothed her flaming brow. Something had given her the strength to fight death's grip and struggle back to life, and he felt powerless next to it.

William de Severin, the man who had died on the field of honor three years before, only knew that he was part of her fight for life and nothing he did or thought could change that.

The pain!

Deep, searing, like flames through her, tearing at her strength until she could fight no longer.

At first, she tried to struggle against the pain, to claw her way up through the darkness, toward the light she could feel at the edges of her existence. Then she realized that in the darkness was numbness. And numbness was relief from the rippling waves of anguish that seemed to have no end. So, for a while, she sought the comfort that the darkness offered.

Then a voice pierced the darkness. A soothing, warm voice that called to her, urging her to fight, telling her not to surrender to the darkness. Sometimes the tone was soft and sometimes powerful, but never could she ignore it. Although there was no pain in the bliss of the darkness, the voice called her from it and when she had gathered enough strength, she followed it.

She knew not how long she had remained within the darkness or how long her journey through the pain took. She simply listened for that voice to guide her, to give her courage and to sustain her when fear attacked her resolve.

At some time in her struggles, the urge to know and to find the source of the voice overwhelmed her and she forced her eyes to open. As she did, even more pain coursed through her body and she hissed with the intensity of it. Deciding she had not the strength or courage needed yet, she slid back into the darkness and waited.

Had she made a sound? William moved closer and drew the covers more securely around her. A chill not uncommon for this time of year had spread through the area and he remembered Wenda's instructions to keep the woman warmed enough. As he brought the lamp nearer to her, he saw no sign of waking on her face. If her breathing had changed, it was even once more.

He paced the small room. It had been three days since her fever had broken and Wenda told him that every day she spent in this limbo was an indication that she would not recover. A deep sadness filled him at the thought that she would simply drift off into death without him even knowing her name or her story.

'Twas at times like this that memories of his sister Catherine came to mind. There were days and nights at the convent in Lincoln when he thought she would simply give up her hold on life. The good sisters who cared for her urged him to speak to her, even in her unconscious state, and to talk to her of things mundane and comforting. And he did. He spoke of happier, carefree times when she was but a child in a household and family that loved her. He spoke of her dreams and urged her to fight. Recent letters passed to him from the convent spoke of her recovery.

William found himself using the same tones and the same words each night before he sought his own rest. He spoke to this woman, called her to fight and to survive. And for the first time since he'd disappeared from the court in England three years before, he allowed himself to care what happened in his life.

Chapter Two

Her eyes were green.

He had not realized he was curious about her features before the attack until he glanced down at her indrawn breath and saw the emerald-green color.

She was looking at him.

She was awake.

A moan escaped her lips as he shifted her head higher onto his shoulder to feed her from a bowl of broth. He could only imagine the pain that still afflicted her from the many wounds she'd suffered. He whispered to her as he lifted the spoon to her mouth, urging her to comply with his directions. After a moment's hesitation, she swallowed the soup without resistance.

Even as he tamped down an initial desire to ask

her the questions that had plagued him in the weeks before, he knew that she must have just as many questions of him. William carefully and methodically fed her the broth, giving both of them time to adjust to her awakening. He finished spooning the entire helping into her mouth and then paused for a minute. He planned his next move to cause the least amount of pain to her, but he realized she would suffer nonetheless.

"I am going to move you now," he whispered. "Do not try to move yourself."

William began to slide from behind her, holding her head in his hand to support her. Pushing some pillows in to replace his own body, he took care with every movement so that it was slow and did not startle her into resisting him. Soon he had her sitting up on the pallet, with pillows and rolled blankets surrounding her. William moved a few steps away and crouched down next to the sleeping platform.

"Welcome back to the living," he said with a cautious smile. He wondered if she knew what she had gone through in recent weeks, how close to death she had been. "Do you have need of anything?"

She blinked her eyes several times and then

looked around the room slowly. 'Twas not so large a room that it took much time at all. Soon her gaze was back on him. Questions clouded those emerald eyes and pain filled them, too.

"Some water? Mayhap the broth was too salty?" He stood and retrieved a cup of water from the jar he kept. Lifting it to her lips, he tipped the cup to let her drink. She tried once to lift her head to meet the cup, but the moan that escaped told him how painful such a movement was to her.

"Here now, rest back and do not fret. I am rushing you, I think." He pulled a stool close to her side and sat on it.

She closed her eyes and he was not certain if she was still awake or falling back to unconsciousness. But, after a few moments, she looked at him once more. Her breathing was ragged now that she was awake. Any relief that the sleep of the unconscious had given her was gone now. She forced a word out with great effort.

"Who…?" she gasped.

"Ah," he said, nodding in understanding. "I am called…Royce."

Would he ever not trip over the name he used? It was his middle name and one he was familiar with, but the urge to say his real name had not lessened in the three years he had not used it.

Her eyes closed again. This time he waited, realizing that she was dealing with the pain. When her eyes opened, confusion and agony filled them.

"You are in my cottage near the village of Silloth-on-Solway Firth." Before she could ask, he answered what he thought would be her next question—it would be his. "You have been here for three weeks. I found you, or rather my dog found you, in the woods some distance from here."

Her gaze became cloudy again and he waited. He could only imagine how much strength it was costing her to stay awake and not scream against what she must be feeling. He had suffered his own wounds in battle and in tournaments and had developed a tolerance for most pain, but this woman could not have experienced anything like this before.

"Would you like to rest?" he asked, ready to stave off his curiosity until she was stronger.

With obvious great effort, she shook her head slightly and mouthed the word *no.* She swallowed again and tried another word.

"I…hurt."

Her voice was strained and husky from disuse and probably from damage, as well. He noticed that her left hand clutched the blanket as she tried to speak.

William looked at her, examining her once more and seeing the bruises and scars as though for the first time. She did not need to know everything at this first moment, he decided. He did not want to scare her into a faint with the extent of her injuries.

"Your face was cut and a few ribs were broken. The worst of it is your leg, but Wenda says it is set well and it should heal as straight as it was before."

Her face lost more of its already pale color so he stopped detailing what had been done to her. "I am tiring you. You must rest and then we can talk again. I am certain you have more questions and I have some for you."

He leaned down to straighten her covers. The touch of her hand on his surprised him—her grasp was stronger than he would have thought she could have accomplished. William did not pull from her, but waited. Her mouth moved several times as though she could not choose the words she wanted. Then she spoke.

"Who…am…I?"

* * *

The darkness threatened to claim her once more, but she needed to ask that one question. Upon regaining consciousness a wave of panic moved through her, removing any coherent thoughts. Only this man's voice had calmed her mind and spirit. It sounded familiar and soothing and safe. But nothing else she could see or hear did.

As he finished feeding her and moved from behind her, she followed his instructions. The pain was so great that truly she had no choice, but his gentle handling made it easier to put herself in his control. 'Twas as he was staring at her that she realized she did not know who she was.

Searching through the thick fog of her memories, there was only black. She saw no faces, heard no voices and smelled no aromas. Only a black void existed where her life should have been.

She needed to know her truth. Who was she? Where was she? And who was this man holding her and caring for her? Was he her husband? Brother? It had been his voice speaking in the hellish darkness; his voice guiding her and soothing her. Why?

The first word she could form and force out had

really been about herself, but the man misunderstood and gave his name.

Royce.

A kingly name for this rough warrior before her. Then another wave of darkness surrounded her as she realized the importance of him sharing his name with her. If he told her his name, then she had not known him before. Had he known her?

Every breath hurt. Just moving her mouth to speak took all of her strength. But she had to know…so many things. And she needed to know now, before the panic that pushed in on her from all sides took control and she lost all thought.

She used the pain to focus her thoughts and her efforts. It moved through her in waves, some more powerful than others, but like the relentless sea, it did not stop. More a statement than a question, her words were forced out of her by the torturous anguish.

"I…hurt."

He did not want to tell her the truth. She read the coming lies in his silver-gray eyes before he spoke the words. Now fearful of knowing, she listened to the sound of his voice and did not pay attention to the content. Her wounds were grievous; she knew that from the inside out. A retelling would simply make the pain more frightening than it already was.

A question filled her mind and she realized it would be the last one she would ask. The strength she had used to push herself back into consciousness was waning quickly. He stood and came nearer, tending to her. He was leaving. He was leaving and she still did not know who she was. Her hand moved on its own to keep him close.

"Who…am…I?"

The words she most feared at this moment were out now. He would tell her who she was and the chaos inside her would calm and she would remember. She would remember her life and her family and her name. She waited.

The confusion she felt now filled his countenance. She watched as he looked over her face again and again. Now he struggled for words and, as she recognized the import of this, the darkness surged forward to claim her. Losing herself to its grasp, she barely heard the words he whispered in answer to her plea.

"I know not."

She was truly lost.

* * *

'Twas not the first time he had felt this helplessness in his life, but he prayed to the Almighty that it be the last. As he watched her eyes close, his gut gripped. Had she died? Her body slumped back as she gave up the fight to speak.

William reached down and removed the bolsters from behind her, laying her flat on the pallet. He watched for the rise and fall of her chest even as his own tightened. It took a few moments, but then he saw it. Letting out his own breath, he watched hers become slower as she slipped further and further into unconsciousness.

This was a fine muckle, as Connor the Scot would say. The burly warrior from north of England's borders had a saying for every situation.

Had he himself caused her faint with his words? He thought not. Covering her with another layer of blankets, he sat back and thought about this mystery.

William had hoped she would awaken from the sleep of these past weeks, tell him her identity and then he could return her to her people. Well, that was not the complete truth. A part of him was certain that her death was the motive for the attack on her and returning her to her people would not be the safest thing to do. Someone had tried to kill her, had almost succeeded and would try again if her survival was known. The warrior he was knew this for a certainty.

Who would want to kill a woman? And with such savagery?

From the smoothness of her hands, he suspected she might be a noblewoman. But what woman of noble blood could simply disappear and have no one know? If she were titled, someone would be searching for her. Lord Orrick would have known if there was a search being carried out, especially on his lands.

No, he was mistaken about this. Shaking his head, he circled the cottage and prepared for the night. Not of noble blood. Then who? And more importantly, why?

In his travels before settling here in the service of Orrick, he had seen many unfortunates throughout England—women who had been deserted, abandoned or marked for some failure on their part. Divorce was not possible, so men would simply force an unfaithful or unwanted wife from their home, taking everything from her but for the clothing she wore.

And sometimes, not even granting her that

much. If marked as a whore, the woman would find no sanctuary and be forced to accept whatever living she could. Although this cruelty was infrequently seen, it existed nonetheless. Orrick did not permit it on his lands, but other less scrupulous lords did.

William sat on the pile of blankets on which he slept and watched her in the low light thrown off by the vestiges of the hearth's banked flames. He was probably worrying for naught. This first awakening after so many days asleep must simply be one filled with confusion for her. As she regained strength and did not have to fight against the pain he knew coursed through her with every breath, her mind would clear and she would know herself.

Wenda and young Avryl would arrive just after dawn and he would tell them of this brief period of alertness. Wenda would surely know what to do for the confusion that plagued the woman, for the healer knew a potion for all ailments.

Aye, Wenda would know what to do in the morning.

"Royce."

The strangled whisper of his name was like a scream in the silence of the night. He was up in an instant and at her side before she could say it again. He did not need to see her to know she was awake. He could hear the uneven pace of her breathing and the turmoil in her restless movements.

He lay down beside her and whispered to her. Careful not to lean against her and cause more pain, he gently stroked her forehead and urged her to calm herself. The words flowed easily for he'd said them to her many times before in the darkness and privacy of the night. Softly, over and over, he spoke the words. Finally he felt the tension leave her body and he thought she slept once more.

As he began to move away, her voice pierced the night again.

"Stay?" It came out on a hiss. A plea, not an order.

William settled back on his side and did not move. The morning's light found him still there.

Chapter Three

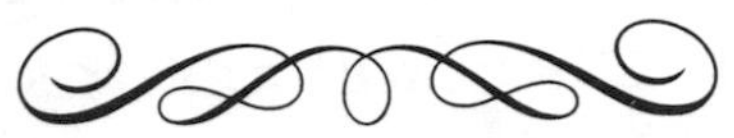

"'Tis a good thing then?"

William had moved away from the group of men he sat with at the table and waited to hear Wenda's advice. Lord Orrick had asked him for a report on the stranger in his care and William did not want to delay. And he wanted to know for himself.

"That she has awakened? Aye, 'tis a good thing." Wenda nodded. "But this confusion is not."

"Will it go away? Surely, her memory will return?"

"Mayhap it will and mayhap it will not." The old woman shrugged at him. "I have seen this but once before and that in a man wounded in the head during battle. He recovered his mind after a few days."

"Surely it will be so for her?" William was

frustrated by the healer's words more than he was satisfied by them.

"I have heard stories of those who have never regained their memories."

"Nay!"

His words and tone were a bit more vehement than he had planned so he paced away from the woman and tried to sort out his thoughts. He would not believe that this stranger would live in a state of confusion and without identity for the rest of her life. Last night had been her first time awake in weeks and this fog must be normal, a natural part of healing. But if it were that, the nagging thoughts in his head told him that an experienced healer such as Wenda would know of it.

"Royce," Wenda said. "We must simply wait to see if she continues to heal or if this is a pause in a decline. Time will tell us something more with each day."

"And is that what I tell Lord Orrick?"

"That is all we can tell him for now."

William let out the breath he held and looked toward the high table where the lord he served was at his meal. Orrick was a fair man and would not begrudge a stranger a small measure of care after an attack such as she had suffered. Once she was stronger, her thoughts would clear and she would know herself. Once she was stronger, she could move to the keep and be tended by the women there. Once she was stronger, he would lose her.

Shaking his head at his own foolish thoughts, he thanked Wenda and walked forward at Orrick's behest. Her recovery would be a slow one and be filled with pain and struggle. It would be best if she was moved as soon as possible since his many duties for Orrick took him away from the village frequently. 'Twould be easier for all if she were not in his cottage. He thought himself convinced so no one was more surprised than he when his first words to Orrick were a request to keep her where she was.

The rest of the day moved too slowly for him and he found himself wondering how she would be when he returned home. Wenda said that Avryl would continue to come each day to take care of her needs while he was at his duties. Wenda would visit often and Orrick had given his permission for things to be this way until the stranger either recovered enough to give an accounting of herself or until she succumbed.

Finally his duties were finished and he took up his weapons and walked through the village toward the stream. Following it for a few minutes, he soon stood in the doorway of his small croft. It was quiet within. Young Avryl stirred a pot on the hearth and his guest lay sleeping. He fought a smile when he noticed that her hand rested on the head of his also-sleeping dog. She had found a champion after all.

William dropped his sack next to the door, gaining the attention of the girl before the fire. Avryl was really older than a girl, nigh to ten-and-seven if he remembered correctly. He watched her graceful movements as she used the edge of her skirt to shield her hand from the heat of the pot and then poured some of the stew into a bowl on the table.

She would not meet his eyes as he thanked her for the meal, and William noticed the blush creeping up her neck and face. He remembered Avryl's mother trying to make a match between them after his first year in Silloth in the service of Orrick. A new bachelor in the close-knit community, especially one high in the esteem of Lord Orrick, was fair game for any unmarried woman. He had done his share of dodging those who would try to tie him into matrimony.

He could afford no entanglements of that nature. Nothing that endangered his anonymity or threatened to reveal his past could be allowed. He became practiced at brushing aside the matchmaking. He waited for her to finish putting food and drink out before turning his attention to the woman lying on the pallet.

"She has been awake for some hours today," Avryl answered the question before he could ask it.

"Does she know herself yet?" William crouched down to be nearer to the woman and inspected her for signs of worsening.

"Nay. But she spoke a few times to Wenda and to me."

"Has she eaten?" William looked at the bowl of steaming food. It was probably too hearty for her.

"Aye, she had something not long ago. Wenda gave her a potion for the pain and said she might sleep the night through."

William nodded at the information and stood. "My thanks for your care of her."

"I could stay longer…?" Her voice softened with a question and he did not miss its true meaning.

"'Tis been a long day for both of us." William pushed the door open and stood next to it. "Would you like me to walk you back to the village? The dark is growing deeper."

Avryl gathered a few items together and put them in her sack. Slinging it over her shoulder, she shook her head. "I can go back by myself." He could also hear her unspoken words.

Looking at this young woman who invited him to walk with her, William felt much older than his years. In another life, he would have been seeking out young women, wooing and bedding and marrying an appropriate one. Avryl would have been suitable for the wooing and bedding but not the marrying, if he'd stayed in his former life. Now, she was suitable for someone in his station.

He sighed, letting out some of his frustration. *He* was now the one not suitable for marriage, so he took his pleasures discreetly when he felt the need. Never with the wife of another man. And he never encouraged any of the women in the village or within the purview of Lord Orrick to expect anything more.

William would not let her work go unappreciated, so he walked to the stream with Avryl and waited for her to make her way a good distance before returning to the cottage.

Looking around his home, he noticed that Avryl had been busy during her time there, and not just in tending to the sleeping woman. His stores of oats and other food supplies kept in jars were neat and the shelf that held them was now clean of any crumbs. His floor was swept clean and a pile of clothing lay on the table neatly folded. Busy, indeed.

"She likes you."

He turned at the words and found his guest looking at him. How long had she been awake? He moved closer to aid her in sitting up, but she shook her head slightly.

"Eat."

"Do you need something? Water? Broth?"

"You eat." Her focus turned to the table and the bowl of hot stew sitting there.

William nodded and sat on the bench next to the table. It placed his back to her, but he did not move it. He concentrated on the meal and finished the thick stew, chunk of bread and cup of ale in a few minutes. Then he cleaned out the wooden bowl and cup and placed them up on the shelf in the corner. Lifting the pot from the hearth, he placed it on the floor to cool. Covering it with a battered lid, he knew that there were at least two more meals left within it.

When no other tasks lay before him, he paused before facing her. Nervousness grew inside him and he knew not the cause. This was the feeling that usually accompanied a new challenge or going into a fight, but he had neither planned. He only needed to face this unknown woman who was in his care. In his home.

Aye, that must be it, he thought. No other woman had spent the night here since he first moved from the keep. And he had not slept beside a woman in a very long time. Especially to sleep only. He had done that last night and now confusion over the way he felt about it filled him.

Finally he turned to his guest and found her watching his every move. He pulled the bench from the table, placed it next to her pallet and sat down. How do you begin when someone has lost all memory?

"Catherine?" He paused to see if she reacted. None. "Alyce? Emalie? Mary? Eleanor? Margaret?" None of the names elicited more than the lifting of her brow and a blank stare as she listened.

"I do not remember," she whispered. "None sound like my own."

"What do you remember? Any faces? Anyone else's name?" How *did* you go about helping someone regain their memory?

"Would you help me up? I want to sit for a while."

Her voice was soft and refined. Once more the suspicion that she was noble reared itself in his mind. The dog roused and moved away as he reached down and supported her head and shoulders to help her to sit. After packing the blankets behind her to keep her steady, he moved away and let her settle.

She clearly battled pain, for she held her breath and bit down on her lip. He watched her hands clutch and release the blankets over and over again. Since he could do nothing for her, he waited for her to gain control. A minute or two passed in silence as she gained some measure of relief in not moving.

"Voices?" He tried again to focus her thoughts.

"I know only you and those who were here today," she replied.

For a moment, his heart threatened to stop beating. She knew him?

"Me?" He must know. An icy chill shivered through him as he waited. Had they met *before?*

"Royce. Last night, you told me you were called Royce." She frowned as she spoke and he realized that all was well. Had his panic shown? He pushed his hair from his face and nodded. He must move away and focus the attention back on her.

"Shall we try a few more names? Mayhap one will trigger a memory?"

"I do not think so. Avryl has been doing the same thing each time I wake."

"Really?" She nodded slightly, pain still clear on her face. "Would you simply like to pick a name you'd care to be called until we find out who you are?"

"Isabel sounded nice when Avryl mentioned it."

"Well, then, Isabel is it." He smiled and let the name settle in his mind. *"Isabelle."* He repeated the way he used to say his mother's name.

"You speak French?" she asked.

He cleared his throat and nodded. No use denying he spoke the language of the court. Many did, not just the nobles who existed within its hierarchy. He gave away nothing by admitting the truth. Then she shocked him by speaking to him in that language.

"Have you always lived here?" she asked in flawless French. Then she blinked several times, surprised at the words she'd spoken. "I speak French?" she asked in English once more.

"Apparently." He turned the conversation back to her instead. "Do you remember traveling there or speaking it?"

She—nay, Isabel now—closed her eyes and sat quietly. Myriad emotions crossed her face, none staying for more than an instant. She shook her head. "No."

William felt the disappointment as she uttered that single word. Surely, when her injuries healed, her memory would return. Surely.

"Do not dwell on that. For now, rest and regain your strength." He stood and prepared the cottage for the night. She said nothing as he moved from spot to spot, placing his sword and sharpening stone on the floor next to his sleeping place and wrapping a rope around the knob on the door.

"Would you like to sit or should I help you lie back down?"

"I would stay up for now. Will it disturb your rest?" she asked.

"Nay. Sit as long as you'd like. I have to work on my sword, so I won't go to sleep right away."

He sat down and gathered his tools closer. Wrapping the well-oiled cloth around the blade of his sword, he wiped it clean. Then he picked up the stone and began to smooth away any roughness caused in the day's practice. Over and over, he slid the stone down the length of the sword in even strokes, putting a fine edge onto the steel of the weapon.

The movements tended to soothe her as she watched the motion of his hand and the sword in the shadows thrown off by the hearth's low flames and allowed her thoughts to roam more freely. She had many questions she wanted to ask him but feared interrupting his work. He had already done so much for her and the last thing she wanted was to annoy him.

"I am not tired," she whispered across the room. Her black hair fell over her shoulders as she shook her head.

Royce looked over at her and nodded, his movements never slowing or altering. "You have slept much in these last weeks. I am certain that some restlessness must be expected as you heal."

Restlessness? Was that what she felt? Although she knew he would not hurt her, a measure of absolute panic ran through her. How could she not know her own name? Could someone survive in this state, never coming back to themselves? The shiver of fear ran deep and threatened her hard-fought-for control.

"Are you cold?" he asked, putting his weapon aside and beginning to stand. "Let me build the fire up."

She raised her hand to stop him. It took all her strength to move it, but she was pleased to know her body was coming back under her power.

"I am not cold. And I do not want to disturb your work." Her movement was not without a price to her for it caused the pain to flow and ebb through her. She waited and took another breath. "I am fine."

"Not fine, but not cold is more like it," Royce said, settling down on his pallet. "I suspect you will not be fine for some time more."

He inspected the blade and checked its sharpness with his thumb. He moved the stone over one side and then the other, repeating the action and checking every few minutes. The silence in the room was not uncomfortable and she watched the muscles in his arms ripple as he worked.

"Will you tell me of this place?" She, *Isabel* as

she would call herself now, had many questions to ask.

"This land belongs to Lord Orrick. His family has been here for decades and descends from the Norse invaders who took control of this land many years ago."

"We are near the coast?"

"Silloth is a small holding on the south end of the Firth of Solway. How did you know?" His hands never slowed as he spoke.

"I did not know," she answered. "It was more of a feeling of the air around me being different."

"So you come not from the coast but from inland?"

"I…do…not…know." The terror welled from its place deep inside her. It was building stronger and soon would be unmanageable. Not knowing, not recognizing, not being someone. It was too much.

In an instant he was at her side. Royce sat carefully next to her and brushed the hair from her face. Although her panic was strong, she did not fear him at all. He lifted a cup to her lips and she sipped a small amount. It was ale.

"Shh… Do not fear, *Isabelle*. No one can harm you now." He whispered the words, but she sensed the promise of them through her whole being. Tears gathered in her eyes and she felt weak. Too weak and too weary. But the most haunting questions still remained. She would ask just one more before surrendering to the exhaustion.

"Why? Why would you do this for a stranger?"

He looked at her and lifted a corner of the sheet to wipe her tears. A sad smile crossed his face and it made her want to cry even more.

"You remind me of someone who needed the help of strangers and received it." His words were poignant with some emotion. Her own chest tightened in response to the haunted tone of his voice.

"Your appearance here reminded me that we cannot always avoid what the Almighty throws at us."

He turned away from her and as he stared into the fire she could see his profile, a profile that did not hide the pain he suffered. He left her side and moved back to where his sword lay. Silently he sat and returned to sharpening, the stone gliding on the edge of the metal until she thought he would speak no more. A crackling block of peat drew her attention for a moment, and then he did speak.

"Your survival reminds me that sometimes we must force ourselves to live even when we would like to die. That is why I took you in."

Chapter Four

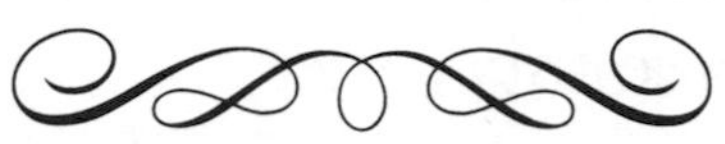

Two more weeks passed until Wenda finally pronounced her out of danger of dying. Isabel still slept more hours than she'd like to, but her body had decided on its own that rest was more important than discovering her identity. Since she spent most of the hours of the day awake and struggling to function on her own, she could not keep awake when Royce returned to his cottage. Wenda assured her that this was the way of healing, but it was pure frustration for her.

Wenda and Avryl shared women's talk with her; she felt as though she knew everyone in Lord Orrick's keep and village without ever having met them. Wenda promised her a trip into the village once her leg mended more and Isabel looked forward to that with great anticipation.

For now though, little steps such as sitting up without support were the mainstay of her days.

And although she hesitated to sound ungrateful, she wanted more and she wanted it quickly. She wanted her self back. Isabel looked out the small window in one wall and noticed the darkening sky. Royce would return soon and she would be awake this time.

She watched as Avryl finished her tasks and prepared to leave. 'Twas obvious with each passing day that the girl was giving up hope of having a relationship with Royce. Avryl tarried no longer than necessary when the end of the day approached.

Soon she was gone and Isabel listened for the sound of Royce's approach. The scurrying of Royce's dog as he greeted his master brought a smile to her face. Although she could not see out into the clearing from her place on the pallet, she could hear the noises of man and dog frolicking. Isabel wondered if Royce smiled while throwing the stick back and forth.

His gruff voice came closer until his shadow fell against the half-opened door. He shushed the dog at the doorway and peered into the cottage. If he was surprised to see her awake and sitting up, he did not show it. He nodded, pushed the door open all the way and placed his sword and sack on the floor next to it.

"Are you well?"

"Better."

"'Tis a good thing, considering," he said, his voice so low that it sounded like a whisper to her.

"Just so. I am making progress. At least Wenda seemed pleased with me."

"She is a kind soul who is generally pleased with everyone. Even me."

Isabel looked at him and saw a twinkle in his eyes. "And why would you be a trial to her?" She knew so little of him, even her probing questions were deflected easily.

"Knocking on her door in the middle of the night. Dragging her across the village and into the woods to what she knew not…"

Isabel felt the heat in her cheeks and lifted her hands to touch them. He was teasing her for the first time.

"I must be getting well or you would not abuse me so."

The corners of his mouth rose ever so slightly, but it was close enough to a smile for her liking. Although a rough-looking man with his long black hair and beard, his manners and movements were more refined than his appearance. Due to her loss of memory, he was a mystery to her, but she suspected that he gave little away about himself to others, as well.

Avryl was a perfect example of that. After days of trying to get closer to him, through caring for Isabel and working in the cottage, the girl had given up her efforts at a match. Wenda's gossip had hinted that there were other women before Avryl and some who would try after her to gain this man's attentions.

He crossed to the hearth and lifted the pot's lid to smell its contents. Isabel watched as his experience at living alone became obvious—he filled a bowl with stew, poured a mug of ale from the jug on the table and found a small loaf of bread sent by Avryl's mother. Sitting on the bench, he arranged his bowl, cup and spoon and was about to begin when he caught sight of her watching him.

"Are you hungry still?" he asked, beginning to rise from his place. "There is plenty in the pot."

"Nay. Eat while 'tis hot." She shook her head and smiled. Her face did not hurt now when she smiled or grimaced. The skin felt very tight where the stitches had been placed, but at least there was no more of the burning sensation when her skin moved against them.

Royce sat back down and began to eat. "So, tell me of your progress."

"I am awake." He probably had no sense of how much strength it took to stay awake each day. "And I have been sitting up for a few hours."

"No mean feat," he said. "Wenda tells me the stitches will come out in a day or two."

"Aye. And then a bath." She knew her desire for a bath was frivolous, but after weeks of being wiped clean, she craved the comfort of submersing herself in hot water until she was clean.

"You must be improving if that is all you think about." He lifted another spoonful of stew to his mouth and stopped. "Do you like baths?"

"I do," she answered without thinking about her words. "A steaming bath with rose-scented soaps…" Her words drifted off as the feeling of soaking in such a bath overwhelmed her. The quiet soon gained her attention and pulled her from her reverie. Royce stared at her with a frightening intensity.

"I have suspected that you are not a serf or villein. If you remember the luxuries of bathing with rose-scented soap, you must be wealthy enough to afford them or belong to someone who is."

"I…"

She could say no more. She did remember baths. She remembered that her favorite scent was that of roses. She could almost smell her perfume now, the one she saved and wore only on special occasions. Her maid would…

He watched the confusion and memories cross her face. There was obviously a slight crack in the darkness of her past. Her mannerisms, even though she was not aware of them, had aroused his suspicions that she was noble-born and raised and now these fleeting memories seemed to confirm it.

He recognized the distress in her expressions and did not pursue the subject. She was trying so desperately to remember her life that she was fighting the memories, grasping instead of waiting for them to flow freely. William could not imagine the terror within her, but he knew he did not want to cause more of it. He paused, eating more of the stew and watched her for signs that the panic was abating. When she was breathing more evenly, he attempted to draw her attention back.

"After a bath, what is your next goal?"

"Next?"

Her thoughts were still confused. He nodded. "Any good battle plan must have a series of goals. Smaller steps taken toward the greater one. Recovery is your larger goal. A bath is your first smaller one. What do you want after that?"

William watched as she began to think on his words. He smiled to himself, pleased that she was the type of person who was accustomed to organizing her thoughts and plans. Another sign of nobility? Someone who oversaw a keep would need to be organized in their manner. A chatelaine would need to supervise many people and tasks. Was that her past?

"In truth, there are several skirmishes I must win before I can attain that bath," Isabel answered, looking him full in the face. "The stitches must be healed completely, the day must be warm and I must fit into the washtub that Wenda can bring out here."

The laugh that burst forth from him was a surprise. He could not remember the last time he had found someone's humor so pleasing. And she did have a sense of humor. He finished the last of his food and stood before answering her.

"Ah, commander, but you have no control over those encounters. How will you win?"

"As Wenda has mentioned on several occasions, I have no patience," she said. "My first battle must be to, as Wenda says, bide my time."

"As one who suffers from that same flaw, I know how difficult it is."

"You are impatient? And how do you win over this in your own self?"

"I bide my time."

She laughed and the sound rushed over him. He had lived alone for so long now that simply talking with another person was a chore. But he enjoyed this brief conversation, with its insight into the personality of his guest.

Isabel was intelligent, stubborn and had a sense of humor. She had the manners and speech of a noblewoman. And she had no memory of her life or her people. Her presence struck fear in the part of him that had worked so long to detach himself from those around him, the part that knew he had not suffered enough for the evil acts he had committed against the innocent, the part of him that must remain dead for the rest of his life.

She was dangerous to his well-ordered life and he would be wise to tread with care and not reveal much to her during this brief time they shared. He was tempted to laugh once more when she proceeded to pry into his life anyway.

"How long have you lived here?"

Not answering her would be the best way to keep his own life, but how could he avoid such direct questions? Deflect, distract and avoid. Tactics of fighting that could be applied to anything in life.

"You must be getting tired? Can I get anything for you before sleep?"

She opened her mouth to say something, but no words came out. Her eyes narrowed and he knew that she understood what he was doing. She gave him a smile that did not quite reach her eyes.

"I have need of nothing else."

William nodded and rose from his seat to clean up his meal. As he did so, Isabel began shifting her position. A silent grimace on her face was a constant indication that the discomfort was still strong. He waited for her to request help from him. Moments passed like days as she turned her body, slid down from the wall and lay back onto the pallet. He'd held his breath as he watched her, just waiting on a word from her, but the word was never spoken. Her own breathing was labored when she finally ceased moving and closed her eyes.

"Isabel, I would have helped you had you but asked." He stood over her as he spoke. "I am surprised you could move that much."

"As I said, Royce, I will have a bath and there are things I must do in order to have it."

"And this was one of them?" He secured his door, walked to his pallet and emptied his sack to retrieve the implements he needed to work on his sword. Sitting down, he placed the sword across his lap and began to smooth its surface. She did not answer. Peering over at her, he noticed the uneven rising and falling of her chest.

"Every moment is one of them," she said with great effort.

Memories of his first days after his battle with Christian Dumont and his almost-fatal neck wound filled his mind. Once he had passed the point when his survival was not in question, he'd struggled with the choice to survive or to live. The reverend mother at the convent where he recovered assured him on a daily basis that God had kept him alive for some purpose.

Once he knew his sister was safe and that the earl had pledged his support for her, William had not cared enough about himself at all. He'd left Greystone and everyone he knew and walked off into the wilderness. At that time, he cared not if he lived or died, if it was night or day, warm or cold. He would go for days without eating because nothing mattered to him.

It wasn't until later, when he'd survived an attack by outlaws in a forest in Scotland, that he had even tried to think about why he had been allowed to live. The earl could have cut his throat with a flick of the blade, but chose to injure and not kill. He was alive for a reason, one he could not discern and still sought.

William stared across the room at Isabel. Was she the reason he had been saved from death? Was saving her life his purpose? Would it atone for the sins of his past?

He nodded at her words, understanding the pain involved with living. "Are you settled for the night?"

"Yes. I will try not to disturb you."

Little did she know, but everything about her disturbed him. He listened to her as she slept. He wondered about her while carrying out his duties to Lord Orrick. Soon, once she could stay upright and begin to walk, she would move to the keep or to one of the villagers' cottages that was closer to the keep. Then his life would return to the sameness he had endeavored to create. Nothing unexpected. Nothing eventful.

Nothing.

William decided to seek sleep and put his sword and tools aside. He rose to bank the fire in the hearth, and then claimed his pallet. His dog moaned mournfully, looking back and forth, from him to Isabel. Traitor that he was, the mutt chose to lie at her side for the night. Oh, well, 'twas for the good, he thought. She still needed the comfort of the mongrel's warm body next to her and he had grown unaccustomed to it in the weeks since her arrival. He could feel sleep claiming him when she spoke.

"Have you no squire or lad to care for your weapons?"

William sat up and looked at her. Sweeping his arm, he gestured around the room. "See you a squire? Do I look as one who would have the services of others for my care?"

"For certain you are a knight."

"A knight, you say? And how do you know that?"

"The way you carry yourself. Your speech. Your habits. All of those bespeak a man who has attained and enjoyed some level of rank or privilege."

William wondered if she knew how much about herself she gave away with her words. Now that she grew stronger, her conversations were showing her truths as well as hunting for his. He had deflected the villagers and even Lord Orrick from his truths and he would not be tripped up now by a woman with no memory of herself.

"I am simply a man who works in the service of Lord Orrick. No more and no less." To accentuate his words, he lay back down, turned his back to her and pulled the blanket over his shoulders. There. That should end her questions.

"Simply a man in service, my arse!" she whispered across the room.

William learned the limits of his self-control in those next moments as he fought the words that threatened to spill out of him. He had not hidden his secrets for nigh on three years to give them away now for the asking. His sister's safety was still in question if his life was revealed.

And so, with the greatest of efforts, he closed his eyes and slowed his breathing and waited for sleep to come.

Chapter Five

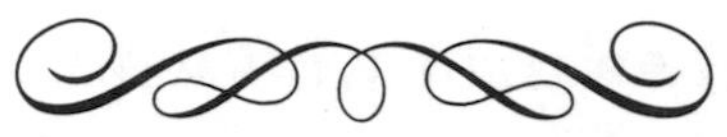

He was a coward.

With the cold dampness seeping through his blanket and into his exhausted body, it became clear to him, and he smiled grimly as he realized the punishment for his cowardice. The torments of being on this road escorting his lord's wife on her pilgrimage to Carlisle Abbey was probably as torturous as staying behind and facing the prospect of Isabel in her bath. Turning onto his side and pulling the meager blanket tighter, William knew assuredly that one hell was just as bad as the other.

William's plans had been to leave before Wenda's arrival at the cottage the next day. His services, already requested to escort the lord's wife for a visit to the convent where her sister was prioress and her niece was a nun, was his ready excuse. He'd accepted the lord's assignment with a speed that surprised even himself. Mayhap he'd known what was to come?

William de Severin, champion of numerous jousts and tournaments all over the Plantagenet kingdom on the continent and in England, was a coward after all. The victim of visions of a woman and a bath. It was all her fault, after all.

He'd been able to think of her as an injured stranger for all the weeks when she lay in his cottage, helpless and ailing. But when she spoke of her anticipation of a bath, a simple bath, his mind was suddenly filled with her as a woman.

He'd been able to fight the images until she asked for his aid in getting off the pallet that next morning. Isabel wanted to be seated at the table in order that Wenda could decide about removing her stitches and so the old woman would have to lean down no farther.

Placing his hands on her waist, he'd lifted her easily from the pallet. When her knees buckled at this first standing and his hands slipped up from her waist, he'd been granted a hint of the womanly attributes still hidden under the loose shift and gown she wore. The reality of the woman shocked him, for he had thought only of her as a stranger and never looked at what was in front of him all those weeks.

His attention followed his hands' course and then her indrawn breath drew his attention. Without loosing his hold on her, he moved to her side and held out one hand for hers. Balancing her weight as in the step of a popular court dance he once knew, William eased her to the bench and guided her down to it. They were both out of breath when she settled on the bench.

She would not raise her eyes to him immediately, but took a few moments to position her splinted and trussed leg. From the way her lips pressed together and her brows wrinkled, he knew she was battling the significant pain of being on her broken leg for the first time.

William left her and came back with a mug of water. Isabel gulped it down in two swallows and the mug thunked back onto the table.

"Is there aught else you need?" he'd asked her. A strange awareness had been created in that moment of touch and he'd felt the strong need to be away, as though threatened in some way.

"I will just sit until Wenda arrives. My thanks for your help, Royce." She lowered her eyes and fumbled with her skirt, rubbing on her leg to ease what he knew must be tightness and discomfort.

And then he ran.

Oh, he knew to outward appearances he strode purposefully from the cottage with his sword and scabbard in hand. He knew that he'd maintained a directed, self-composed pace until he'd reached the cover of the trees, and then he'd run as though chased by demons.

Or by the thoughts of a full-breasted woman within his embrace.

William shifted again on the hard ground where he lay and waited for the dawn. There would be no sleep this night, not with the memories of the soft-bodied woman who lay asleep in his home while he lay here. Sitting up, he slid back and leaned against a stout tree. It was not much later when Lady Margaret's maid approached him with her lady's call.

Lady Margaret sat within the dry, well-appointed travel tent that he and his men had erected the night before for her comfort on the road. 'Twas obvious that Lord Orrick supported his lady wife's need to go on pilgrimage and had made her frequent journeys as comfortable as possible. That this was opposite of what was normally expected of pilgrims on their way to holy places for prayer and contemplation had surprised him the first time his escort had been asked. Now he'd grown accustomed to the many ways in which Lord Orrick indulged his wife.

"I seek your counsel, Royce." Another of the indulgences of Lord Orrick was his lack of opposition to his wife calling his men by their given names. In many circles at court, this would have been an indication of some untoward attentions being given, but not here within Lord Orrick's sphere of control.

William considered it another of the many eccentricities that seemed to govern life on the fringes of the Plantagenet kingdom in England. Left on their own, close to the wild Scottish borders, those who held land and power lived their lives according to their own standards. So long as their tribute in fighting men or in wealth of one kind or another arrived when requested, the king and his brother bothered them not. With King William of Scotland and King Richard's agreement some years ago, the north of England lay in relative quiet while chaos in the kingdoms to the south, on the continent, held Plantagenet attentions.

"How may I help you, my lady?" William

dropped the tent flap behind him and stepped closer.

"I rely on your opinions, as does my lord husband, and have a question for you." The lady changed from the rough English tongue and now spoke to him in Norman French, their native language.

He nodded and waited for her question. She played this game often—speaking in a language not heard in the mostly Saxon northwest. If she had revealed this practice to Lord Orrick, he knew not, for Orrick never mentioned it to him and she did this only in private, with her maid as the only witness.

"While at the convent, should I mention or seek out information about a woman having been beaten and left on our property? So many people pass through its gates that surely someone may have heard or known the woman you harbor."

William thought about her words. Since the prioress of the Gilbertine Abbey was her sister, Lady Margaret would have no problem seeking out information about such a woman. But he knew, just as surely, that someone did not want the woman now called Isabel to live. And that someone might very well still be in the area or be waiting to hear of anything that could link him to the attack. No, until Isabel had some sense of herself, the danger to her life still existed.

"I would listen, my lady, but ask nothing at this time."

She smiled and nodded. "I understand, though what bothers me is the harshness of this. 'Tis easy enough these days to rid one's self of an unwanted wife by putting her aside and placing her in a convent or other religious community. Having her killed is a bit excessive."

"One would think so, my lady." He had enjoyed her irreverent sense of humor since he'd been introduced to her. She was very different from Lord Orrick in temperament and upbringing, but it seemed that opposites did attract in their case.

"Then, unless words are offered, none will be given about this woman. Has she spoken of her life? Know you anything yet?" Lady Margaret motioned for him to sit in a chair next to her and he did so. Her maid offered him a cup of ale.

"She continues to live without knowledge of her past, or at least, none that she can speak of." Lady Margaret nodded at him.

"But you suspect what?" Another thing he respected about the lady—her intelligence.

"She speaks as one noble-born. She has fleeting memories that speak of wealth. She knows of knights and squires and she knows our Norman French."

Lady Margaret's eyebrows rose at those revelations. "Is she aware that you know these things?"

"The French, yes. We exchanged a few words in it when she realized I understood it."

He waited for the Lady Margaret's reaction, for no one but she and her maid knew this about him. He'd sheltered his past from all in Silloth. She chose, and he recognized it for the conscious decision it was, to ignore this weakness on his part and offer her own suspicions.

"A lord's bastard or leman? Both could have that same background—raised or living near the noble-born, exposed to the wealth and privilege of those in that rank."

It was his turn to raise a brow. Never had she come so close to speaking of her truth to him before. He knew it, of course. He had heard the story many times both in his homeland of Anjou and at the court of Eleanor—although no one would have ever spoken of it in the queen's presence. Then called Marguerite, she was the bastard of one of Henry's closest allies in Anjou and her beauty and wit drew him like a bee to honey. She'd been Henry's mistress for a number of years before overstepping her bounds and demanding marriage of the king.

Henry had, in his own way, said yes. But he'd married her off to Lord Orrick, in thanks for services rendered in his service in the north of England and Marguerite became Margaret. So far as he knew, she'd been the perfect English wife to the powerful lord. Her tale had been used for years to caution those women hungry to gain the royal gaze and attentions that, regardless of his volatile relationship with his queen, Henry would never voluntarily give up anything Eleanor had brought to their union.

"That is a possibility, of course. Until she remembers more, there is no way for us to know."

Lady Margaret stood and handed her goblet to her maid. "Tell my husband when you return that she should be moved into the keep and placed in my care. When she is able, that is. Let Wenda guide us on that. As my sister would say, she has been delivered to us for a reason. We should be responsible in our care until we discern the Almighty's reasons."

"Aye, my lady." He rose as she did and handed his cup over as well. "We will break our fast and be ready to leave anon."

"I shall be ready, Royce." When the last words were spoken once more in English, he knew their discussion was over.

There were no more private meetings during the rest of their two days of travel through Thursby and into Carlisle. William and his men delivered Lady Margaret to her sister's abbey outside Carlisle and left the next morning to return to Silloth. If he forced the group to travel more quickly on their return, no one remarked on it. All knew that their pace was faster due to the lack of women, but William also knew he wanted to get back to see how Isabel was progressing. As Lady Margaret had said, he needed to be responsible in his care of their injured stranger.

They arrived later than he had planned and he was drawn into several hours of discussions with Orrick about the news from Carlisle and the building of the new stone wall around the keep. He accepted Orrick's standing invitation to stay the night, but the dawn found him awake. In spite of Orrick's assurances that a man had been sent to guard her, William could not fight the urge to return to his cottage and see to her safety.

It was an hour after dawn when he approached his home. As he dismounted from the horse that made his arrival sooner rather than later, he heard voices from inside. A man's and a woman's. No. Two women's voices—Isabel's and Avryl's. William walked to the door and opened it.

The first thing he noticed was that she stared at him with wide, jade-green eyes and did not look away. Then he realized she was sitting up, on a chair in front of the hearth. And after nearly three years of taking notice of little and having even less interest than that in the way of things, he saw that her black hair reached to her hips.

The silence rose between them and he was aware of Avryl and young John who stood and watched. No words came to him. He searched for something to say and nothing happened. Except that he felt the rising tension in the room and knew he must stop it. Finally he took a breath and blurted out his first thoughts without censoring them for the others present.

"By the look of things, your bath went well."

He watched the blush spread over her face, down her neck and below the collar of her gown.

Isabel blinked several times and looked away from him. He listened to Avryl's sudden intake of breath and tried to ignore the choking sound that young John made. The gangly youth with the scruffy growth of a first beard on his face stood protectively near Isabel. With a sinking feeling in his gut, William realized the personal nature of his words.

Inappropriate and personal. Well, they would be if he had not been taking care of her for weeks. Confused by the reaction in the room and the change from cheery to uncomfortable, William sought to explain himself.

"I did not seek to embarrass you, Isabel, and meant only that you look well. How are you feeling?"

He moved across the room and crouched in front of her, focusing on her. When closer to her, he could see the results of her injuries. Wenda had removed the numerous stitches from Isabel's face, but the angry scar still outlined her from scalp to chin. More of the redness and bruising would go away with time; however, the area looked sore right now. Her nose carried a bump from its break that would never go away. William fought the urge to reach out and touch it.

"I am well, Royce. Avryl and John have been

attending to me these last few days while you were gone."

He stood and nodded at the two as they watched the exchange of words with some interest. "My thanks for looking after our guest." The urge to sweep them out the door grew in him and they must have sensed his desire for them to leave. With a few murmured words of leaving, they rushed out of the cottage and strode off in the direction of the keep and village.

"John's father made this chair for me. Wenda thought it might be more comfortable to sit in rather than lying on the pallet."

"'Twould seem to make sense. This gives you much more support than the bench." William sat on the bench himself. Looking over her face once more, he was surprised again by her appearance now.

"Now, without the blood and stitches to hide them, you are taking note of all of my flaws?" Her lips trembled with a nervous smile and he knew his answer was important to her.

Such things were of importance to a woman.

A woman! Dear God!

He stood and began to clean up the bowls from the table, thinking about this situation as he moved. Hiding beneath the blood and healing for these weeks, right under his gaze and care, was a woman, complete with the fair face, soft, full body and intelligent, quick mind God had given her. Their world had shifted with his notice of her gender. How had he fooled himself for this long?

He had certainly known in those first weeks, when he took care of her needs during the darkest of nights. He had seen and touched most of her body, but realized now that her unfamiliarity and his despair of her not surviving had allowed him to ignore the fact of her femaleness.

"Royce? Have no fear, for Wenda has told me the truth of my injuries." Isabel lifted her hand to her face and outlined the scar that had cut so deeply into her skin that it reached down to the bone beneath. "'Twill fade, she said, but never be gone. And even now the hair at my scalp grows in white."

He turned at her words to see what she spoke of. He moved out of the sun's rays, which poured through the open door, and stood next to her. His eyes could see nothing but the even blackness of her hair and it reminded him, in its brightness, of the shiny ebony and onyx jewels he'd seen on the queen. Isabel lifted her chin a bit and pointed at the place where the scar ran into her hair and disappeared. A tuft of white now grew from there.

A mark to remind her of the terrible battle for survival that she fought and won. He didn't realize he'd said the words aloud until she replied.

"I am ever the warrior?"

"A warrior of some success, it would seem. Do not belittle your survival or the strength of will it took on your part."

"Or your part in my survival."

This was getting much too dangerous a way of discussing the simple topic of her scars. He needed to bring the conversation and situation under control…under his control.

"I am happy I was able to bring you in from the forest and get Wenda's aid for you."

She scrutinized his face for a moment and nodded. "You have my thanks for that and more."

Knowing when to retreat was as important in a battle as knowing when to fight. And William knew, as soon as he was looking at her and noticing her features, her face, her hair and her form that he was in over his head. 'Twas as if he could feel the crack in the shell of his well-ordered, well-controlled, empty life begin in his soul. Once begun, 'twould matter not if the break came from within or without.

"If you need naught from me, I must return to the keep."

William waited for her reply and, when she shook her head, he searched through his storage chest for something, anything, that made it look as though he had come to retrieve it. Taking out a small wooden box, he turned to her.

"I told Lord Orrick I would bring this to him. I shall return later."

He left the cottage and made it into the trees before the mocking words in his mind clarified how low he'd sunk.

Coward was repeated but joined by another word.

Liar.

Chapter Six

Exhausted from the past three days' efforts at sitting, standing and bathing, Isabel spent most of the day on her pallet. The frustration was building within her as each new day gave her no more insight into who she was or where she had come from. Or how she had gotten here, to this lone cottage in the woods some distance from Lord Orrick's keep. Avryl had returned for the afternoon and Isabel enjoyed the tales of those who lived under Lord Orrick's protection.

That would be her next goal—to be strong enough to visit the keep and the village. And then…then she would… No thoughts came to mind after that. For the one thing she wanted most was that which eluded her grasp still.

Pushing away the not-so-pleasant reality of her

life, she decided that she was done with self-pity for the day and would try to sit up in her chair to eat supper with Royce. Avryl's very fragrant fish stew was on the hearth, bubbling and soon to be done. A small loaf of dark, crusty bread sat wrapped on the table. It was her intention to set out the bowls and cups by herself—a minor accomplishment in any woman's day but a more monumental one for her.

Isabel lifted the covers off her and sat up. Forcing her breaths in and out as she moved, she turned onto her side, then her knees. Using all of her strength, she grasped one arm of the chair and pulled herself onto her feet. Taking a moment to regain her balance, she shuffled a few steps until she was closer to the chair, careful not to put too much weight on her still-healing leg.

Rather than sitting down, Isabel stood and stepped closer to the table. Reaching up to the shelf above it, she took down two pottery bowls and cups and placed them on the table. After another moment of balancing, spoons joined the ensemble. Then, placing herself midway between the table and the small cupboard, she managed to grasp and lift the jug of water and then the jug of ale kept there.

Exhausted but pleased with the results of her

efforts, Isabel stumbled over to her chair and sat down with more of a thump than she would have liked. Her leg ached, truly it ached terribly, but the sharp and burning pains were gone. She smiled, another battle won. Soon she would walk without pain. Then she could…

Her next thoughts were lost to her as she caught sight of him outside the open door. His eyes met hers and she knew he'd been watching her for some time. There was more in his expression however than just simple curiosity. Something deep within his eyes spoke to her of loneliness and need and denial and a hunger so strong it nearly took her breath. It was something so personal and so personally devastating that it disappeared as soon as he knew he had shown too much to her.

Her heart sped up as she watched him walk into the cottage. He took over the space of the room with his presence and his size, for he was much taller than she and had the build of a true warrior, one who battled with swords and strength of body. He wore the simple clothes of a man in the service to another, but Isabel could almost imagine him in the fine dress required at the royal courts. A deep red tunic would bring out the silver in his eyes and the darkness of his hair….

She blinked, trying to regain control over her wayward thoughts. Royce walked over to where she sat and looked at the table she had prepared.

"You have been busy this day. Were you not supposed to rest?"

"I did rest," she said, her words stumbling a bit as she spoke. "I am following Wenda's advice of adding a new challenge to each of my days."

He crouched down nearer the fire and lifted the lid of the pot. The smells of the seasoned stew floated through the air and her stomach grumbled in anticipation of it. He looked back and smiled.

"Nothing increases your hunger so much as pushing yourself to your physical limits. You must be famished."

Embarrassed by her noisy stomach and by a sense that a lady should not reveal her appetites, she only smiled. When she would have stood to move to one of the benches, he stopped her with a motion of his hand. Royce surprised her then by lifting one edge of the table and dragging it over in front of her. Her plan to serve the food was at an end since she was now trapped behind the table. Part of her was disappointed, but a larger part of her was grateful for his intervention.

Royce moved the pot to the edge of the embers and ladled out two bowlfuls of the stew. He gave her the same portion as his and she thought to protest, not needing so much, but the set of his chin gave her pause. Then he reached for a skin of wine that hung from the cupboard; he poured some in her cup and handed it to her. Instead of arguing, she sipped it before tasting any of the food.

"Wenda said that the herbs in this will ease your pain and help you sleep better."

"Without making me lose consciousness like her last brew?"

He smiled. "She assures me so. She said you have no tolerance for some of the herbs she added last time."

Isabel nodded at him, lifted a spoonful of the thick stew to her mouth and savored its well-cooked taste. After a few minutes of silent eating, she wanted to talk to him.

"I have been eating Avryl's cooking, or that of her mother, for all these weeks and have yet to taste two of her fish stews or soups that are the same."

"'Tis true. They are good at cooking." He shoved another spoonful of stew into his mouth and chewed it.

"Fish is plentiful here?"

"It is a mainstay of our diet. Even the fish-days of Lent are no hardship, as the women here lack not in ways to cook it."

"Because we are near the coast?" Wenda had explained where the lands of Lord Orrick were located and the general surroundings of the area.

"Aye, and because Lord Orrick owns most of the sea lathes to the north where salt is produced. So, fresh in summer or salted in winter, fish is always on our tables."

"I think I like the sea." Isabel could see an image in her mind of the ocean, with its salty scent and its waves crashing wildly onto a sandy beach. Then she could see two young girls frolicking on that beach, one with black hair and one with blond. They splashed along the edge of the ocean, their gowns dragging on the wet sand as they ran in the shallow water. They were held back from running in completely by the stern warning of—

"Isabel?"

She closed her eyes, knowing that she wanted to keep the scene she'd watched in her memory, for it was important in some way. But, to her despair, the sounds and sights grew dimmer until it was gone.

"Isabel? Are you well?" Royce touched her hand and she opened her eyes.

"I saw…I remembered." Her throat clogged with tears and she could not get the words out. He held her hand under his and squeezed it gently.

"Do not fight these memories, Isabel. Let them flow over you when they happen. Grasping too tightly simply forces them away."

She swallowed to clear her throat. "How know you of such things?" Did he not speak of his past because he could not remember it? Was that how he could seem to understand her every struggle against this overwhelming darkness?

"A very wise person counseled me about this. I yield to her knowledge, not my own." He nodded at her and lifted his hand from hers. Returning to his meal, he did not speak again.

Her knowledge. Wenda? But, if Wenda was this wise person, why had he not simply called her by name? Because he spoke of someone else. Someone in the past that he held close to him and that he shared with no one here in Lord Orrick's estates. She was certain of it.

They finished the rest of their meal in silence. It felt so different to her to be sitting up at the table and eating instead of reclining on her pallet. It felt wonderful.

"So, you are happy with your successes this day?" His voice was deep, even when lightened by his tone.

"I am. I was able to get to my feet alone, to stand and even to walk a few steps from chair to table and back again. I expect to be battle ready by the end of the week."

He laughed at her nonsensical boast and she looked at his face as he did. Most of the time he wore a frown, deeply troubled by something or worried over something. His manner was always intent, focusing on his duties or the activity that held his attention. The laugh altered his countenance and showed her a man much younger than she had thought him to be. Her curiosity won and she blurted out her thought to him.

"You are a score and ten?"

His gaze narrowed on her and she thought he would not answer, but he did.

"Nigh to that. And you?"

"A score and five."

He nodded at her words and then she began to

tremble. She had not considered his question at all before answering it. The words had simply escaped from her. His hand on hers, when it happened, was comforting against the fear.

"I have five and twenty years," she repeated, now more sure that it was true when the words came out.

"And?" he asked.

She tried to search her memory but it was dark. Nothing came to her. She shook her head.

Royce stood and moved the table back to its place by the side of the hearth, near the cottage's lone window. She watched as the task was accomplished with little effort on his part. The strength of a warrior. Then he pulled a bench next to her chair and sat on it, leaning down and closer to her.

"Tell me what you remembered before. We spoke of the ocean and you were watching something in your thoughts."

She was almost undone by the kindness in his manner and tone. She felt the tears gathering in her eyes when he took her hands in his and held them.

"Fear not, Isabel. Simply close your eyes, take a breath and tell me of your ocean."

She did as he told her and thought once more

about the ocean and its waves. Soon the scene from before filled her mind and she watched as though she were on the shore. Isabel saw the two girls with their gowns growing wetter as they ran along the length of the rocky beach. Darting into the water and out again, they raced each other, always laughing and screaming at the coldness of the water on their bare legs.

"Tell me what you see," he whispered.

"Two girls, one with black hair and one with pale, running on a beach."

"How old are they?"

"They have not ten years yet." She watched as they darted among the boulders that crept up to the ocean's edge. She smiled. "They run like the wind."

"Tell me of the day."

Isabel looked around the scene before her and noticed that the sun was hovering above the sea, gaining strength. "'Tis only after dawn, for the sun just now rises over the edge of the sea. We sneaked away to play pretend on the beach."

Royce noticed the change in her view, for now it was "we" and not "the girls." "What do you pretend you are?"

"Maidens running from Viking warriors. We

pretend that we can see far out to sea and watch their ships approach from the north and east."

She was on the east coast of England. And, if she was correct, she had a blond-haired sister, although many people whose hair was light as children darkened with age. He suspected that it was her sister who played pretend on the beach.

William nearly let out a laugh of his own when he realized that his own Viking forebears would have licked their lips over such a prize unguarded on an English beach.

"Who is with you on the beach?" He watched as her eyes moved behind closed lids. He still held her hands in his.

"My sister and our maid. See her there?" Isabel turned her head to one side.

William marveled at her ability to see these scenes. 'Twas then he noticed her empty cup on the table. Were Wenda's herbs causing this? Could this be a way to encourage her memory to return?

"Isabel, what is your sister's name? Call out to her now." William waited for a response. If he discovered the name of her sister, it might be possible to trace her family after all.

Her face lightened first as she began to call out a name, but none came, no words were said, no names called. She turned her head from side to side as though seeking someone.

"They're going!" she shouted. "They're going away," she whispered mournfully. Tears glistened as they rolled down her cheeks. "Please…"

Her sorrow and frustration tore at him. He had thought to help to guide her to some memories, but had only caused her more pain. William released her hands and let them fall to her lap. Taking her by the shoulders, he called out to her.

"Isabel. Open your eyes, Isabel."

Her eyes fluttered and then slowly opened. Her gaze was vague, as though lost in some other place. He was not certain she even recognized him.

"Isabel? Can you hear me?" He shook her gently to rouse her. A look of resignation filled her now.

"Royce? What happened?" She put her hand up and touched her forehead. "I feel so dizzy."

"Here," he said, putting his arms around her and lifting her from the chair. "I think you pushed yourself too far today. You are overwrought."

William carried her the short distance to her pallet. Kneeling down, he gently placed her on it and stepped back. As he watched, she shifted on the blankets and positioned her leg before lying back.

"Try to sleep," he told her. "And on the morrow, try to pace yourself."

"Yes, commander," she whispered, calling him the name he had used for her just a few days before.

"I did not mean to give you orders, Isabel. I but sought to suggest…"

She reached out for his hand, stopping his words, and when he leaned down and gave it to her, she squeezed it. "I thank you for your care of me, Royce. I know I would have been dead without you."

He reached over her and took another blanket from the pile next to her. Shaking it out, he placed it over her. He did not trust himself to say anything, for her gratitude had caused a strong reaction inside his soul. She did not know, could never know, how much her presence brightened his sorry life. Never know how much life she had brought into his existence even as close to death as she once was. She could never know that she had made him think about a future in spite of the fact that she certainly could not be in any future of his.

William was not as strong and aloof as he would have wished at that moment, for before he stood and went about cleaning up the cottage for the night, he allowed himself to reach out and touch the smoothness of her cheek. And he allowed his thumb to brush over the softness of her mouth as he enjoyed, for a single second, the guilty pleasure of imagining that he could kiss her lips. When she turned into his palm, as she had many times during her dark, unconscious nights of pain, he knew he would remember it for years after she was gone and when his life was as it was before her arrival.

Before going too far to turn back, he asserted his control and stood up. "Sleep well, Isabel."

She must have seen his struggle or recognized it and been frightened by the desire in his eyes, for she simply nodded and turned on her side. 'Twas a good thing, for his hard-won self-control was waning and any sign of welcome from her would be his complete undoing.

He followed his routine without thought, gathering up the dishes, covering and moving the pot for the night, hanging the wineskin back on the cupboard and putting everything in order. He needed some distance to regain his equilibrium and decided to walk to the stream while she fell asleep.

"I will return anon, Isabel. I need to fill the jug of water for the morning."

She did not reply and he had hoped she would not. Escaping with the jug under his arm, he snapped his fingers to call the dog to follow him. This time, the mutt heeded his call and ran at his side through the trees.

Sometime later, after tearing off his clothes and swimming in the frigid water, after cursing himself for the fool he was becoming, he returned to the cottage to find Isabel asleep. He watched the even movements of her shoulders for a few moments and then, convinced she was soundly asleep, he brought in the small leather-covered box he had taken from his storage chest. It had all been a ruse that day, an attempt to make her think he'd been there for a reason other than to see her. He would never show anyone, especially Lord Orrick, the contents of this box, for it exposed his secrets in a terribly painful way.

But he kept the papers inside, for they strengthened his resolve when he faced a weak moment like this one. When he thought that mayhap he should seek a life, or seek to share his existence with someone else, he was drawn back to this collection of parchment.

Passed from Gilbertine convent to Gilbertine convent by way of messengers and travelers, the letters had made their way from near Lincoln to the place where Lady Margaret's sister was prioress. He knew not if his lord's wife was aware of the letters passed on to him by her sister, but they never spoke of them or of his need to receive packages from the prioress.

William lit a candle and placed it on the table. Sitting with his back to Isabel, he opened the box, took out the top letter and, with the greatest of care, smoothed it open. The reverend mother's words of greeting gave way to a report on the status of his sister Catherine. Although her physical recovery was wonderful news to him, the rest of the letter tore him apart, for he was the one whose actions had destroyed Catherine's life and made her the target of the evil machinations of a dark prince of the realm.

If only he had given in without a struggle, Prince John would never have sought out Catherine as a weapon of control over him. If only he had stood up to John and revealed his plans to the Earl of Harbridge, Gaspar Montgomerie. Montgomerie had strong allies and could have, would have…

William leaned on his elbows and cradled his head in his hands, rubbing his eyes and pushing his wet hair back. He had made so many mistakes and so many others had paid for them. Now, his chance to let them live their lives and the chance to somehow redeem himself was threatened by the presence of a woman who could not know how great a danger she was to him and all he had put in place over the last three years.

He owed it to his sister, his former betrothed and to their daughter to never let anyone know of his existence. The price of their lives was his death and he would continue to honor his agreement with the new earl. Rereading the indignities and dishonor his sister had to accept in her life, being passed off as the orphaned cousin of the countess instead of the heiress and pampered daughter of a noble family that she was, William renewed his own inner strength.

Isabel would be ready to move to the keep and take a place within Lady Margaret's circle of women until her memory came back. Her future would be out of his hands, her life no concern of his. And his future? William looked once more at the reverend mother's letter and knew the answer.

William de Severin would remain dead and buried and Royce of Silloth would simply continue to exist on the fringes of the English kingdom. There was no future for him at all since any exposure could endanger Catherine or Emalie or…

No future at all.

Sleep did not come easily or well for Isabel. Mayhap it was another reaction to Wenda's brew or mayhap the memories of the girls on the beach had stirred something deep within her. Whatever the cause, her restlessness even scared Royce's dog away. She turned once more and faced the open space of the cottage, limited though it was, and let out a sigh.

As exhausted as she was, the thoughts in her confused mind would give her no peace. She tried to simply relax and let the physical exertions of the day force her to sleep, but that hadn't worked. And even more than the vague memories that tugged at her from an unknown place within, Isabel could not erase the expression on Royce's face when he'd first entered the cottage that morning.

In some way known to women, she'd read the stark wanting in his eyes. And Isabel had felt it when he gently touched her cheek and slid his thumb over her lips. But it was so much more than simple physical desire; 'twas as though she offered him everything in the world he wanted…and could not have. And it tore her up inside that just being here somehow caused such pain to the man who'd saved her very life.

Soon her jumbled thoughts drifted off and she saw the girls on the beach once more. The cold water splashed on her feet and legs and she gathered the edges of her gown to try to run faster. The sun that had shone down now turned dark, and the crashing of the waves receded in the darkness. Looking around for her sister, Isabel knew she was alone.

Instead of the beach, she now stood in the spongy murkiness of the marshes. The black mud pulled at her legs and gown and she struggled against it. When she peered down at its surface she saw the legs of a woman and not a child. Through the fog, voices called for her, but they called another name she could not understand. She only knew she must flee.

The fiery pain in her leg and the dizziness in her head kept her from moving fast enough and soon they found her. Circling her, they taunted her with daggers and fists until she fell into the nearest men. Fists pummeled her and she was passed from one to another until she knew she would faint. Even her screams did not deter them. Then one of them drew out his dagger and, grabbing hold of her gown, slashed at her. The knife's point tore her skin and then her dress and then skin again. Only losing her balance and falling away into the deeper water saved her from further attack.

She knew that she must have appeared dead or they would have made it happen, so she let her body drift into the water, hoping and praying that they would not follow. A man's words came to her in the terrible darkness.

"Let the creatures of the swamp finish her now. Then her death will not be at my hands. Come, my brother will give us more sport than this."

Sinking into the mud and knowing she must remain silent, she cried out in her thoughts for someone to save her.

Save her.

At that moment, the words poured forth and she woke herself up screaming them. Sweat poured over her even while icy chills raced up and down her spine. The panic that she'd managed to keep at bay for days and weeks pulsed through her, stealing her breath and making her heart pound furiously. The muscles in her injured leg seized as terror filled her. When the arms encircled her, she fought them with all her might. Then his voice broke through her darkness and called her to calm.

"*Isabelle,* fear not."

Her soul recognized the voice that had spoken to her in the void of unconsciousness. Her soul accepted the safety his voice and his embrace offered. But it was her heart that knew this was a turning point for them. Then her body accepted the solace and protection he offered and fell into sleep.

Chapter Seven

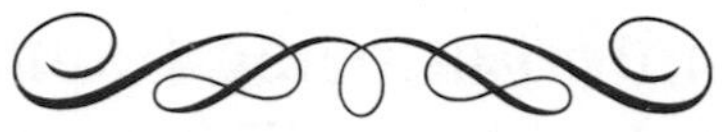

She knew not the first thing when it came to cooking. Oh, Avryl was pleasant enough about it and made light of her ineptness, but nothing about cutting vegetables or chopping salted or fresh meat or deboning slimy fish and making a stew or soup was familiar to her. Or something she wanted to do again and again. Following Royce's example, cleaning their bowls, spoons and the table after meals did not rouse any memories or feel as though she had performed the tasks before, either.

Embroidery did, though, as did the simple sewing of garments. Wenda provided her with borrowed gowns and some additional material and thread and she was able to fashion another chemise and outer gown for herself that fit reasonably well. Sitting in her chair, using the light coming in from the open door, she worked for hours in peaceful oblivion.

Isabel was not happy with the uneasy situation between Royce and her. The feel of being held in his arms through the night had stayed with her over these past few days, although not a word passed between them about it. Or about his obvious discomfort at being found by Avryl the next morning. He'd run like a sinner trying to escape the devil's clutches when the gasp of the young woman had startled both of them from sleep.

She smiled to herself over that sight. Try as he might to slip from their embrace of tangled limbs, he stammered over an explanation. In her own opinion, no explanation was necessary and if Avryl sought one, she had not come to Isabel for it.

A summer breeze blew through the cottage, cooling it and refreshing it with the earthiness of the forest. The dog, sitting at her feet, roused from his favorite position and then fell back again when convinced that nothing deserved his attention. Isabel lifted the heavy braid off her neck to cool the sweatiness caused by the heat and the weight of her hair. Remembering Royce's mention of how close the stream was, Isabel toyed with the idea of walking out to it to seek its coolness from the heat of the day. And to wash her hair again.

Feeling bold after her recent daily improvements, she placed her sewing aside and grasped the newest gift from John's father. Taking a long moment to evaluate her ability to accomplish this, she leaned on the crutch and took the first step. Although the dog looked as though he did not believe she could do it, she tested her leg and found the pain not unbearable.

Realizing she would need a jug and some soap if she was going to carry out this mad idea, she stumbled to the cupboard and took the small pottery bowl of Wenda's soap and the smallest empty jug she could find. Putting one in the other, she stuffed them into the large side pocket of her gown and looked around for anything else she needed. Tugging a length of linen from inside the cupboard, she threw it over her shoulder and faced the door.

More than once she almost turned back. Her leg ached with each step and the folly of her plan became quite clear to her before she had traveled even to the edge of the forest. But each time her resolve wavered, she listened for the sound of the stream, its cool waters flowing nearby. Mopping her face with the linen, she continued toward the rushing brook, one slow and painful step after another.

Royce's dog sat at the open doorway to the cottage and moaned at her progress. He did not follow her but begged that she return and that it be now. She laughed at him as she neared her goal. She laughed again when she walked into the covering of the forest and again as she spied the stream through the trees. Trying to pace herself, she made her way over to its edge and sought a place that would suit her needs. A few yards from her, the water formed a shallow pool and she knew that was the place.

With the dog's mournful noises still calling her from the croft, Isabel maneuvered down to the ground and slid closer to the edge. Testing the waters, she decided to rest a bit before attempting the rest of her plans. Pulling the edges of her gown up to her knees, she unwrapped the splint on her leg and laid it aside. Then she rolled down her stockings, loosened her shoes and slipped them both off. With a great deal of care, she let her legs slide into the pool of water and then could not stop the moan of absolute pleasure at the sensations that pulsed through them.

Isabel knew not how much time passed. She sat with her legs dangling in the cool water and her head thrown back, letting the breezes soothe her from her exertions. Now, taking a deep breath, she readied herself for the next task. Drying off her injured leg, she placed her stocking and then splint back on and wrapped it securely to give it support as she moved. Turning onto her knees, she arranged herself and her supplies and then leaned over as far as she could without falling in. Using the soft soap and jug, she washed her hair, enjoying every laverful of water that she poured through it.

It was as she was twisting the water out of her hair that she noticed the dog's barking. Louder and more intense it grew and Isabel hurried to finish her ablutions and get to her feet. Things did not go well, for she lost the linen she needed to wrap around her hair and then the crutch slipped from her grasp. The insistent barking was now replaced with something else, something that sent fear into her heart and made her stumble.

"Isabel!"

Royce's voice carried through the trees.

Fearing that she was in danger, she stood and looked about for a place to hide. Taking one step and then another, she heard someone crashing through the trees behind and prepared to scream. She would have, but her very breath was knocked from her by the force of the impact…of a large body…a large, hard body…a man's large, hard body. The force carried them both into the water, but she was saved from real harm when he turned and took most of the impact on himself.

Gasping from the cold water and the fall, Isabel pushed away and tried to sit up. Royce's arms surrounded her and he would not let go. Finally he let go of her and she discovered that she was sitting on him, in the water. Then, abruptly, he sat up and pulled her out of the water with him. Still not understanding why she was in the water, she pushed her soaked hair out of her face and looked at him.

"Are we in danger? Has someone attacked?"

"Attacked? No, why would you think that?" Royce stood and carried her to the bank of the stream. Water poured down from both of them.

Cold water. The prior cooling breezes now caused her to shiver. He noticed.

"You yelled my name as though I were in danger. You knocked me into the water."

Sometimes men could be so…male. But it was good that she remembered that much.

"I found the cottage empty, you gone and the dog barking and running in this direction. I thought you were being attacked again!" She watched as he set his teeth on edge and clenched his jaws. And she could not help blurting out how absurd his reaction had been.

"So you pushed me into the water to save me?" Isabel felt her own chin push out in challenge. Royce responded by gently placing her legs on the ground and holding on to her until she stood on her feet.

"I saw you wobbling and falling toward the water. I did not push you in. I tried to keep you from falling in. You can be daft sometimes, Isabel."

His voice softened, as did the expression in his eyes as he looked over her from head to toe. He reached out and gathered her hair in his hands and twisted it to release the water. Of course, this brought him closer to her and his arms surrounded her shoulders as he worked on the mass of sopping curls.

Shivers raced through her again, this time caused not by the chill of the water but by the heat in his eyes. She was torn by the urge to reach up to run her fingers through his hair. Then he leaned in and she thought he meant to kiss her, and for a moment she could not decide whether that was a good thing or bad. Her hands clutched at his wet shirt and she waited.

The moment was broken by the growling of the dog next to them. When she glanced down, she found the mutt wrapped in the linen she'd brought to dry her hair and dragging it to them. She burst out laughing at his antics. Royce released her and chased the dog for the cloth. It was then that the humor in the scene struck her. Royce, finally victorious over the dog, brought the cloth to her and looked as sheepish as the hound.

"I am sorry, Isabel. I thought that you were…" His words trailed off as she took the linen. "Did I cause you further injury? Is your leg hurt?" He looked down at her sopping clothes and for a moment it appeared he would lift her skirts and inspect her leg himself.

"My leg is fine," she said, smoothing the soaked gown against her legs. Now that she thought of it, he had controlled their fall so as not to hurt her. "You thought I was in danger?" He nodded. "I but sought to enjoy the pleasures of the stream…I thank you for your concern."

"Lady Margaret said we should be responsible in our care of you." His gaze became intense again and her breath caught in her chest. "And allowing you to stand here in a wet gown is not following her orders. Here," he said, as he reached down and lifted her into his arms. "Let me take you back to the cottage so you can change."

Isabel decided this was not a bad way to travel and, since the weight of her gown would have made it nigh impossible to walk back, she accepted his assistance. With the dog nipping at his heels, Royce carried her the short distance to the croft.

She tried not to notice the strength of his arms as she sat quietly in them. She tried not to notice the muscular chest that she found herself leaning on. And she tried not to let herself dwell on the fact that he had come to her rescue yet again. Even more, she tried to ignore how easy it was becoming to allow him to be her protector.

"Wait!" He paused and looked at her. "I left everything at the stream. Your jug and my soap and shoes and crutch."

"I will fetch your things once you are settled."

He did not stop until he stood before the hearth

and her chair. She did not sit when he put her down for fear of getting the chair wet.

"Undress," he said, handing her a blanket. "I will spread your garments outside in the sun to dry."

Without pause or another word, he left. Isabel watched out the window as he walked back into the forest, all the while talking to himself, for no one accompanied him. The worthless mutt who had caused most of the misunderstanding stood whining at the doorway.

She disrobed of everything except her shift and wrapped the blanket around her shoulders. Sitting in the chair, she removed the bindings on her leg once more and waited. Royce returned with the jug, soap and her crutch.

"My cottage is filling with Corwyn's handiwork. Does this work?" he asked as he held it out to her.

"I made it to the stream using it." She carefully slipped her hand out of the covering and grabbed the crutch. "And it would have been a wonderful weapon had I been under attack." She could not help but tease him. Smiling, she waited for his reaction. Royce began to laugh. A deep vigorous laugh that she had not heard from him before and her heart felt lighter in hearing it.

"I fear that I did overreact. My apologies for knocking you in the water." He nodded to her.

"And I ask your pardon for my part in this. I did not expect you back so early and thought I could accomplish what I wanted before you returned. Thinking on it now, it may not have been the best plan."

"For many reasons it was not. But we have both survived." He walked to the storage chest, took out dry garments and some linens for them both and laid hers on the table. "I will be outside if you have need of me."

Isabel made quick work of slipping the dry gown over her head and then, using the crutch, she stood and went in search of more bindings to use to put the splint back on her leg. As she passed the window, she could see Royce at his tasks outside. Their garments were strewn over bushes along the cottage and with the heat outside and the strong sunshine beating down, they would dry quickly. She had begun to turn away when Royce loosened his belt and scabbard and dropped them to the ground. Once he reached for the edge of his shirt, she could not force her eyes to look away.

Even though her hands had run over the

muscles of his chest and shoulders as he lifted or carried her in these past weeks, Isabel lost her breath at the sight of him naked from the waist up. A sprinkling of black hair began below his waistband and spread upward toward his shoulders, thickening over his chest and making Isabel's hands itch to touch it. His muscles were well-defined and developed from years of training and working with weapons. Although she had never seen him wield his sword, she imagined it would be a magnificent sight.

Shocked at her boldness and her wayward thoughts, Isabel decided that her gawking was done. Until she saw him stretch to spread that shirt out over a low bush. He turned and his back faced her now. Sculpted and scarred, she watched in fascination at the male beauty in his form. Surely, this was not the first time she had seen a man unclothed? Nay. She knew 'twas not, for somewhere in her mind, she knew she was comparing Royce to others. She knew not who the others were, only that there *were* others.

Lost in her thoughts and trying to let her memories loose, it took a moment to realize that Royce was now facing her once more and staring back at her. Heat flooded her face at being caught in such a flagrant perusal of his form. Not sure how to respond, she smiled. He returned it, but his changed to something she could only describe as wicked. Wicked and filled with pure male arrogance at her inspection. 'Twas only as she noticed his hand slip toward his waistband that she blinked and looked away. His laughter filled the air as she cooled her cheeks with the damp towel in her hands.

Oh, no. How could she face him now after this blatant disregard for propriety? She had looked on him with nothing less than lust. The tingling in her breasts and other places she did not want to think on told her quite clearly that her thoughts had stirred some buried passion within her.

A returning passion, not a first one?

What did that mean? Had she been married? Whatever pleasurable feelings had been initiated by watching Royce now turned to frustration as the truth of her life was still a mystery to her. A mystery buried somewhere within her and one that would not be solved.

An onslaught of emotions grew until she was overwhelmed by them. Fear. Anger. Sadness. Self-pity. It seemed that all the feelings she'd kept at bay since she'd awakened here were fighting for release. She'd centered her thoughts and actions so much on recovering that she had ignored everything else within her. She turned and looked around at Royce's cottage with its true unfamiliarity and felt a wave of tears coming. Unable to stop them, she sat back down in her chair and wept for all she'd lost.

Chapter Eight

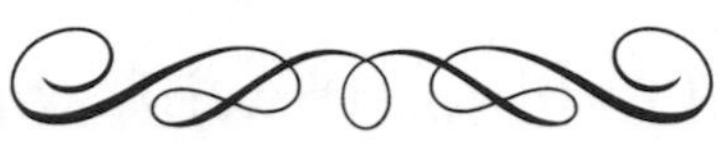

Pulling on a dry shirt, William paced outside the cottage, listening to the sorrow-filled sounds made by the woman inside. He stopped himself from entering at least five times, choosing to wait and give Isabel some time to recover from this torrent of emotions. Thinking to help her and comfort her, he'd first imagined going to her, apologizing to her for his blatant teasing and holding her in his arms and…hell, there was only one way that could end and he could not permit it to happen.

So he waited outside his own home.

And the irony of the situation struck him as a blow—an outsider again. But once Isabel moved into the keep and into Lady Margaret's domain, his life would go back to its structure and regularity.

Ha! He wrung out the water from his shirt and

rebuked himself. The old lies no longer worked for him. His very existence had been changed the night he found her. He drew in a breath and let it out as he tossed the last of the sopping garments over a bush—with too much force, for it went flying onto the ground on the other side of the shrub.

He admitted to himself, with some reluctance, it would take somewhat longer to adjust to her absence than it had for him to become accustomed to her presence. It had taken a fair amount of time to close off his soul when he'd first lost everything. It would take some time to remove the memories of her he had within him. It would take a long time…

He didn't hear the silence at first. William had been trying so hard not to hear the sobbing that he didn't realize she'd stopped. Looking up, the only sounds were those of the breeze that moved the trees and the sniffing of the dog as it hunted for something interesting on the ground.

But no crying.

William fisted his hands and waited a few more minutes to be sure that Isabel had regained her control. And for him to regain his. He did not want to embarrass her by acknowledging her loss of it. And he could not risk losing his.

Or should he? Mayhap this was one of those times with a woman when she needed to be comforted?

Damn! He was sinking into the quagmire of feelings again. William turned and stalked into the trees. He could not do this. He would not do this. It was too dangerous to let her affect him thus. Too many lives, none his own, were at stake here.

He found himself standing at the side of the rushing water, staring at the whorls and eddies moving within it and getting no closer to telling Isabel of the plans for moving her to the keep. Mayhap it would cheer her from her mood to know that she would be among people again and not kept in such a small place without company?

Aye.

That was most likely what she needed—the busyness of the village and the structure of those who lived there. Each knew their place and their duties, be it serf, knight or lord, and Isabel would find the life she'd forgotten, most probably without even trying. Memories were breaking through into her thoughts much more frequently now, even though he knew she did not share them with him. He was certain that even her nightmares were memories, just the darker ones better left unstirred.

Part of him wondered at the wisdom of moving her now, but, to Lord Orrick's knowledge, no one had been searching for her here or anyplace nearby. That meant only one thing to him—whoever had done this to her thought they'd succeeded in their goal. They thought her dead. And so long as she remained that way, she was safe. Lost, but safe.

Like another blow, that irony was not lost on him, either. He must remain dead as well to all who knew him. The difference was that he had made his life and his decision and knew he would abide by it no matter how unpleasant or lonely or painful.

Isabel, however, was dangerous because she held on to life and would not relinquish her hold. She fought to regain the life taken from her. And, if she did, the identity of the person who had taken hers would be revealed. If his suspicions of her background and standing were right, someone would have to pay for the crimes against her. Someone who wanted her dead once.

Someone who would kill to accomplish his goals.

Someone who knew her with or without her memory of them.

William debated the wisdom of her leaving the security of his home for the exposure she'd gain within Lord Orrick's family and people. Although Orrick was himself of Saxon and Norman blood, his father's family had been in this area before England took control of it decades before. And one thing was certain—they protected their own. If Orrick granted his protection to this woman, that would end any speculation of their role in it. No one would carry tales out of Orrick's lands. No one would question her or her presence, at least not openly.

Isabel would be safe enough.

It was time to tell her of the arrangements made for her. He turned back and walked to his croft and found her standing in the doorway. Dressed now and using her crutch for support, she watched him with troubled and swollen eyes.

"I was not sure if you had gone," she said, her voice trembling as she spoke.

"I but searched for anything you might have left behind."

They knew the words for the lie they were, but Isabel did not argue them. She simply nodded and walked back into the cottage, sitting in the chair until he followed her. 'Twas as she was dressing that she realized he had returned from the keep much earlier than usual. From his expression, she thought it must be bad news he carried. Unsure of what his message could be, she took a breath and waited for him to speak.

"Are you well?" His gaze moved over her in a perfunctory way, assessing her. When he met her eyes, she nodded.

"Well enough now that I am dry. What brings you home in the light of day?"

Her words had wounded him in some way, for his eyes darkened and narrowed. Had she insulted him? Been too sharp in her tone? Ah, she had reminded him of why she needed to change garments. "I meant no insult by my words, Royce. Have I caused you one?"

"Not at all. I just did not realize that there was such a pattern to my days."

"You are a creature of habit, Royce. You leave each morning just after sunrise and return just after sunset. You eat your food, clean your table and then your weapons. Then you retire for the night."

He reeled a step back as though struck by a blow. Isabel wanted to slap herself for her foolish words, but was so startled by the truth of it that she waited for him to respond. The way she described his life was no life at all. Surely there was more to him? Was she, her presence here, the cause of his habits?

"I did not even think about it until now, Royce. I have been such a disruption to your life. Surely you do not live in this manner? Have you curtailed your days to care for me?"

His face became like granite and she knew she was stepping farther and farther into some hole that she feared she would not climb out of. How to get out of this? How did this happen?

Something had changed between them. They had moved from caretaker and patient to man and woman and it was making for a growing discomfort. Did not the church teach that that had been the original sin committed by Adam and Eve? The knowledge of themselves had been their undoing. And for her and Royce the knowledge of their natures was making things difficult.

Could they go back? Would they ever look at each other in the innocence of one helping an unfortunate and one receiving that aid? She thought not. Once knowledge was gained, it could not be unknown the next moment. Then he shook his head at her question.

"I have done nothing different since I brought you here. Except to care for you in the night when you had need."

His tone had not changed, but a sharp stab of pity pierced her. He had no one. He carried out his duties to Lord Orrick and otherwise he survived. He did not live.

Angered by the meanness of his existence, she wondered why. Even the lowest serf had family and companions and something other than only the work he did. After toiling for his lord, he could return to family and share the burdens of his life with someone. Royce had no one and it tore her heart in pieces.

Mayhap he did not live here in this croft? Mayhap his belongings other than this one chest and his weapons were in some other place? She'd sensed in Wenda's and Avryl's words that Royce was held high in regard by his lord. That should mean a suitable place to live, especially if one was a knight, as she suspected he was.

She was about to ask him a question, one about family, when the bleakness in his eyes gave her pause. Isabel knew she was prying, seeking information that he did not give freely. Who was she to ask for an accounting of his life? She was his guest, a woman who owed him her life. This was beneath her. She could feel that through her being.

"I owe you so much, Royce. I ask your pardon. My questions have gone astray of what I wanted to ask."

"And that was?" His voice was flat, devoid of all inflection. All emotions. Or was it filled with so much that it just seemed unaffected?

"Did you have news for me?"

He seemed to shake off the bad feelings her questioning had caused and the tension between them seem to ease a bit. He shook his head and finally spoke.

"Lord Orrick told me that Lady Margaret returns in two days from Carlisle. She would like you to come to the keep at that time."

"To meet her?" Finally she would meet those whom she had heard so much of from Wenda and Avryl.

"To stay there while you complete your recovery."

He was getting rid of her. Now that she was healed or mostly healed, she would no longer be his responsibility. As if he'd read her thoughts, he shook his head again.

"Nay, Isabel. 'Tis not that I want to be rid of you. Lady Margaret believes you may remember more if surrounded by the usual things, the people of the village and the life of the keep."

"You have spoken to her of me?" She did not want to be the center of gossip. The very thought made her uncomfortable, like icy fingers on her spine.

"Many times. And to Lord Orrick, of course, as is his due."

The heat of a blush stole into her cheeks and she only knew a deep embarrassment. How did she feel these things? How did she know things about her temperament? About propriety?

He moved toward her and she looked at him. Crouching next to her, he smiled. "As lord and lady, it is their right to know about anyone on their lands. You know that somehow, do you not?"

She did. She nodded her agreement.

"I have been keeping them informed as to your progress."

Isabel surmised he told them much more than was required. "And your suspicions about me?"

"I do not have suspicions about you, Isabel. It is about your past that I suspect many things."

"Such as?"

As if it would take some time, he stood and pulled a bench nearer to her. After taking some time to pour each of them a cup of ale, he sat down and looked directly at her. Isabel trembled, not certain she was ready to hear his words. She lifted the cup to her mouth with a shaking hand and sipped the ale. And she waited.

Chapter Nine

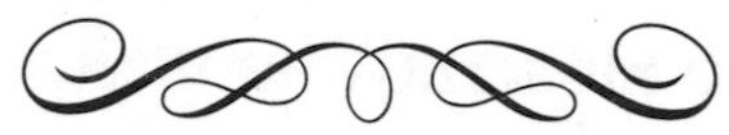

"I believe you to be noble-born and that you have a sister. With blond hair," he added with a smile. "I think you lived on the eastern coast of England as a child."

"Noble-born?"

"'Twould explain much, although I thought that mayhap you were some nobleman's by-blow or leman."

"What? You think me a b…?" She could not say the word.

"You have the soft ways and speech of a noble-woman, and your hands show no signs of working. You gave hints of being familiar with wealth and with power. You know of knights and you speak Norman French, the language of the court."

"As do you." She winced as the words escaped.

"As do I." He nodded his acceptance of her challenge. "I have simply changed my suppositions a bit. I think you are a noblewoman, not a b—"

"Fine!" she said with a bit too much vehemence. "Then why is no one looking for me?"

He smiled with a look of satisfaction. "Ah, the very quandary I have been thinking on."

She took her cup in hand and swallowed all that remained in it in one mouthful. It would not be good information he was about to share. Indeed, something scary was coming in his words. Her fears were confirmed when he took her hand in his.

"You are a noblewoman with at least one enemy. An enemy powerful enough to have planned your death and one who believes he was successful in his plan."

"Why?" was all she could force out. Her thoughts were jumbled at the idea of someone wanting her dead.

"Why do you have this enemy or why do I believe you do?"

His hand smoothed over hers as she leaned against the back of the chair. The roughness of his thumb drawing circles on her skin soothed her in some small measure and she treasured the attempt to calm her that he was probably not even aware of.

"Why do you believe this?"

"No one has searched for you. Lord Orrick said nothing in the letters he's received from the surrounding landowners mentions a missing woman. If you are noble and not where you are supposed to be, someone, your father or brother or husband, should be searching."

She stared out the window, not really looking at anything, as her mind was filled with more questions. A strong shiver pulsed through her. Someone had tried to kill her. Others must think her dead. Did anyone miss her?

"Unless your family believes you dead. Or was convinced by someone that you died."

"But why? Why would someone plan my death?" Tears burned in her eyes as she knew the truth for what it was.

"You must stand in the way of something important. Wealth? Land? Powers? Heirs? Those are the usual goals of subterfuge and machinations."

His words hit too close to the mark for both of them. His voice had trailed off.

"You describe the reasons for marriage, Royce."

He met her eyes now and nodded slowly. "Those are the reasons for most decisions in the world. Someone wants something that he could not or would not or should not have, but covets it anyway. 'Tis simply the way of it."

She thought he was not speaking in general terms now but about something very personal to himself and his life.

"Am I safe now?" She looked around the small cottage and wondered at her ability to ever be safe again. No wonder he had reacted that way earlier when he found this place empty of her.

"So long as you are thought to be dead, you should be."

"Does Lord Orrick know this?"

He nodded.

"And he agrees with you that I should move to the keep?"

"You mistake me again, Isabel. 'Tis the Lady Margaret's plan that you should be part of her women and thereby disappear into her realm. Only when your memory returns will you be in any danger."

"So, that which I want the most could be to my biggest detriment?" Knowing herself could bring knowledge of the one who had planned her death. Could she face that knowledge?

"I fear so. But do not fret over that now. Life

within Lady Margaret's circle of ladies should offer you some diversion from the existence you have been living here. No cooking, but there will be plenty of embroidery to keep your hands busy."

His smile warmed her heart, for they both knew the sorry results of her attempts to help Avryl. "Working with needle and thread is good." She smiled back, their even footing now recaptured for the moment.

"Lady Margaret will see to your comfort and you can trust her with any concerns you might have."

"Why do they do this? For all we know, I could be the daughter or sister or wife of their enemy?" She was feeling worn down by this lack of self and lack of history and of life itself.

"They are good people trying to help someone in need. Give them that chance." Royce stood and pushed the bench back to the table's edge. "I also came to share an invitation with you."

"An invitation?" She'd been so long in this one place that her excitement over this grew quickly.

"Wenda lives on the edge of the village and she thought that with the aid of Corwyn's crutch, you might want to try to walk there and share the evening meal with her and Weorthy."

"Is that her husband? I have not met him yet."

"Well, he is not exactly her husband." She must have shown the puzzlement she was feeling on her face for he continued. "They do not share the bonds of marriage, but do share bed and board. Is that a reason for you to not share their meal?"

There were many reasons why those in the lower classes did not marry. Isabel blinked, wondering from where that thought had come? Did she object? Everything was so new to her, she thought not.

"I would share a meal with them. If she was good enough to save my life, I certainly could not refuse her invitation, could I?"

"I would hope not. She is a good woman."

"You will come with me?"

"I would not allow you to go this first time without an escort." He looked around the cottage and then at her. "If you are rested enough after your adventure to the stream, we could leave now and not have to rush."

"Do I need to bring anything with me?" Since nothing here belonged to her, she did not know what she could offer, but Isabel knew that hospitality should be returned.

"Nay. Only your determination."

"That I always have." She laughed as she stood and gained her balance. "At least as long as you are with me."

Before she could say any other foolish words, she put the crutch under her arm and supported her weaker leg as she walked out the door and waited for Royce to show her the way.

"How many here know of me?"

'Twas a question that had bothered her throughout their meal and conversation with Wenda and Weorthy. Some plans, organized by Lady Margaret had been put in place and would result in Isabel's arrival at the keep on the morrow as a woman sent by Lady Margaret's sister at the convent. No explanation would be given other than that, since none was expected.

Her past, or rather lack of one, was being kept secret from the people here. As Isabel thought about it, it was the best hiding place—out in the open. Those under Orrick's control would see a woman sponsored by his wife. Those who may visit would see only another woman in the group that served the lady.

The one aspect that bothered her was what would be thought of her since no explanation was forthcoming. She would not be presented as noble, since they knew not if she was. She would not be presented as serf, since they were certain she was not. This vagueness would give the impression of illegitimacy, as many bastards of nobles were raised in gentle surroundings with comforts and servants to see to their needs. Even good marriages could come for them.

This round-and-round was giving her an ache in her head. Pressing her fingers onto her forehead, she sought to soothe the pain. Closing her eyes, she tried to let go of it.

She and Royce had arrived back at the croft after a wonderful but challenging visit to Wenda. Although feeling stronger with each passing day, the distance between the two cottages was more than she had attempted over an entire day. Her leg would throb through the night, but the journey and the testing had been worth it. The food and company had been exceptional.

Royce had still not answered her question. She opened her eyes to look at him. "How many?"

"Very few. Orrick and Margaret. Wenda and Weorthy. Avryl, her mother, John and Corwyn. Your presence here was not an open discussion."

She was tired. She was being called on to play

a role when she already felt as though as she was playing one. It took so much concentration to get through a day and deal with only one or two people, how could she manage in the keep and in the village?

"Do not worry on this, Isabel. Lady Margaret's plan is simple and will be easy to follow. She will expose you to various tasks and duties to see if you remember any of them. Just follow her lead if you are unsure."

"And if someone asks me a question?"

"Follow your own inclination in answering it. Isabel, this will work. It is best for you."

"The villagers? The serfs? The servants?"

"Have no place to question anything the lord and lady do. They answer only to God, his bishops and the king." He approached and lifted her chin with his fingers. "No one will question this."

She tried to smile but could not. Now that her emotions had broken through this afternoon, she found that there were many she'd held under check since her awakening. Even though they signified life and a returning vigor within her, it was difficult to stay calm and not react with fear or worry or anger. How many of these feelings were simply reactions to her situation and how many were part of her own person before this, she knew not. Isabel looked at Royce's reassuring smile and decided not to battle against herself at this point.

"'Tis difficult, Royce."

"I do understand how much so, Isabel. As I told you, you are on the lands of a good man. You could not have found yourself a more fortuitous place than this one. Lady Margaret assures me that your turning up here is part of a larger plan and I dare not disagree with her."

Royce stepped back and picked up the large pitcher on the cupboard. "I will fill this for the morning. Why do you not get settled for the night?"

When he returned a few minutes later, she was already on her pallet and could feel sleep drawing her down. But this was her last night here and she did not want to sleep yet.

"Will you go to escort Lady Margaret back from Carlisle?"

He moved around the cottage, finishing tasks. "Nay. Lord Orrick sent Richard and his troop to bring her back. I have been given other duties for now."

"Lady Margaret spends much time at the convent?"

"She travels there about six times each year. Richard or I usually see to her safety."

"She is a pious lady, then? I hope not to insult her practices with my lack of them."

"Not particularly pious, but of strong faith. Her sister is prioress of the convent she visits."

"Lord Orrick is lenient to allow so many visits. Even if the purpose is prayer and contemplation, my father would allow only..." Her words trailed off and she tried to let them flow.

"How many visits was your mother permitted, Isabel?" She heard Royce's voice come closer. "How many?"

"Two each year. She was permitted to go once during Lent and once on the anniversary of my eldest brother's death."

She struggled to sit up. "Royce, I have a brother."

"Two from the way you said it. 'Eldest' usually implies a younger." He seemed to back away from her now, taking a seat on his own pallet near the door and looking at her across the darkened cottage. "And a sister."

"And parents," she added. An overwhelming

sense of loss filled her and threatened her control. "Why are they not seeking me? How can I not mean anything to them?"

His voice filled the darkness but still he moved no closer to her. Part of her ached for his arms to close around her and offer the protection and solace that he had many times before.

"I believe they would, if they knew or even suspected you to be alive. They have been fooled by someone they have no reason to disbelieve."

"Thank you for that," she whispered, truly grateful for his efforts.

"I wish I could offer you more, Isabel."

There was more to his words than that simple declaration. He spoke so clearly of more than just words. His words gave her a glimpse into the part of him that longed for more than he had here. He wanted more than this solitary existence that she'd fallen into, but he would not grasp for it. What did he fear so much that living, existing, this way was preferable? She dared much but asked her question anyway.

"Have you no family, Royce?"

The space between them filled with so much tension that she knew she had crossed a tenuous line. He would not speak, had never spoken freely, of his own past. Isabel slid down once more and listened to the sounds of night that surrounded the cottage, hoping that they would calm her enough to allow rest.

Her thoughts were filled with the new memories she'd discovered—a brother alive, a brother dead, a mother and father and a sister. She could see only her sister and then but as a child, running on the beach with her. Caught up in her own thoughts, his words surprised her.

"I had a sister."

"Is she dead?" She held her breath, waiting for some explosion from him for treading too far into his life with her questions. The softness of his denial tore into her much more.

"No. She is not dead."

Isabel sensed there was more, but it came not. Quiet once more ruled and Isabel found herself drifting to sleep.

But I am.

The crack into his control, into the emptiness, was growing deeper. Not content with making him feel things he'd not permitted in almost three years, now she forced words from him to confirm things he did not want known. To anyone.

Determined to ignore any more of her dangerous questions, he turned away and cursed himself in his thoughts. He had withstood any number of challenges in these past years. So many times, the reverend mother's words made him want to return to Harbridge and to take his sister away from those who would demean her. So many times, the anger and the loneliness had crashed in on him and he thought to go back and challenge the prince, to clear his name and to return to Catherine all she had lost, all he had lost. So many times that he'd lost count of them.

'Twas a good thing that Isabel was leaving on the morrow. He needed time to rebuild the walls around himself so that he could continue on his chosen path. Wanting more, wanting someone he could not have, was too dangerous.

She was a hazard to be avoided. Her memories pointed to a plot to kill her, and to her own nobility. He could afford to be involved in neither the vengeance that her attack demanded nor the trappings of the life she left behind. Once her identity was revealed, actions would need to be taken and not by him. For exposure to anyone associated with or familiar with the Plantagenet courts could reveal his existence. Too many barons and earls and counts and knights knew him and would report his survival to John. The hedonistic, vengeful, distrustful, unstable scion of the royal house would not cease until an insult was answered and the insult William had dealt him would never go ignored.

How could he fight her incursions? How could he resist the lures of a woman in need and a woman who had no idea of the appeal she offered him? In another time, in another life, they would have been perfect for each other. Now there was no hope of more than this passing alliance. For, in the end, he knew she was a noblewoman and he was damned.

Turning onto his back, he listened to her breathing, even and deep. Content to know she slept, he planned out the next two days and considered how to strengthen his guard against her. Satisfied that she would soon be ensconced in Lady Margaret's solar and out of his path, he startled at her scream. He sat up and watched her fighting something, someone, in her dreams. Her pleas grew stronger and more impassioned until he could not stop himself from going to her.

Gathering her in his arms, he lay down next to her and held her while the nightmare terrorized her. She turned to him and burrowed next to him, clutching at him. He held her, soothing her with soft words until she quieted.

This would be the last time he held her. She would leave and he would never have her this close again. He could let go later, but he decided to allow himself this passing pleasure for the night. Then he would go back to his dead life.

Alone.

Secure.

Empty.

Safe.

Chapter Ten

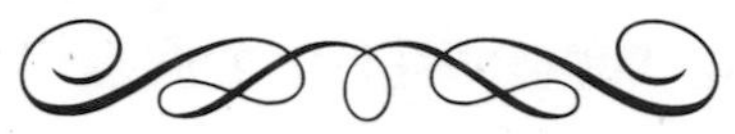

After ripping out the stitches she'd placed for the fourth time, Isabel knew her mood could find no peace in needle and thread. Royce had said he'd return by midday to bring her to meet Lady Margaret on the road from Thursby and that time had passed. And another hour and then another. She looked around for something else to do to fill her waiting.

The blankets of her pallet had already been shaken, aired out and now lay folded on the storage chest. Royce's bowls and cups and jug were back on the shelf in the cupboard. All was in order and there was no sign that she had ever been here.

None.

She'd brought nothing here and took but the clothes on her back with her. This lack of a marking, this lack of presence, bothered her in some way. But, within knowledge of herself, what could she leave behind?

The sound of horses approaching drew her attention and Isabel made her way to the window. 'Twas Royce, riding one horse and leading another. She pulled the door open and walked out to greet him. A fretful feeling passed over her, her heart beating in anticipation and her hands sweating with nervousness. Wiping her palms on her skirts, she tried to put a smile on her face but could not.

The sight of him on the huge stallion took her breath away. He was born to it, she had no doubt. He guided the horse with his knees as he tugged a smaller horse along with them. He reached the clearing and dismounted in one smooth motion.

No matter how he denied it, he was a knight by training and probably more. It was in his bearing; it was in his ease with the horses; it was even in the arrogant smile he wore at times when he was in his element, as now. Yet, he said only he was in the service of Lord Orrick. A man in service could not afford this magnificent horse and its care.

He tied the horses' reins to a tree and strode over to her. "Did you eat something bad?"

Puzzled, she shook her head.

"Does your leg pain you? Oh, wait…"

Before she could answer, he turned and walked back to the smaller horse. She watched as he loosened a leather satchel and a small wooden stick and brought them to her.

"This is why I am later than I said I would be. Wenda said the crutch was slowing you down and so Corwyn made this instead. Try it." He held out the stick to her and she traded him the crutch she held under her arm for it. "Wenda said use it in your left hand so you have your right arm to balance with."

Nodding at his instructions, she grasped it and leaned on it. 'Twas truly much easier to walk with than the crutch. And her leg did not pain her when she used it to support her weight.

"So, 'tis as Wenda said?" He watched her every move.

"Aye, Royce. Much easier."

"Will you smile now?"

His soft words caught her unaware and she tried to smile.

"'Tis as I thought, you ate something bad."

She laughed at his silly words and tried to banish the worry from her thoughts. "I admit to some small measure of fear at this moving."

"Isabel, I would expect that. Try to look upon this as a good thing." He tilted her chin up and looked at her closely. "Lady Margaret will be there to help you."

When tears began to gather in her eyes, he turned his face to the sky. "Here now, we will miss her at the appointed place if we do not hurry a bit. She said that all you need is in this bag."

She followed him back into the cottage and watched as he emptied the bag on the table. A longer shift, a dark brown gown, a leather belt, and some head coverings. Lifting the veil and inspecting it, she realized that her hair had been uncovered all this time. A woman's hair should be covered at all times. What other rules had she conveniently forgotten or disregarded in her blissful ignorance here?

"Necessity dictated your garb, Isabel. Do not fear that you have shamed yourself in this." He'd read her thoughts again.

"I should ready myself for the journey. Can you give me a few minutes?"

"*Certainement.*" He nodded and pulled the door closed.

She exchanged her old gown and shift for the new ones and felt different once she wore them.

The material was far superior to the gown she'd worn. This new one was not a servant's dress. The belt fit around her waist twice and she draped the second loop down lower near her hips. Then she reached up to fix her hair.

With a familiarity of years of doing so, she braided her hair tightly, twisted it and tucked the end inside so that it stayed wound around in a bun. Isabel took the barbette and wrapped it around her chin and fastened it on the top of her head. Then the veil went into place and she felt somehow at ease.

Covered.

Proper.

Protected.

Folding the gown and shift she'd worn, she left them on the table. Isabel walked the few steps over to the door and pulled it open. Taking a deep breath, she crossed into the clearing and waited for Royce to see her. It was a moment or two at most before he turned to look her way.

Had there ever been a moment when he had doubted her noble birth and place within society? Now, faced with a properly garbed lady, he knew what he had known from the moment she first spoke to him upon awakening—she did not belong here in this peasant cottage. Any more than he did.

William walked to her side and extended his arm to her. “Let me help you onto your mount—”

He stopped the words “my lady” just before they escaped. He felt her unease from where she placed her hand on his arm to the way she held herself away from him, careful not to touch anywhere but their arms. Reaching the horse, he did not ask, but only lifted her over it so that no undue weight was put on her leg. She sat as one practiced at riding and arranged her skirts.

“Isabel?” He wondered if her memory had returned as well as her manners.

“Aye.”

She looked down at him and he saw the same fear and sadness, the same Isabel, just dressed in something different. He decided that any reference to her clothes would embarrass her so he simply handed her the reins of her mount and climbed onto his.

“The ride will not be long or strenuous. You must tell me if your leg pains you.”

He watched her face as she gathered the reins into her grasp and then threaded them between and over her fingers. As he’d suspected, putting her into situations that she might have been exposed to in her life brought her past to light. Oh, she might not consciously remember it yet, but it was there for all to see. She nodded and he led the way to the path that would take them toward the road to Thursby.

It took about an hour of riding to reach the place where they would meet Lady Margaret's party as they returned from Carlisle. William slowed his mount and directed her to a shady spot under some covering where they could not be seen from the approaching road. He lifted a water skin from next to his saddle and held it out to Isabel before taking a drink himself.

His mount sidestepped, moving his leg and hers together. When he would have edged his horse away, she stopped him with a stroke of her hand on his thigh. Her eyes met his and she offered him a smile as well as the soft touch.

"I would thank you for all you have done for me, Royce. Somehow my words do not seem enough for all of your kindnesses."

He could say nothing in reply for his throat tightened and burned. A simple touch and soft words of thanks from her and a rip began in his core that threatened his very existence. He could not let this happen and yet his hand moved on its own to claim hers. Did his flesh hunger so much for the touch of another?

He covered her hand with his, lifted it from his leg and brought it to his mouth, turning it as he did. Without releasing her gaze, he placed a kiss on the soft inside of her wrist. 'Twas as much of a touch and a taste that he could allow for himself, though his body clearly wanted more. He noticed that she held her breath but she did not pull away or object. Only the sound of horses interrupted the moment.

William remembered himself and the role that had been designated for Isabel. With more regret than he thought possible, he placed her hand on her own lap and guided his mount a few steps aside.

She blinked a few times and then reacted to the impending arrival of Lady Margaret and the others by turning away from him. The loss twisted in his gut, but it was made worse as he watched her steel herself for the meeting.

The group, with two of Orrick's men-at-arms in the lead and with Richard riding next to Lady Margaret, came around the bend in the road and William touched his horse's sides to move forward. Hailing them, he raised his arm in greeting and motioned Isabel to move with him.

If he could get through the next few minutes, he could turn her over to Lady Margaret's attentions and begin to resurrect the life he wanted. He would go back to the routine he set for himself, back to the safety of being solitary. Away from the temptations of life.

Away from her.

Away from the constant wanting her presence had encouraged in him.

He never looked back. She waited and watched his face, but he did not meet her eyes once the others joined them.

The ache and wanting caused by his kiss were strong within her when Lady Margaret arrived. With few words, Royce greeted the traveling party, introduced her to her new hostess and rode off alone. His haste to rid himself of her was unseemly and noticed by those around her.

Isabel didn't trust herself to say more than was required of her and the rest of the ride to Orrick's keep was accomplished in silence. After days of anticipation of seeing the village and the keep and meeting those about whom she'd heard so much from Royce and Wenda and the others, her enthusiasm dimmed as she faced them without him.

With little explanation or hesitation, Lady Margaret gave orders to the servants about her care. Prompt and efficient, the servants carried out her instructions and placed Isabel in a small room of her own, delivered trays of food at appropriate intervals and presented her with a young maidservant to see to her other needs. The next days sped by without her even noticing.

On the morning of her fourth day there, she received a summons, or invitation, to join Lady Margaret in her solar. Isabel, now well rested and ready to seek out clues to her previous life, followed her maid down a hall to a corner room in the tower keep.

Upon knocking, the door opened and she stepped into a well-appointed room, complete with a table, four chairs and a hearth that filled half of one wall. Lady Margaret occupied the grandest and most comfortable of the chairs and worked on a large tapestry to her right. Isabel drew nearer, careful not to block the light that streamed in through an impressive window set high in the wall. Lord Orrick was quite wealthy to have such expensive features in his keep. The image that Lady Margaret embroidered was a garden scene, with two lovers seated on a bench.

"Good day, Isabel. Are you well?"

"I am, my lady." She dipped into a polite curtsy and rose again. Lady Margaret nodded and, with a wave of her hand, dismissed both servants. Once alone, Isabel waited for the true subject to be raised. She was more startled by the manner in which it was raised.

Lady Margaret began speaking to her in the language of the Plantagenets—Norman French! Unsure at first whether she should respond to her question in it, Isabel waited.

"Royce told me of your knowledge of the Norman dialect. Do you know Latin as well?" She had switched into Latin with the question and Isabel understood her.

"'Twould seem that I have learned Latin as well, my lady," Isabel answered in that tongue. "I can read both and write them fairly well." She only just remembered those abilities.

"Your use and skills in these bespeaks of education, Isabel. I think that either your family is well-favored with wealth or you were in a convent, perhaps? Or both?" Lady Margaret raised an eyebrow at her question.

"I do not believe my education came from a convent."

"Pray, be seated and tell me why." Guided by the lady's motion to one of the other chairs, Isabel sat down and tried to explain.

"'Tis more of a feeling than certain knowledge, my lady. I do not believe my temperament is suitable for a convent."

"Many noblewomen retire to the convent after they have completed their duties to family. 'Tis not so uncommon, Isabel." Lady Margaret shifted in her chair and her eyes became unfocused. "My sister is one such lady."

"I meant no disrespect, my lady." Isabel stood, worried that her words had caused an insult.

"None was taken, my dear." She smiled with a look of true compassion. "Besides, a woman would not be beaten near to death in a convent. No matter how unsuitable her temperament was."

"Royce thinks it was someone I knew."

"I know of his suspicions and my lord and I share them. That is why we moved you here rather than leaving you in his cottage."

Isabel had not spoken of him or heard his name

in the four days since she'd arrived here and did not know until this moment how much she missed him. Nay, that was not true. She had not admitted even to herself how much she missed him.

"He is a difficult man to fathom, Isabel. Think you not that his manner was in some way caused by your presence or behavior."

She must wear her thoughts on her face, for Lady Margaret had spoken them back to her. Isabel decided to take advantage of the lady's knowledge to find out more about her protector.

"Has he been here for many years, my lady?"

"What makes you think he has not lived here his whole life?"

"You two must be related," Isabel mumbled under her breath. Realizing that Lady Margaret was listening, she answered louder. "You and he handle questions in the same manner, my lady, with evasion and deflection."

The lady laughed at her comment and pushed the embroidery frame away. "Isabel, a man's past is his own business and he will tell what he wants known."

"And a woman's past, my lady? Whose concern is that?"

"Everyone's concern, my dear, whether it ought to be or not. And you were correct, for your temperament would not be suitable for a convent, unless you were in charge."

Isabel knew not how to respond so she looked at the lady. The twinkle in her eyes and the smile that threatened on her mouth told Isabel all she needed to know. It would take much to anger Lady Margaret.

"'Tis time for you to leave your chamber and mingle with our people. Look about you, see and feel the life of the keep. Surely something will assist you in remembering your life before. Edlyn will be a fine guide to show you around my lord's keep and village."

"My lady? I would like to do something in return for your hospitality and care. Is there something to which I can apply myself? Some tasks or errands I can do for you? This idleness does not feel right to me and I would earn my place here."

Isabel looked at the frame of the tapestry. "The only thing familiar to me is working with threads. Mayhap I could help you on this?" She walked over to it and examined it more closely. The work was skillfully done and the results would be a spectacular image to grace the wall of some hall or room. "Or mayhap not since I doubt my skills are as good as yours in this work."

"Although my lord's hospitality is freely given and no payment is expected for it, I would welcome the help for I fear I am beginning to lose interest in this one. Let us plan to sit after dinner for a short while and work on it together. We can review your day and determine if any progress is being made. What think you of this?"

"I am pleased by your invitation, my lady. I can see that I will learn much from you."

"Eat the evening meal in the hall with us, then, and we shall begin your adventure."

Lady Margaret stood and nodded. After curtsying, Isabel walked to the door of the solar.

"Please send Jehane in to me," Lady Margaret requested. "And tell no one of the Norman French we spoke between us."

Surprised, Isabel could only nod. Leaving the room, she found both maidservants in the hallway and sent Jehane into the solar as requested. Edlyn waited for her instructions.

"Lady Margaret has given me leave to move about the keep and village now. Would you accompany me around the grounds now?"

With a curtsy and a nod and a small bit of encouragement, Edlyn took the lead but set a slow pace through the buildings that were Silloth Keep. Isabel found her commentary to be enlightening about the history of the families of the surrounding areas as this part of England moved back and forth from English to Scottish and back to English control over the last century. Edlyn's family had served the noble family who held this land for decades.

Not overly picturesque, the square-tower keep provided stout protection for the lord and his family from the weather and from any intruders, as well. With four floors, the top floor housed the family, the great hall took over the third floor, the second held the kitchens, storerooms and some small sleeping chambers, and the lower floor, built partially under the ground, was where the lord's fighting men were housed. Even more important to the safety and security of those living here was the freshwater well that Edlyn told her lay on that lower level, protected from attack by its very location.

She did not go to the lower floors, but instead relied on Edlyn's very clear descriptions to familiarize her with them. There would be plenty of time in the next weeks to visit all the places within the keep that the young girl mentioned. And although a visit to the kitchen and storerooms would be acceptable, Isabel knew she would never go where the men were housed.

Growing tired after walking so much, Isabel decided there would be time enough to see the village on the morrow, and the two women made their way back to her chamber to rest. 'Twas as she turned into the hallway outside the solar that she saw him. He stood leaning close to the door of the lady's room, as though listening to someone inside. Her steps, with the clicking of the wooden stick on the stone floor, drew his attention.

Royce looked at her, stared for a moment and turned back to the person he spoke with at the partially open door. Then without any acknowledgment of her presence, he pulled the door closed and walked away down the corridor.

Although she had no claim to him or his attentions, Royce was the only constant in her unstable life, the only one she knew she could depend on. And he was walking away as though she was nothing, without even acknowledging her, without saying a word. She'd thought the world must be a cruel place, if someone could destroy her life and not be held accountable for it. Now, as she felt her heart break, she knew it was true.

Chapter Eleven

Trapped between Lady Margaret and Sir Richard, Isabel fought to remain calm and prayed for a swift end to this torturous meal. Noises and smells threatened to overwhelm her as the hall filled with Lord Orrick's people. Surprised at how accustomed she'd become to the simple fare and fresh air at Royce's cottage, she struggled with the many choices of food and drink and the attentions of so many at the high table.

The pain and tightness in her head increased with each course until Isabel knew she could not remain in the company of so many. Richard's polite comments and questions swirled around her, making no sense to her. She smiled and nodded as much as she could. Finally she closed her eyes and tried to block it all out.

"Isabel?"

She blinked several times trying to regain her focus and turned to face the lady.

"You look pale and tired. A breath of air before retiring may aid you in resting better this night. My lord," she said looking at her husband, "with your permission, I would ask Richard to escort our guest for a short walk before bringing her to my solar?"

"My lady, I thank you for your consideration, but I would like to retire now. By your leave, of course?"

Isabel stood and gathered her skirts, moving around the bench on which she sat and bowing to the lord and lady. The commander rose as she did and waited on his orders.

"'Tis a warm night. I would favor a walk after this supper as well, my lady." Lord Orrick smiled warmly at his wife as he spoke. True affection shone in his gaze as he considered Margaret's request. "Richard, to the chapel and back should not tax our guest too much on her first night out of her chambers."

Accepting that this was a command, Isabel returned their smiles with less enthusiasm and knew she was walking outside with Sir Richard whether or not she wanted to. Placing her hand on Richard's proffered arm, she allowed him to lead her down from the table and out through one of the side doors to the stairway. Without her voicing it, he seemed to know that she could not walk far or fast, and he slowed his pace even more on the steps.

It took hardly any time to reach the door to the courtyard and Isabel breathed in the cooler night air as they did. Using the walking stick and leaning little on his arm, they strolled between the keep and the smaller outbuildings. She could estimate the chapel's location from Edlyn's description earlier today, but her explorations had been limited to the inside of the keep and not out here. Soon they approached the stone chapel and Richard guided her through a gate in the fence surrounding it and to a bench next to the door.

"I know of your recent infirmity, um…"

"Please, call me Isabel," she said, sitting down on the seat. She knew of Lady Margaret's practice of familiarity, but she offered him her given, or taken, name since she knew not what else he should use.

"You must call me Richard, then." His pleasant smile and soft eyes made being in his company easier. Completely the opposite of Royce, he was personable and friendlier at the start. No, that wasn't quite a fair description of Royce.

"You cannot call me Richard?"

Isabel did not even realize she'd been shaking her head until he asked her. She bumbled through a reply.

"You have worked many hard hours to earn yourself the right to be called 'sir.' I would dishonor your accomplishments to call you less." Sir Richard warmed to her compliments and Isabel decided she was not above plying him with more of them to find out about those who lived at Silloth Keep. "Pray sit by me and tell me of your duties here in service to Lord Orrick."

Richard's eyes lit up with enthusiasm and in but a few minutes, she learned much about how things worked here. Richard and Royce shared the duties of overseeing keep and village and men for Lord Orrick. Richard's talents lay in provisions and provender, storehouses and salt production. Royce oversaw the safety of the family and the security of the keep and the training of the men-at-arms. They each led their own small company of men, hand selected, to guard or escort the lord or his lady when traveling, although Richard confided to her that Royce stayed much closer to Silloth while Richard himself preferred the longer journeys when necessary.

"And how did you come to serve Lord Orrick, Sir Richard? I have not heard you mention a connection by family." Isabel wanted to learn more about Royce and this would be her chance.

"I am the second son of one of Lord Orrick's vassals. My lord was pleased with my abilities when I fostered here and I pledged to him once I'd earned my spurs."

"And Royce? Did he foster here with you? You seem to be of an age…" She waited and hoped he would continue to share his knowledge with her.

"Royce has five more years than I, Isabel, but I have been here longer. Two years more than he." She heard a hint of something under his words. Anger? Jealousy? Something indiscernible to her right now, but it was there.

"Sir Royce is family, then?" Isabel offered the most reasonable explanation for favoring one man over another. "Or his wife is?" She nearly choked on the word, but it was an acceptable means of advancement.

"He wishes not to be called 'sir' although I am

quite sure he has been knighted." Richard rose and held out his arm to her. Mayhap she had pried too much with her questions? "And he is not married."

Isabel stood and positioned her walking stick, preparing herself for the walk back. Planning a retreat so as to not draw attention to her interest, she changed the topic and sought a safer one than Royce.

"I have heard that the lord and lady have a son?"

Richard nodded as he guided her steps back toward the keep. "Aye, little Alain is fostering with Lord Orrick's cousin near Chester."

"So far?"

"'Tis the only issue on which Lord Orrick has remained firm when it comes to indulging his ladywife." Richard lowered his voice in offering this confidence.

"How so?" Although Edlyn had explained that there was a son, it had also been made clear that he was not to be brought up to the lady. This might help explain why.

"Lady Margaret wanted to keep him here for another year, but Lord Orrick insisted 'twas past time for the boy to be set upon learning his skills.

There was an argument...." Richard's words faded off as he seemed to be remembering the words spoken. He looked back at her and finished the tale. "As is his right, Orrick sent him away and the lady was inconsolable, Alain being the only one of her three sons to survive to this age."

"'Tis the way of things," she answered, knowing it for the truth it was.

"Just so, Isabel. Now the lord grants every whim and wish his lady asks. Some say it is too much laxity in a man."

"And what say you, Richard? Is Orrick too lax with his wife?" Royce's voice broke into the conversation, startling both her and Richard.

"Royce, I heard not your approach." Richard's embarrassment at being overheard was clear in his expression. He stepped away from her and looked back and forth between Royce and her. "'Tis the lord's decision to make, of course. No one would question that."

Ah, but he had been and Royce had heard it. Would this cause a problem for Richard?

"I fear that my hunger for knowledge has caused Richard to misspeak. I asked of personal matters and Richard sought to give me answers."

When she looked into his eyes, it was as if they

were alone. The air between them crackled with the tension and the fury emanated from his very flesh. For a moment, she thought he was going to strike out.

"You push too hard and in the wrong directions, Isabel." The coldness of his voice belied the message in his eyes. He was angry, very angry, at her. This had little to do with the lord and lady's son; his words warned her about asking more about his past.

"I but seek the truth."

"You ask too much."

It was the flash of fear and vulnerability that she witnessed in the depths of his soul that made her flinch. He was not angry at some supposed breach of etiquette. He was terrified of her seeking out *his* truths, asking him for more than he could give. Gone in an instant, Isabel wondered if she had seen it at all. Richard, shifting his stance between them, drew her attention and she cleared her throat of its tightness.

"Sir Richard, I fear Lady Margaret is kept waiting for me in the solar. Mayhap 'tis time for you to take me there? Unless you would be so kind?" She turned to Royce.

"I have my duties to attend to, Isabel. And

Richard should carry out his." With a curt nod at them both, Royce turned and left.

Rebuffed again by his callousness, Isabel could not speak. Richard stepped closer and offered his arm. Accepting it, she walked silently back to the keep while considering Royce's words. The puzzling aspect of this was that she knew not why this tension existed between them. Looking up at Richard's profile as he guided her steps, she wondered at his reaction to this.

"Do not fret, Isabel. Royce is known for his dark temperament."

"And does he inflict it on everyone around him or are we special in some way to receive it?" A distinct sensation of being harassed by words came over her and Isabel grew frustrated at being a target. Where these feelings came from, she knew not, but they were real to her. Were they memories from her life?

Richard let out a deep, hearty laugh. "He shows us no favor by this. Indeed, everyone here has been gifted at some time by his…intensity."

"Not temper? Surely, he shows this not to Lord Orrick."

"I have worked with him in many situations these past three years and have rarely seen a temper flare with him. But, once on a task, he clings to it with a single-minded intensity that can border on obsession."

So she was simply an object of his obsession to carry out his duties. Found on Orrick's lands, she must be protected. There was nothing else between them, no matter how much she believed it so. Or how much she might want it.

Her head pounded once more and she ached for her bed and sleep. Ever the attentive host, Richard noticed her weariness.

"This has been too long a walk for you. I will escort you to your chamber and then tell Lady Margaret you are indisposed. Fear not, the lady is gracious and will not require your attendance on her if you are ill."

All Isabel could do was nod. The pain grew worse so she let Richard take her back to the chamber, where Edlyn awaited her. Assuring her that he would go directly to Lady Margaret with an explanation of her absence, the knight left her after bowing politely.

She endured the attentions of her maid only to hasten her descent into sleep. Within minutes, she undressed, washed and settled herself in bed and then waited for the growing silence of the keep and the night to soothe her to sleep. Edlyn would return later and share the small chamber. Still, this measure of privacy and luxury was a joy, unknown to most. Only the lord and lady enjoyed such privilege, if space were available for separate chambers.

Isabel felt herself falling into sleep's grasp when the visions came. Loud words shouted at her. Reprimands and rebukes, on and on until her head ached from them. Accusations of not fulfilling her duties, not completing the terms of an agreement. Not always in a man's voice, the haranguing went on, the tone never changed, the target never changed.

It was her. She failed at her duties. She failed to meet her part of the bargain. She failed to…

Trying to flee from the harsh blame aimed at her, Isabel ran until she found herself once more on the beach on that bright, sunny morning. Her sister grabbed her hands and they spun around and around until they were too dizzy to stand. Their gowns twisted around their legs, they fell back onto the sand and laughed. They tried to stand and ended up rolling on the beach until their maid stopped them.

Pulling them to their feet, she shouted at them

to stop their foolishness. Her face, always kind, changed into something monstrous and scary. Her hands became claws, clutching and tearing Isabel's skin as she tried to pull away. Then Isabel saw the dagger ripping her gown and felt its burning path through skin and down into her core. Struggling against the attack, she pulled herself away and tried to run.

The first blow broke her leg. She screamed at the anguish that cut through her as the club snapped the bone and threw her to the ground. Staying meant death and she was not ready to die. Pushing herself up, she dragged her body along until she could use a sturdy bush to stand.

They laughed at her efforts. So many of them. Her hair had come loose in the chase and she pushed it out of her face so she could see their attack coming. Panic threatened to overwhelm her as she faced her death. Then the scene froze and a different voice came to her.

"I will always be there for you."

"And I for you," she answered as always. 'Twas the pledge of two sisters. The words of promise spoken over joined hands by two who had shared the same womb, the same birth.

They were twins.

Isabel came awake in an instant. Covered with sweat and with her chest heaving raggedly, she tried to remember the dream, or rather the memories. Her stomach rolled and bile threatened as the visions faded and her tears fell. Isabel despaired of ever seeing her sister again. Remembering her only as a child helped not, for she did not resemble the dark-haired girl in the dreams.

Tugging away the blankets that covered her, Isabel climbed out of bed. A moment of fear engulfed her as she felt the spasms in her leg and thought it broken again. Waiting for them to subside, she sat on the edge of the bed and wiped the tears from her eyes.

How could she continue in this way? Would her life ever be her own again? Her thoughts jumbled and she felt brainsick from it. Would she never sleep in peace again? Standing now, she straightened her sleeping gown and tried to replace the covers on the bed in some semblance of order. Edlyn had not returned yet, so Isabel knew that no more than an hour had passed.

She then walked over to the small window that was covered with wooden shutters and pushed them open. Peering out into the night, she could hear the sounds of the ocean on the other side of the keep's wall.

With its place high on a sea cliff, Silloth Keep commanded a strategic place at the opening of the Solway Firth. With one side facing the sea and three sides guarded by hill and wall, it was also formidable against attack. Edlyn had told her that on a clear night, the lights from fires on the Scottish side of the firth could be seen.

Watching the fog moving across the courtyard, Isabel wondered how she could survive in this purgatory. When no answer came to her, she tugged the shutters closed and climbed back into her bed, hoping that a less fitful night awaited her.

The expression on the guard's face told him that the young soldier had considered refusing his order to open the gate. The hesitation lasted only a moment after William strode into the light of the torches that were set in the wall next to the barred doors. The standing orders were that none left the keep after the gate was closed and barred, but since he'd been the one to issue those orders, the soldier must have realized that to gainsay would be useless.

William waited until the gate had been secured

and then walked through the village and down the path that would lead to his cottage. Hoping to burn out some of his frustration, he jogged a part of the way. Every time his thoughts turned back to the sight of her, he knew that putting some distance between them was the best of ideas.

Seeing her at the table with Margaret and Orrick and their other guests renewed his belief that she was born to the high table. Then he witnessed her growing paler until she closed her eyes and he thought she'd fainted. Lady Margaret recognized her distress just in time, for he was about to leave his place, hidden from Isabel's sight by the crowd, to take her to her chambers.

What would she think if she knew that he had watched her as much as he could since turning over her custody to the lord and lady? William admitted to himself that he'd created errands and duties that kept him close to her in the past five days. After telling himself that ridding himself of her presence would repair the damage she had done, he added that to the long list of lies he'd told to himself and others since he had found her that night two months ago.

When he had followed Isabel and Richard too closely, his blood had boiled at their light and teasing tones. He found his hands fisted and even discovered one on the hilt of his sword. This physical reaction to her had to stop. He was losing more of his control with each day, and soon there would be so little left as to not signify.

He forced his feet to walk out of Silloth Keep every night for fear of following her to her chambers and kissing her the way he wanted to. He closed his eyes and looked away when he saw her talking to another man, especially Richard, since women seemed to find both his manners and his appearance pleasing.

She was temptation incarnate to him and he thought more than once that he would have to leave Silloth, to leave the people who had accepted him and the place that had given him sanctuary in his time of need. If she did not remember her life and return to it, he would not be responsible when the time came and the facade broke, freeing the monster he knew truly lived in his soul…the one who would not be denied anything, anyone he wanted. The fiend without conscience, without a soul, who had destroyed innocents in his quest for power and wealth.

Once in his cottage, with his gear stowed and

his preparations for night completed, he reached for his protection, the only thing that seemed to still hold sway over his emotions and over the evil that he knew still lived within him. William carefully opened the top two letters from the reverend mother and took a deep breath to ready himself for the pain that always came with reliving the life he had damned his sister to with his actions.

Hours later, after burning several costly candles, his soul was still not at peace. The pain that usually cleansed him was fading and he feared its power would be replaced by something else, something he'd avoided for just over three years, something that would alter his life in an unpredictable way.

"He follows her whene'er he can."

Orrick watched from a place high atop the keep as Royce trailed many paces behind Isabel. From here on the roof, he could see at least a league in all directions on a clear, sunny day. His courtyard he could see on any day. Now he stood and waited for his ladywife to make her thoughts known on this situation.

"And she hungers for any mention or sight of him, but will not say his name."

"Hungers? Then this will pass as other passions do?" Orrick turned to his Margaret. "He has had other women."

"He has not had her."

Orrick was surprised by this. Anyone with half a brain and a pair of eyes could see the fire between Royce and Isabel. Surely his commander had… "You think not? Is that the problem, then?"

Margaret walked to his side, but would not look over the short wall that formed the edge of the towering keep. A fear from childhood kept her from enjoying the perspective he gained from these heights.

"There is more than one problem here, husband. They belong together."

"And that's a problem, Margaret? I see none, then, between them." He was goading her plain and simple, he knew, but he was losing his patience with the man he'd come to trust and this unknown woman who was upsetting Royce's life. He smiled when his wife whispered something under her breath, something foreign about men.

"He does not see her for the soul mate she is to him. He sees only the threat." She was gritting her teeth now.

"Most women are threats to men in one way or another, my dear." Orrick was pleased when she began to swear at him in French. The signs of her temper being riled were pleasing to him, for when full of life and emotions, Margaret intoxicated him. These months without Alain had saddened her deeply and it pleased him to see her take an interest in something or in someone finally, even if it presented difficulties in managing.

When her words involved slicing off certain male body parts, he grabbed for her and pulled her into his arms. She was startled but did not resist his embrace or his fervent kisses.

"If you do that, my love, think of the hours and hours of pleasure you would deny us."

When she opened her mouth to argue, he kissed her deeply, his tongue tasting her as he plundered her lips. He felt her surrender to him and pulled her closer to stand between his legs so that she could feel the effect she had on him, even after their years together. Their passion, each for the other, once inflamed those many years ago had not waned at all.

Before he lost the capability to speak, he remembered their subject. With his hands on her shoulders, he leaned her away from him. "And what of him to her?"

Margaret took several breaths before answering. Ah, he thought with a strong sense of manly pride, he had not lost the ability to stir his wife's feelings.

"She would be more to him, but she cannot until she knows her past." Margaret released his hauberk and stepped farther from his grasp. "And she shows no sign of remembering it."

"None? She remembers nothing?" Orrick had never seen anything like this before, in spite of Wenda being familiar with the condition.

"Daily life, she remembers. How to make candles and soap, how to tend the garden and which herbs do what, she remembers. But whose daughter or sister or wife she is, she does not."

He was going to ask about her methods when she stopped him with a look. "I have taken her into the village and we have watched many of our people in their duties. I have exposed her to names and to the many responsibilities of a lady and she knows much, but knows little."

"And now? What do you plan now?"

"It depends on you, my lord husband."

He knew he was in trouble now. She never called him that unless she was dragging him into some scheme of hers. "Go on," he said, waiting for her to disclose the details to him.

"If her memory does not return, she has two choices. She could marry." Margaret paused and the glint in her eyes warned him in advance that he would object to this coming portion of her plan. "If you or I would claim her as a distant cousin, a suitable husband could be found for her. Probably right within your own knights."

"You would have me count a complete stranger as my own? For what purpose other than subterfuge and deceit?"

"Because Royce needs her. She is the burst of life he has been running from during these years in service to you." Margaret's brows tilted and her eyes gazed into his with a soft look that promised much. "Or she would make Richard or even Hugh a good wife."

He burst out laughing as he realized her real plan. Richard and Hugh were simply distractions.

"So Royce is your true target of all these machinations, then? But you mentioned two choices. What was the other?"

Margaret smoothed her gown down and rearranged her headpiece. "She could enter the convent."

Orrick laughed out loud again and earned another disgruntled look from his ladywife. “And tell me, fair Margaret, which convent would you suggest she enter?” He crossed his arms over his chest and tapped his foot.

“Fine. Fine!” she shouted. “You can see my plan, but I will say it anyway. I think that she could enter the Gilbertine Abbey outside Carlisle. She could live as a lay sister until she knows if she is clear of conscience to take vows or not.”

Where her sister was abbess. ‘Twould give Margaret another reason to spend more time away from him and he would not give her that. Better to seek a husband for the lady than to put her away in a convent. He did have several suitable men to suggest, men high in his regard whom he could gift with land when they married.

“I think we should consider suitable husbands for the lady and wait until her memory returns before forcing any decision on her part.”

She looked as though she would fight him on this, but he stopped her with a pointed finger. “You will yield to me on this, Margaret. ‘Tis my decision as lord.”

Margaret capitulated to his power and nodded her head. “I accept your decision, my lord husband." She took a few steps toward the stairwell and turned to him before entering it. "My solar is empty now, my lord, if you would like to join me there?"

The soft swing of her hips and the seductive wink she gave him caused an immediate reaction within him. He lost all thoughts of decisions and could only think of sinking into the softness she offered and claiming her once more as his own. A niggling suspicion, and one that lasted but a few moments, worked its way into his thoughts. Had he fallen into some trap she'd set for him?

And as the promise of passion became a reality, he knew for a certainty that she had let him think it was all his idea. But, at the moment when their bodies joined and their hearts beat as one, Orrick could think of nothing but his lovely Marguerite.

Chapter Twelve

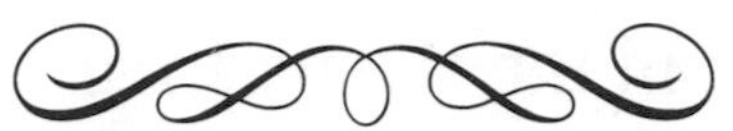

"Come, Isabel. There is an easy path down to the beach over here."

The tall, blond knight waved to her and she touched her heels to her horse's sides to make it follow him. Sir Hugh's invitation to ride on this sunny afternoon promised a chance away from the scrutiny of those who lived in the keep and so she accepted it with little delay.

Isabel trailed Hugh and his larger stallion down the path that led away from the keep and down to the beach. On one side of the keep, this beach was more sand than rocks. Once the land curved around the keep, only rocks and boulders and a sharp cliff lay between the sea and the tower.

The rays of the sun hit her as they came out of the shadows of the tree-lined path and she tilted her face to the heat and light. She longed to tear off the headpiece that covered her hair and her stockings and shoes and run bareheaded and barefooted through the warm sand. That, however, was not acceptable behavior for a lady and especially not with this knight in her presence. So she contented herself with walking and breathing in the fresh sea air.

Hugh carried with him a large cloth and a basket of food, generously suggested by Lady Margaret. The lady knew that meals, in the great hall with so many around her, were taxing Isabel's strength and had recommended this quiet, informal meal to her. Hugh spread the cloth over the sand and assisted her in sitting down. After arranging herself and her skirts, he handed her the basket of food.

Isabel examined the knight as she placed the roasted chicken, haddock, hard cheese and brown bread on a trencher between them. As was expected, he tore off pieces of each of the foods and served them back to her. A fine example of knighthood and gentlemanly behavior.

He was fair to gaze upon, she decided, and his manners and treatment of her were filled with concern and care. With his blond hair and mustache and tall, muscular form, he was all things in a man that a woman would want in a husband. And although he was a second son like Sir Richard, they were both of noble birth and from good families.

Isabel shook her head. Why was she thinking of these things? Marriage? It had no place in her life now. Until she discovered whether or not she was bound to another, she could make no promises or commitments. Lady Margaret had other ideas and she knew what they were, but without a clear conscience, Isabel would not even hear any discussion of marriage.

"I've been uncaring, haven't I?" Hugh said. "The sun is directly in your face." He rose and repositioned the food and then her so that she could look on him without squinting.

"Your concern is most welcome, Sir Hugh."

"Isabel, you must call me Hugh. Here with you, I am simply a man, not a knight."

This was heading off in a direction that Isabel did not intend to go. "But you are a knight, whether we are together and alone or not. However, when we are sharing an informal meal as this one is, I will call you Hugh."

He seemed placated by this compromise, for he

smiled. "I understand, Isabel. Formality and manners are all you have to guide you at this time of uncertainty in your life. You must cling to what you know while you seek out the truth of your life."

Now she was certain—Lady Margaret was behind this after all. Hugh had repeated her words almost exactly. The lady was setting up these encounters and counseling the knights of her household in how to treat her and the limits of her health and her knowledge of her past. Isabel was also sure that Lady Margaret was not sharing this personal information with the rest of her household. To do so could invite ridicule and embarrassment to Isabel and she knew the lady wanted no such thing.

But this new attempt to break free her memories was disconcerting to her, for it encouraged these good knights to think of her as a candidate for marriage. Isabel was filled with unease about this.

"I do not seek to speak of something so personal," Hugh said softly. "I simply wanted you to know that I am mindful of your situation." He picked up a small slice of cheese and offered it to her. "For today, pray leave your worries behind and enjoy the sunshine and this food."

Deciding to accept his offer of a truce, Isabel reached for the food and enjoyed their meal. The rest of it passed in a companionable silence. After sharing some of the sweet comfits packed in with their food, Hugh asked her to walk. He stood and helped her to her feet. Feeling quite daring, she paused to tug off her shoes and stockings and wiggled her toes in the sand. If she shocked him with such behaviors, he did not show it.

She led him down to the water's edge and, after gathering the length of her skirts up, she ran into the icy waves. Isabel indulged herself for only a few minutes and then walked back to where Hugh stood watching.

"I would end up with wet, sagging hose if I followed your example." He pointed down to his knee-high boots and the hose that she knew began at his feet and continued up to his waist.

"I have wanted to do that ever since I saw how close to the beach Silloth Keep was." Using her hand to guard her eyes from the sun's glare, she peered up at the top of the sea cliff to where the tall stone tower sat. "Look. Someone is on top of it." She pointed to the small figure she could see walking on the roof of the keep.

"'Tis either Lord Orrick or Royce. The view

from there is good and on a clear day, you can see to the edges of Lord Orrick's lands."

"He can see us?" She suspected it was Royce watching them from high above.

"The entire beach can be seen, as well as most of the cliff," Hugh explained. "To the north and east you can see all the way to the salt marshes."

Images of the dark, swampy land, with the icy water sucking her down filled her mind. The rancid smells filled her nose again. The cries of the curlew and loon filled the air around her as she struggled to escape the grip of the water. Pain and terror threatened to overwhelm her....

"Isabel?" He shook her again. "Isabel? Speak to me."

She blinked several times and realized Hugh was holding her by the shoulders and gently shaking her. "I am fine now. Truly," she said, pulling back from his grasp. "My thanks for your concern."

But she was not fine. The nightmares were now invading the daylight hours, haunting her even when she was awake. Would she ever discover their message and have peace?

"You are pale and shivering, Isabel. Come, I will escort you back, for Lady Margaret will have my head if she thinks I have caused you ill."

She did not argue with him but only stood and watched as he gathered up the remnants of their meal and packed it in the basket. Then he guided her to the horses at the edge of the beach and helped her to mount. Her throat tightened and her eyes burned with tears at the ruin of such a beautiful day. Clinging to the reins, she retreated into her thoughts and tried to make sense of the scene she'd witnessed.

'Twas not the first time the marsh had appeared in her dreams. The smells and sounds so clearly told her that her attack had happened there. But who were her assailants? Why? As had happened before, the harder she tried to sort out the memories, the faster they slipped from her grasp. She wanted to scream out her frustration, but this was neither the time nor place to do it. If Hugh was already alarmed by her actions, that would send him in search of a priest to exorcise the demons from her.

Isabel pulled her thoughts together and tried to calm herself on the ride up the path to the keep. Getting upset would gain her nothing. She must remain calm when these memories broke through or she would not be able to remain here. Lady Margaret had suggested that she consider visiting her sister's convent on the other side of Carlisle. Mayhap she should think on that suggestion more carefully, for alerting the rest of the people here to her lack of a past and to the heinous attack she'd suffered would put her in more danger.

William was waiting for them as they entered through the gates. Isabel's color was poor and anyone could see she was upset by something. When he had seen Hugh lay hands on her from his perch on top of the keep, his blood had boiled and the roar in his ears was louder than even the crashing of the waves on the beach. He tried to convince himself that Lady Margaret would never have permitted this interlude if she thought that Hugh would take advantage of Isabel.

From the looks of it, the lady had been wrong.

William fisted and released his hands as he strode over to where they dismounted. Hugh continued his sham act of courtesy, even assisting Isabel from her horse, until William approached. Grabbing his shoulder, he shoved the man out of the way to get a closer look at Isabel.

"The lady is unwell, Royce," Hugh argued, shoving back. "Give her space."

William wheeled and pushed him again; this

time his blow made Hugh slip back away from her. "And what part did you play in this? Did you press your suit too ardently? I saw you grab her on the beach." William clenched his jaw and waited for the denial.

"So, 'twas you watching us from the roof. And what else did your eagle eyes spy?"

That was all the goading he could take. He threw the first punch and was pleased to see Hugh land in the dirt some feet away. William then jumped onto the knight and pummeled him thoroughly. When some of the anger within him was quelled, he got to his feet and dusted off his hands. Hugh would not accost Isabel again, he was certain of it.

Isabel.

Isabel?

Where had the woman gone? She did not look as though she possessed the strength to walk off, but it appeared she had. Looking at the faces in the crowd that gathered around him, he could not see her. Pushing his way through them, he searched the courtyard again and still there was no sign of her.

She could not have disappeared into the air. She looked so pale and so lifeless he could not have imagined her going anywhere without help.

"You there," he called out as he pointed to one of the kitchen servants. "Where did the lady go?" He motioned back to the riderless horse. Shrugs and more shrugs were the answers he received.

He felt his control slipping. Like the day he had returned to his empty cottage after learning that outlaws had been reported on Orrick's lands. Nowhere, she was nowhere to be found. Again. His chest tightened and his breathing labored as he tried to find her.

"Isabel!" he yelled. When those around him quieted more, he called out again, even louder. "ISABEL!" Everyone in the courtyard stopped and stared and he knew he was acting like a madman, but he needed to find her.

"The chapel, sir. I think she went into the chapel." A soft voice spoke behind him and he whirled around to find its source. A young girl stood before him, eyes wide with fear.

"My thanks," he said.

He noticed the stares and the silence and knew he had let his anger and worry get out of control. Waving them on, he urged the onlookers back to their duties and ran to the chapel to see if Isabel was there.

Vaulting over the low stone wall, he approached

the door. Taking in and releasing a deep breath, William pulled the door open and peered into the dim coolness of the church. A small figure sat on one of the benches against the side wall. With a sigh of relief, he entered and walked to where she sat.

She gave no sign of hearing him come near. With her eyes closed and her head leaning against the wall, she looked to be asleep. 'Twas then he noticed the dark smudges under her eyes, making her skin look even paler. He could not fight the urge to smooth his thumb over them and, as he did so, he prayed they would go away.

"Leave me be," she whispered.

Of all the things he thought she'd say, that was not one of them. "I sought only to help you, Isabel. You do not look well."

"You beat Sir Hugh to a bloody pulp to help me?"

Put in that manner, his actions did not seem to make sense. But William knew his reaction had been sound. If Hugh had not yet overstepped the bounds of good behavior with Isabel, it would happen soon. And now Hugh had a clear understanding of the consequences of such actions.

"He needed to know his place." There. He had

explained it to her. She would realize the correctness in his reaction to seeing her upset.

"And shall I warn Sir Richard not to share the evening meal with me for fear of being attacked by you? Will all those who eat supper with me be in danger of a thrashing by Orrick's captain of the guard?" She opened her eyes. "Shall I warn my maid not to come too close?"

"Isabel, 'tis not like that." She must see that he did it for her. Did she not know she was trembling when she rode through the gate with Hugh? Could she not see that he was there to help her? "I but tried to help you."

"You ignore me and shun my company and conversation for a week and now you want to help me? Forgive me for being dense and not understanding."

William winced at the sarcasm in her voice. Stated as she had, his behavior did sound bad. But that was not the way it was for him. He had fought off the desire to speak with her and to be near her. Every night he forced himself to leave before the evening meal, for watching her with the others, especially the knights who Lady Margaret encouraged to pay her attention, was tearing him apart. Some nights, still craving the sight of her, he stood outside the hall and watched her from the darkness.

Could he tell her that? She should not think that his actions were of her making. Isabel had enough problems and did not need him heaping more on her. The urge, the need to tell her the truth grew and he wanted more than anything to share his burden with her. Swallowing against the words, he focused on regaining control over himself and over the feelings she engendered in him.

"I pray you will believe me, Isabel. I do not ignore you."

She did not take her gaze from his and 'twas clear that she was waiting for more. He could not give her that which she wanted, so he changed the subject.

"You do not look well. Are you not resting?"

Something flared within her depths and he watched as she accepted the limit he had placed between them. Closing her eyes again, she leaned back again.

"No."

"You look tired now." He stepped closer and sat next to her. He tugged off his leather gauntlets and took her hand in his. William knew the cause of her exhaustion. "The nightmares keep you from sleeping?"

She blinked several times, fighting off the tears he could see gathering in her eyes.

"Come, I will take you back to the keep. You should rest." He began to stand, drawing her with him, but she pulled her hand from his.

"I was enjoying the quiet here, Royce. You can leave if you do not wish to be in my company."

When he looked into her eyes, though, he read the silent plea within them. He sat back down and moved closer to her. Taking her hand and guiding it under and around his arm, he tugged her until she rested her head against his shoulder.

He did not bother her with words. He allowed the silence to grow and when he felt her slump against him, he knew that sleep was finally overtaking her. Sitting with her, he simply waited, trying not to examine this too closely for the discomfort it would cause him.

Sometime later, the door of the chapel opened and Edlyn entered. With a finger to his lips, he warned her to keep silent. With another motion of his hand, he dismissed her. After an initial expression of surprise, she turned and left.

He shifted on the bench, drew Isabel closer and

relaxed back against the wall. Then, resting his chin lightly on her head, he waited for her to wake.

"They are where?"

His wife shushed him, but he could not help being surprised. Many reports had been given him of the scene in the courtyard on Hugh and Isabel's return. Including that of the disappearance of Isabel and Royce shortly after the fistcuffs occurred.

"In the chapel, my lord." Isabel's maid lowered her eyes to the floor.

"Asleep, you say? In the chapel?" Orrick could not understand this. "You saw them there?"

"Aye, my lord. He was awake the first time I went in, but not the second."

He thought to ask her again to make certain she was telling the truth, but Margaret intervened and, after cautioning her not to carry tales about her mistress, dismissed her to wait on Isabel's return.

"What think you of this, Margaret?" Orrick knew his wife had already made up her mind on how this would work out. "I cannot remember Royce ever losing control before. I have seen him in battle and under pressure and not once has he acted thus. I even thought him devoid of emotions."

"Not empty of them, Orrick. He has too many and too much within himself and thinks to control them by cutting himself off from the world. For three years he has succeeded. Until Isabel turned up at his door in need of him."

Orrick walked to his wife and sat in the chair next to hers. "Has he revealed his past to you?"

"He has told me nothing that he has not told you."

"Is this a wise thing to do? The meddling in their lives?"

"As I said to Royce, she was delivered to him for a reason. Either for his good or hers or both. 'Tis our task to discover the reasons."

"You have spent too much time at that convent. You are sounding like a philosopher or worse, a nun." Orrick knew he'd gone too far, but her more frequent absences were not to his liking.

"Would you change our agreement, then?" Margaret's lips tightened as she waited for his reply.

"I would never go back on my word, Margaret. But I must say that I have no liking for the ever-increasing time you spend there."

"There is so much less for me here. And Genevieve understands."

He knew her heart was broken without her son

here. But an order from the queen could not be denied.

"I am here," Orrick whispered, taking her hand in his and squeezing it. "And your duties to this household have not stopped or lessened with Alain's departure." She stared off at the wall and would not give him the agreement he wanted to hear from her.

"You are my strength in this, Orrick. Never think otherwise." He felt her hand squeeze his in return. "I just cannot bear the thought of my son being under the queen's scrutiny without me there to protect him." She faced him now and her eyes were bleak. "I paid the high cost of my sins against her. Why does she still seek to punish me for the transgressions of my youth?"

He decided to turn her fears and make them work for her. "Do you say that you fear her? Marguerite the Fair of Alençon? You who stood boldly before her even when she knew the truth? Bah! I cannot believe you would buckle to her now."

His words lit a spark in her, for she sat up straighter and took a deep breath. When she met his eyes again, he could see that her determination to be strong, even if only on her son's account, was growing within her.

"You have no idea how much I love you." Tears rolled down her cheeks and he reached out to wipe them.

"And you always have my love." Mayhap something in the water was making everyone in the keep so maudlin? Or was it the emptiness he also felt for their son?

"Not always, husband." Margaret tugged a square of linen from her sleeve and finished dabbing at her eyes.

"Ah, but forever after that day. As I promised." Orrick leaned over and kissed her softly on the mouth.

Neither spoke for some minutes. He needed to regain his composure as much as his wife did. He decided to try to bring her attention back to the matter at hand—discord among his knights over this woman.

"What is your next step to bring Royce to his knees…to the realization that he needs this woman as much as she needs him?"

Orrick winked at her as he purposely stumbled over his words. She needed something to give her attention to and if it was two lovesick fools who knew no better, then so be it. At least it would keep her busy and *here.*

She cleared her throat. "I think that Royce should take the place he deserves as captain of your guards and commander of your defenses. Mayhap at your table tonight? What say you, my lord husband?"

He laughed out loud. Royce stood no chance now that his wife was on the march. No one, not even this man who had held himself apart from all, could withstand Marguerite of Alençon when she was determined. Henry Plantagenet had never been able to and this man was no Henry.

Chapter Thirteen

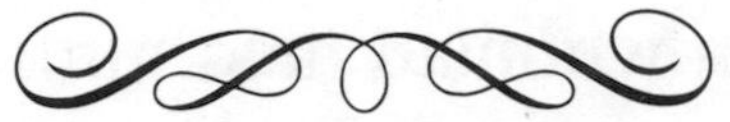

Devilment was in the air at Silloth Keep. Led by its lord and lady, they all turned against William, and the progress he'd made in these last years was for naught. Every bit of separation between him and them came crashing down in the next week.

First, his presence at meals was commanded. When this order was directed at all four of the other knights in residence, he thought that mayhap he was not the object of the lady's scheming. Then, Orrick suggested, commanded rather, that William move into a chamber on the second floor across the corridor from the great hall. The worst was Lady Margaret's grooming directives. Then he knew he was the true target, for Richard, Hugh and the others already met with Margaret's approval.

All of the knights who attended meals must be

dressed appropriately, she said. When he argued that he never claimed that title, the black look on her face truly scared him. She proclaimed that court style demanded no beards and shorter hair. His expression must have been suitably dark, for she softened that demand a bit. No chain mail at table, no filthy boots, no crude talk. When Lord Orrick did not gainsay her, William was convinced that the lord was indulging his lady too much.

William had planned on wearing the better of his surcoats the first night, but when he arrived in his newly assigned chambers, there were three new ones in his chest. The biggest surprise was a boy named Cadby. Even though the boy stuttered nervously, William understood his orders clearly—this was his new page. And in spite of his young appearance and stammering speech, Cadby stood his ground even when William yelled for him to be gone.

He had cornered Lord Orrick and demanded an explanation on the second day. One never-ending meal, filled with niceties and mindless chatter was more than any man could endure and he was determined to put a quick end to this. And since his chamber was in the midst of all the activity of the keep, never was there a moment of quiet, except in the deepest part of the night when all lay sleeping somewhere else.

"My lord? A word, please?" William had followed Lord Orrick to the roof of the keep. 'Twas a place they used often for consultations, since neither the height nor the wind bothered either of them.

"Royce. Come, have a look over here." He walked to the edge of the northern side of the keep and looked where Orrick pointed. "I think we should fortify that section of wall next."

After a few minutes of discussing the defenses, William broached the true matter at hand.

"My lord, I would speak of our agreement. Have I not lived up to my part of it, serving you as you require and swearing fealty to you?"

"You have been ever vigilant on my behalf, Royce. How have I failed you, for your words give rise to that accusation?"

"I did not mean an insult, my lord. I am simply saying that I am used to my privacy and find that moving into the keep, and the other changes instituted by your ladywife, are making that difficult." Had he just insulted Lady Margaret? This was not going as he'd like it to go.

"Margaret felt that some conditions needed to change."

"And I am one of those conditions? I need not her attentions." William rubbed his hand over his face. He had slept little in this new chamber, with noises around him and the little snorer sleeping by his door.

"You would rather live in a hovel in the forest than here in some measure of comfort?"

"There is payment due for these comforts, my lord, and I fear I am unwilling to pay it."

How could he make Orrick understand? He could not risk accepting these things, for soon he would be accustomed to them again and then he would begin to covet that which he did not have. Only deprivation and a solitary existence gave him the strength to control the miscreant who lived within him.

"I ask not for your soul, Royce. Only that you be clean of face and wear the garments I provide when you sit at my table. Is that too high a price to pay?"

William turned and began to walk away when Orrick spoke to him. "Damn me, but I love her, Royce. She is withering without Alain and I would do anything in my power to rouse her spirits. Can you not cooperate until Alain's return? A short time, to be sure."

He knew there was no time frame for Alain to return to Silloth and his parents. "My lord, if I could go to Chester and bring your son home, I would. But we know that is not going to happen until the queen decides otherwise." William did not know the particulars but could recognize another Plantagenet plot when he saw it. And Eleanor had taught all of her sons the fine points of a good scheme.

"No. You are correct, Royce. 'Tis by the queen's order that Alain was called and 'twill be her order to send him home."

Orrick's face clouded and he walked away from William after that admission. He was certain that the boy was safe. Oh, Eleanor was pulling strings and keeping the parents in line, but William did not think she would make the child suffer for something she blamed on his parents.

Now John was another story.

He followed Orrick once more. They stopped on the section of wall that overlooked the courtyard. In silence, the two men watched as Lady Margaret, Isabel and several other women made their way back from the village to the keep.

"Once our guest comes back to herself or submits herself to the convent, Margaret will relent. For now she needs to believe she is helping."

"Convent? Isabel would seek the convent?" This was new. He had never really considered her options if her memory did not return. Of course, even when it returned, she may need to seek the sanctuary of convent walls to protect her from those who would cause her harm.

"I do not claim to know how it will turn out for her, but I know that for the first time in months, Margaret is interested in something. I ask you to cooperate for this short time."

William heard the plea of a friend, not the order of a liege lord, in Orrick's words. Orrick had offered him a place to live and duties to fulfill and saved his life in so many other ways. In spite of the danger to his own soul, he would do this for the lord and lady. 'Twas the least he could do.

"I would have your permission to seek refuge from time to time in my *hovel*." At Orrick's nod, he joked, "And I fear that I have forgotten the manners of high tables."

"Nay. Once bred into you, those never leave." William startled at his words. What did Orrick know of him?

Orrick clapped William on the back and laughed. "I have never asked of your past and will not begin to do so now. You have nothing to fear from me."

As they walked to the stairwell, William felt fear deep inside his soul. He would see her every day. Not only that, they would interact in many ways each and every day. He must tell himself that it was a temporary thing—as soon as her memory returned, he would have his life back again. Fear dragged an icy finger down his spine as, for the first time in three years, he was not certain which life he wanted back.

"Know that I would never keep you in my service should you desire to leave, Royce." Orrick held his attention as he spoke. "You saved my life and I sought to reward your actions by offering you a place here. If you cannot stay, I will accept that."

He knew he must choose at that moment and he knew how much the cost would be. But just as something had put his feet on that path one night over two months ago, something pushed him once more to agree. God help him if this did not work out.

"I will stay."

* * *

That declaration had been made two days ago and he regretted ever letting the words leave his mouth. Due to being called away at times by his responsibilities, he was placed at the end of the table at meals. From his seat, he could see everything Isabel did and everyone she spoke to and even what foods she ate or was fed by the obliging male at her side. He could also see she was in distress.

At each meeting, her eyes seemed more haunted and the black smudges darkened each day. She was not sleeping. He overheard Edlyn telling Lady Margaret of the nightmares and screaming that woke her several times each night. Wenda was called and offered different brews, but none worked for her.

Isabel did her best to take part in the midday meal, but he watched as she began refusing the morsels offered to her. Her appetite was affected as well as her sleep. She needed rest. Remembering their encounter of a few days before, he knew what to do.

Rising from his seat, he explained his plan to Orrick, who nodded approval. Making his way down the dais, he stood at her side and held out his hand.

"Walk with me." He knew it sounded more like an order than a request, but he could not soften everything about himself.

Isabel glanced at the lord and lady, waiting for their approval, and at their gestures, she looked back at him. "I am in the midst of a conversation with Sir Richard. I wish to stay."

She was playing some game, for not even her refusal carried much conviction. He moved his hand closer and repeated his words, trying to ask this time.

"Walk with me, Isabel."

This time she lifted the napkin from her lap and laid it on the table. Standing, she placed her hand on his arm and followed him as he guided her away. Soon they stood before the chapel.

"I thought you could use the quiet of the church for a short time."

They had not spoken of their last visit here. He assumed she was too embarrassed or proud to admit her need to him or to acknowledge his care of her. She turned to face him before he could open the gate.

"You do not need to do this, Royce."

"I think that I do."

"I am in Lady Margaret's care now. Your responsibility for me is finished."

"This is not about responsibility, Isabel."

He saw her chin go up and her eyes hardened. "You have washed your hands of me and I can accept that, Royce. But please do not play with me this way."

Surprised by her words, he stood and watched her walk through the now-opened gate and into the chapel. Without him. Well, she would not have the last word in this. Especially when she was wrong.

She took refuge in the back corner of the church, far away from the altar and the windows behind it. Even with the midday sun shining outside, this room tended to remain darkened and it suited her mood right now. She'd discovered the truth about Royce and it was better if they not have anything to do with each other. She could not count on him to help her any longer.

He walked in and stood at the door. When he saw her, his long strides brought him there in only two paces. Confronted by well over six feet of angry male, she backed up against the wall until she could move no more. Isabel looked up from his chest, higher and higher until she met his eyes, his very angry eyes. She could not suppress the shiver of fear that pulsed through her for he could hurt her with just a blow of his hand.

At that moment, Royce reeled back as though struck himself. Turning away from her, he walked a short distance before facing her once more. "You believe I could strike you?"

"No!"

"Your look said differently, Isabel." His voice softened. "I would never harm you."

She swallowed once and then again, and tried to make him understand. "I felt overwhelmed. By your height, by your strength, by your nearness."

"I will never harm you, Isabel." He repeated his words and they sounded more like a vow to her.

She nodded and accepted them. But she'd heard so many other things. That it was his idea to move her to the keep. That he guarded his privacy almost to obsession and did not want her in his cottage, invading his place. That he only came to meals and only spoke to her when ordered by the lord.

"Is bringing me here simply another of your duties?"

"What are you talking about, Isabel?" He looked as confused as she felt. She wanted to be more than that to him and yet, at the same time, she had no right to be. No right to even think about those kinds of things.

"I have heard that your compunction to carry out your duties is the thing that guides your life. Is that true?"

"I have not thought on it in those terms, Isabel. But, yes, I feel a deep responsibility to fulfill my commitments." She watched as he frowned. "Is that what you are asking?"

"Did you keep me in your cottage only on orders from Orrick? Did you bring me here on his orders? Do you stay at meals and live in the keep only on his word?"

"Aye. No. Both? Neither?" He let out a deep breath and walked over to her. "'Tis no secret that I live alone. I prefer to and chose to three years ago when Orrick took me into his service. Yes, your arrival was an upheaval for me. No, I have not dealt well with it." He reached out and lifted her chin with his finger so that their gazes met. "This, however, I do in disregard of orders and for no one but myself."

His mouth covered hers and all she could feel was the desire and heat pouring from him into her. His lips were firm on hers, pressing against hers, then she felt the tip of his tongue run over her bottom lip. When she chuckled at the tickling sensation, he took advantage and dipped inside to taste more of her mouth. She clutched at his surcoat to keep her balance as the kiss went on and on.

'Twas only when she realized that he was not, other than their mouths, touching her, that she dragged her lips from his and leaned back against the wall and looked at him. In spite of what she knew was mutual enjoyment, he did not appear to be happy. The magical moment passed quickly. Royce stood back and walked away. Sitting on the bench they had shared the last time they visited here together, he looked at her with bleak eyes.

"That was wrong."

"Was it? It did not feel wrong to me."

She knew what he meant, but for that one moment when their mouths met, she knew it was him kissing her. Not a man in service carrying out an order or doing something as a favor to a friend. A man and a woman. And, as it had in the past weeks, that realization brought them both to their senses. He patted the bench beside him and she sat next to him.

"I do have some soft feelings for you, Isabel,

but you must know that there can be nothing more between us. Can you admit that much?"

"I am not asking you to…"

"You ask more than I can give you. Even if not for the loss of your memories of the life you had before the attack, I cannot offer you more. I have wished on many occasions since finding you that it could be otherwise, but it cannot. It will not be."

How had she allowed herself to care for him? Without her past or his, they had no hope for a future. But apparently love took no measure of suitability or other lives when it came into your heart. Or if it was free to be given or belonged to another. She swallowed to clear her tightening throat.

"How do we go on from here?"

He took her hand in his and lifted it to his mouth. Kissing her wrist as he had once before, he smiled sadly. "As friends? Know that I will do everything possible to aid your recovery. And I am here if you need me."

She could only nod as he explained. "But if my memory returns, we may…"

"No matter what your life was before, I cannot make you part of mine now, Isabel. I knew that when I found you and I know that more with every passing day. You cannot be mine."

She nodded and closed her eyes. He tugged her closer and she leaned against him, taking in his strength, his power, his love.

"*Ma chère,* rest a while here. No one needs us."

Isabel found she did not have the desire to move away from him. Exhaustion claimed her and she allowed herself to fall asleep next to him, knowing that he would protect her from the terrors that lurked in her dreams.

He would always protect her.

Chapter Fourteen

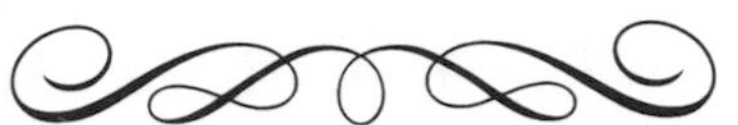

"A bad one is brewing," Rosamunde, wife of Sir Gautier, commented. "When my fingers ache like this, the storm will be memorable."

Isabel opened her eyes and looked around her in the solar. She had been working on Lady Margaret's tapestry until the need to close her eyes had grown too strong to ignore. She needed rest, but it would not come to her. There was only one way to sleep and after the words and kiss they had shared in the church, she and Royce avoided such private times.

"The last time you complained about your fingers, the storm lasted over a sennight. Pray, do not be right this time," Jehane added.

The rest of the women in attendance in the solar laughed, but it was tinged with some soberness at the danger of such storms. "Edlyn, see if my lord has returned yet from his business with the brothers at Holme Cultram. I hope that he arrives before the storm does."

Isabel watched as her maid left to seek out what the lady had asked. Lord Orrick owned the rights to mine sea salt in this area and Henry had gifted the brothers at Holme Cultram with a share in those rights. It provided much income and was Orrick's responsibility to oversee. He spent several days a month over in Abbeytown meeting with the brother prior and was due back from just such a trip that afternoon.

"Isabel?" Lady Margaret called to her. She smiled back.

"Why do you not go and rest for a short while? You have been dozing off for the past hour and your bed would be more comfortable than that chair."

She had considered doing just that except that she had been troubled by scenes from her attack again and feared what she would see in her dreams if she allowed herself to go fully asleep. "Thank you for your concern, my lady, but I am well."

The chamber quieted as they all awaited a response from the lady, since she was known for her short temper lately. Isabel realized what she had done and looked at Lady Margaret.

"I mean not to disobey you, my lady, but sleep offers me no relief from the exhaustion that plagues me or from the terrors that follow me into my dreams. I am at a loss about what to do."

Lady Margaret stood and walked to her side. Lifting her hand, she stroked Isabel's cheek. "And none of Wenda's concoctions have helped you?"

"Nay, my lady. They do seem to put me to sleep, but nothing keeps me asleep when the nightmares come."

"And they come more frequently?"

"Aye. And they are stronger, as well," Isabel added.

"The only thing that helps me when I have bad dreams is my Gautier," Lady Rosamunde said. "He wraps himself around me and I forget about those dreams in but a moment or two."

The ladies laughed at the bawdy comment, for none of them missed it. Isabel smiled at the attempt to lighten the subject. She turned back to Lady Margaret but stopped when she saw the frown on the lady's face.

"A moment of privacy, if you please?" It took

no time at all before Isabel was alone with Lady Margaret. The lady sat back down and looked at her intensely before speaking.

"I think mayhap I was wrong to try to force Royce to express his feelings for you. My judgment has not been sound of late and I beg your forgiveness for causing this rift between you."

Expecting some suggestions about her sleeping problem, Lady Margaret's words surprised her. But more than the admission of her behavior, her belief that Royce cared for her sent Isabel's heart reeling. And just as quickly she remembered Royce's own words—*no matter what your life was before, I cannot make you part of mine now.*

"My lady, you caused no rift between us." At Margaret's disbelieving look, she continued, "Royce and I have simply come to understand that with my situation and his, there is no chance of a future together. We have accepted this and remain on good terms." Did she sound even half-convinced of this as she spoke the words? She waited for the lady to proclaim her a liar.

"I understand you not being able to make a commitment because you know not if you already have taken vows, but I do not claim to know his reasons. In the three years since he arrived, we have spoken more in this last week than ever before."

"I know little of him, as well. Has he always lived alone?"

"Yes. He gained the promise of his own cottage from my husband early on. It was strange to us, but the least we could do for the man who nearly lost his life protecting my lord's."

Her words explained some of the scars on Royce's back. He was an enigma. Hiding from some secret yet living as honorable a life as she could imagine. Who was he?

"And for saving my Orrick, I will be in his debt forever," Lady Margaret said. "I did not plan to meddle even more into his affairs by broaching this with you, Isabel. I seek but to help you both at this confusing time you are in."

The concern shown by Lady Margaret all through her stay here, and now this, touched her deeply. She was not certain anyone had ever cared about her in this way.

Except my sister.

The vision of that pale-haired girl, dancing with her on the beach, returned and Isabel waited to hear a name. All she saw was the joy in their faces and then the joining of hands in a pledge.

"I know, and I cannot tell you how I appreciate all you have done. Taking in a complete stranger, providing for my health and comfort and trying to help me recover my memory are more than anyone would have expected."

Lady Margaret patted Isabel's hand. "'Twas Royce all along. He was and has been your champion here."

"Royce? But I thought he was trying to get rid of me?"

"Rid of you? Oh no, my dear. He convinced Orrick to let you stay with him even after Wenda said you were well enough to be moved. Royce argued that it might not be safe, until you were strong enough to face the challenge of living here with no memory to guide you. And now I am unsure if we gave you time enough."

"I think that these dreams and the headaches are signs that my memory struggles to return."

"I will pray that you regain your memories so that these fears and pains resolve for you." The lady stood and looked out the window. The wind was getting stronger and the sky filled with dark and churning clouds.

"Isabel, one more thing before I seek word of Orrick's return. I did not place our knights in your path only in order for you to consider marriage with any of them. If you noticed, each is of a different coloring and temperament. I thought one or more might be familiar to you—in the tone of their voices, the color of their eyes or their disposition."

"So you have many purposes for your plans, my lady?"

"That makes me sound so scheming, Isabel. I do not know if I like that or not. Mayhap when I was younger and more foolish, but not now that I am older and wiser."

They laughed and then Margaret called to her servant outside the door. Jehane entered and gave them word of Orrick's return to the keep.

"Go and try to rest for now. I will send Edlyn to watch over you."

Whether it was the gloom of the impending storm or just her own dark mood, Isabel decided to retire to her chambers, not to sleep but simply to rest her eyes and try to get rid of the nagging pain in her head.

The bile forced its way up and out and she turned to vomit on the ground. It only made her head worse. They were closer now and she would not survive if she passed out again. Scrambling to her feet, she grabbed whatever was near to help her stand.

Where was she?

This was not the way they had come and she knew only that they approached the sea. The smell of the marshes was growing stronger. The crunching of the tall grass behind was the only warning she got before they were on her again.

She screamed when he struck her with the club, but it did no good. Instead it drew the rest of them faster. Too late. Too late for her to escape. With her blood streaming down into her eyes and the swampy ground pulling at her, she knew she would die.

The pain of their attack poured over her until she fell back into the water. Even her sister's words could not save her now. But she did not want to die. She let herself sink below the surface of the water until they turned their attentions elsewhere.

Come, he said, my brother will give us better sport than this. Thinking her dead, they would kill him now. The wound from the sword was not a killing one. She saw him fall from his horse onto the ground, blood pouring from the hole in his gut, but he was not dead.

Yet.

He would be now, for they had to make certain he was dead.

They would kill him now. Kill him.

She barely made it to the basin before vomiting again. Spirals of pain and terror quaked through her. She was not their only target. They needed to kill him. Kill who? Another wave of nausea and her stomach heaved as she watched him sliced by the sword. Who was he? She rolled to her side on the cold stone floor and tried to think. The memories took hold of her again.

She could not aid him or they would kill her. He was dead, mayhap not now, but no one could live after a destructive blade slash to his gut. No one. She must save herself.

Gaining her feet, she struggled against the pain in her head and her leg. She must get away. She must find…she must find…

Royce. He promised to protect her. She needed to get to him now. He would help her. He had promised.

Isabel limped down the corridor and down the stairs to the second floor. She had not visited his chambers, but she knew where they were. The keep was deserted, as most of those who lived there were preparing for the approaching storm. She ran to his room and pushed open the door.

The young boy named Cadby sat on the floor, tugging a piece of cloth out of a dog's mouth. He got to his feet when she called out for Royce, pushing the dog aside.

"This is Royce's dog."

"Aye, mistress. He said I should play with him and feed him and walk him, too. 'Tis my job."

Even in her hysterical mood, she could hear the pride in the boy's voice at being given such responsibility. "I must find Royce. Do you know where he is?"

"He said he needed to close up his cottage in the forest. He told me to stay here and await his return."

Isabel turned to leave then realized she did not know where the croft was. They had come to Silloth Keep on a different road, one from the direction of Abbeytown and Thursby.

"Do you know where the cottage is? I must go there now."

"But mistress, the storm is coming."

"I know, but I have to go there now, before the storm begins."

Cadby did not look as if he believed her or

agreed with her plan. The dog finally recognized her and began to bark and jump at her, pawing her skirts and whining the way he usually did.

"Does he know the way? Can he lead me there?"

Part of her urged her to calm down and wait for Royce's return. But a wave of pain brought back the memories. She moaned against them, but they did not cease.

"There has been a change to our plans, brother."

He did not see the sword being taken from its scabbard due to the way his brother turned his body and hid most of his movements. The moon shaded itself behind the thickening clouds as she watched the deceit unfold before her. She tried to scream but nothing would come out.

In the shadows she saw the sword pierce his stomach and come out through his back. It could not be real. It could not. His brother would not attack him. But she watched as he clutched his side and caught up his own blood in his gloved hands.

"Brother?"

'Twas when he looked in her direction that the others seemed to remember her. One grabbed the reins of her horse and the closest knocked her to the ground. Landing hard, she lost her breath.

His body came to rest next to her on the ground and he whispered words to her that she could not hear for her ears rang inside. Hatred poured from his eyes and she realized she was the real target. He had wanted her dead and now was dying instead. Not instead, in addition to.

She must run or die. Now!

Jumping to her feet, she ran into the grass on the side of the road. It would be difficult to find her there. She never saw the club as he swung it from behind her. She only heard the sound of the bones in her leg cracking and felt the anguish as she fell.

"I have to find him now. Have you a rope to leash him with?"

Cadby looked as though he would refuse, but grabbed a length of rope from the bed and tied it around the dog's neck. "I will come with you, mistress. You might need help."

Even as he said the words, she knew she should heed them. But overpowered by the memories and the terror, she needed only Royce. She had to find him. He could save her. He had saved her.

"Nay. Nay!" she said, tugging on the rope. "You must stay here."

Waves of pain pulsed in her leg again as she remembered the agony of the injury. She knew the dagger was coming and knew only Royce could stop this. Limping and running as she could, she did not heed the calls for her to stop. She pushed her way through the crowd at the gate as those in the courtyard tried to leave the keep and make it to their homes in the village before the rains.

The wind tore at her headpiece and her clothes as she ran, and it howled as it moved with them down the hill from the keep, through the village paths and into the forest. Then she loosened her hold on the dog and urged him on to find his home. Not bothering to look at where they went, she trusted the mutt to find his owner.

Some turns of the path looked familiar to her, but it was too late. The skies of green and gray opened and dumped torrents of rain out. Lightning cut slashes in the clouds and she covered her ears against the roar of the thunder. She lost hold of the dog and he ran off faster that she could follow. She saw the rope trailing behind him as he darted through the bushes.

Her leg and stomach cramped and she fell, landing in a rut in the dirt path. Trying to breathe, she heard the insistent barking of the dog. He ran back to her, sniffed, barked and ran away again. She gained her feet and listened for the sounds of his barking. Stumbling in that direction, she watched in horror as lightning struck a tree next to the path. She screamed for Royce.

Frozen by fear and unable to move, she stared as a large branch above her came tearing off the trunk of the tree. Was this how she would die? Just moments before it struck her, she was pushed out of the way and into the bushes. The dog had come back and now barked even louder at her. Unable to breathe, she turned to the side and vomited again.

Forced to the ground by the power of their blows, she felt every fist as it pummeled her. She tried to push them away, but they surrounded her. They toyed with her; she knew this was not their worst. As if they'd heard her thoughts, the leader who'd stood back through most of the attack, walked closer and drew out his dagger. As the moon came out from its hiding place, the dagger glinted in its rays and she knew the end was coming.

He grabbed for her, but only took hold of her robe. He slashed with the knife, not caring what he cut or ripped. An evil smile told her he would continue until she did not. Backing away as much as she could did not help.

This time the knife's tip gouged deeper into her arm and the blood felt warm as it rolled down and dripped onto her sleeve. His next blow aimed higher, at her face, and soon she could not see for the blood pouring down. She fell back into the water and let herself sink below its surface.

The water was colder than she remembered it and instead of flowing over her, it pounded her with the fury of a storm. She blinked against it and opened her eyes. He stood above her, sword in hand, ready to strike the death blow. Darkness surrounded them and only the flashes of lightning outlined his form as he swung his weapon. At least this time the dying would be quick. She closed her eyes and gave up the fight.

Chapter Fifteen

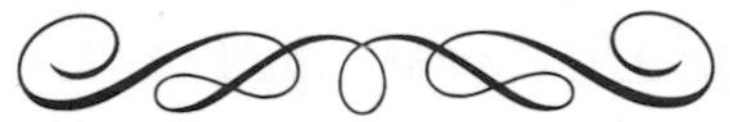

He prayed as he never had before in his life to the God who always seemed to ignore his pleas when he saw the lightning strike above her and knew he could not reach her in time. Royce followed the dog's barking and could not believe that Isabel stood there, in the raging storm screaming out his name.

Luckily the dog jumped on her, knocking her to the ground and out of the way of the falling branch. Drawing his sword, he hacked his way to her side. She was incoherent when he found her, her eyes wild, darting over his face and fixing on his sword. He swung once more and she was freed.

She was also unconscious.

He sheathed his weapon and scooped her from the ground. The wind tore into him as he decided that the cottage was the safest place to wait out the worst of the weather. Calling the dog to his side, he ran back down the path and to the croft. Pushing the door open and then shut with his foot, he carried her to the pallet and laid her down.

Her skin was frigid and ghostly pale. She moved not at all and he called out to her several times, trying to wake her. Her breathing was uneven and she shivered as he removed the coverings from her face and hair. Peeling off the veil and barbette from around her chin, she saw for the first time in weeks the scar that encircled one side of her face.

He knew now why she chose this head covering—it hid not only her hair and the solid white splash that grew from her scalp, but also the scar. William smoothed the hair from her face and called to her again. She did not react.

She needed to be dry and warm so he began to unlace her bliaut and pulled it off over her head. Soaked through to the skin, he realized he had to also remove the undergown and her shift. He found two blankets in the storage chest he'd left behind and, after carefully undressing her, he wrapped one around her and laid her back on the pallet.

Damn, but the rains had started before he could

bring in more dry peat, so there would be no fire to warm her. He wrung out her garments and spread them over the table and bench and chair. And then knew he must do the same with his clothes, for they were just as wet. He divested himself of mail, hauberk, tunic and trousers. With the other blanket around him, he lay down next to her and brought her close.

Tremors racked her as he held her. He began to rock back and forth, holding her nearer and willing the heat in his body to warm her. Whispering to her as he had those weeks before, he called to her and, God forgive him, he told her of his love for her. He even allowed himself to kiss her softly on the cheek and forehead as he urged her to wake.

After a while, her shivering slowed and her breathing became more regular. William continued to hold her, checking her skin for its color and warmth. A deep shudder and gasp told him she had awakened even before her eyes opened.

"Shh, Isabel, fear not."

"Where…?" Her lips trembled so much that more words did not come out. William adjusted the blanket higher and tighter and rubbed her cheek gently.

"We are safe from the storm's fury in my cottage. I found you in the forest."

"The dog…" Her teeth chattered as she spoke. He lifted his leg, draped it over hers and pulled her nearer. It would kill him, but she needed his warmth.

"The mutt saved you, leading you here and getting my attention with his whining and noises." The dog whined from his place in the corner of the cottage.

"My chest hurts." He felt her hand move to her chest inside their cocoon of blankets. Every touch, even a glancing one, created more heat in him. Holding her this close, almost skin to skin, was pure torture and both punishment for his sins and reward for his deprivations.

"The dog jumped at you to push you from the broken branch's path. He may not be big, but the force with which he hit you was greater than his size."

"He saved my life?" Her eyes searched his face for the truth.

"He did just that. And brought me to you. And I brought you here." A frown marred her face and he decided she must have become conscious of their position and lack of clothing.

Would she object to his embrace? Would she be horrified when she comprehended their state, or rather his state? Another wave of shivers passed through her, moving from her head and face through her body and down to even her feet. She clutched at him and moved herself closer.

What had sent her in such a condition of agitation to seek him out during a dangerous storm? Isabel was overwhelmed even before the rains soaked her thoroughly. What had driven her out of the safety of the keep? To him?

"Isabel, why did you leave the keep?"

"I had to find you. I had to tell you..." She shivered again and he rubbed his hands down her arms and back up again, trying to cause some heat.

"Tell me what? What was so important that you risked your very life coming out in this storm?"

"I was confused, Royce. I tried to sleep as Lady Margaret suggested, but the dreams have been so terrible." She leaned her head against his chest and remained there for a few moments. He waited for her to go on and fought the urge to kiss her head while she was awake and would feel it.

"You are safe. Tell me of the dreams."

She let out a deep breath and spoke. "It was the

attack that I remembered. I was with a traveling party when a small group broke off and headed down a road we had not used before."

"Do you remember where you were going to or coming from?" He hoped his small nudges would help her remember some of the details. She shook her head.

"They stabbed the man. I saw the sword go through his body. Then the blow came, knocking me from my horse and onto the ground."

"What man did they stab?" Her eyes had glazed over as she once again watched the events she described to him.

"It was my fault, he said. My failures had brought him, us, to this. I do not know who he is, but he was surprised by the attack, too. He landed next to me and whispered that it was my fault."

This accusation pained her; he could feel it in her voice as she said it to him. She had been blamed before and had accepted that she was the cause. Of what?

"What was your fault, Isabel? Do you know?"

She shook her head. Her eyes were still focused elsewhere and he waited for more of the tale. Another tremor overtook her and he waited for it to pass.

"I knew they would kill me, so I ran. I could not see much for the moon had gone behind the clouds and I knew not the road we were on. But I could smell the marshland nearby."

Her body was shaking now, but he thought from fear and not cold. William gently rubbed his hands on her back, trying to soothe her as she tried to put the pieces of this memory together again. "You are safe now. I will protect you."

"There were many of them, mayhap six or seven, and they followed me. I did not know how close they were until the club broke my leg and I fell."

He flinched at her words, for she spoke in a cold and unfeeling voice. The horror of this was real to him as Isabel continued. "I dragged myself up, knowing that death was at hand, and I tried to get away. I could not." Another shudder. "They surrounded me and passed me one to the other, hitting me with their fists. Then, one came into their midst and drew a dagger."

"Isabel," he said, even as he dreaded asking her to dwell on this any more than was necessary. He asked because, while fresh and clear in her mind, she might remember more now than when this had passed. "Do you recognize any of them? Are any familiar to you?"

He watched in dread as her eyes moved around those she saw in these memories. One by one, she stared at them and shook her head. Then she did not move her gaze and he could tell that she was looking at someone she knew.

"Who is he?"

"His brother." She began shaking again and he urged her to speak of what she saw. "He slashed at me, not trying to kill me, just…"

He knew what this man was doing for he had done it himself in battle and in challenge. He was playing her, weakening her, tiring her out for the kill. "Go on," he whispered.

"I kept trying to run, but my leg would not hold me up. I dragged it and struggled away until he kept striking with the dagger. He cut at my gowns until my arms bled, then he aimed at my face."

He could not help himself this time. He pressed his lips to the ragged scar and kissed her there. William held her close, touching his mouth to her forehead and waited for her to calm enough to tell the rest.

"As I saw the determination in his face, I struggled with myself. Part of me wanted to live, but part of me was in so much pain that I wanted to surrender to it. I confess that I wanted to die then.

I knew he was not done and I did not think I could face any more of it." She leaned back and looked at him now; she was with him. "I know it is a mortal sin, and may God forgive me, but I wanted to die in that moment."

The church taught that it was a sin. William had accepted long ago that the many times he'd wanted, nay invited, death to visit him had simply added to the blackening of his soul. He feared he was past the point of redemption.

"'Twas the fear in you, Isabel. It overwhelmed you. Surely God knows that and will forgive any transgressions."

"But Royce, if this attack was my fault, how can I be forgiven?"

He shook his head. "Do not believe that, Isabel. Ruthless men will say what they must to avoid taking the blame for their actions."

Guilt stabbed through him as he knew he spoke of himself and his own transgressions of the past. He had blamed those who challenged him or those who had tried to resist Prince John's desires or those who had encouraged his misdeeds. Anyone but himself. For accepting the blame meant acknowledging that he was wrong, that he was guilty of sinful acts and grievous misconduct. It had taken losing everything and everyone he cared about before he could accept that blame. His throat was thick with emotions he thought he had banished when he asked her his question.

"Do you know what he accuses you of? Mayhap that would tell us more about you?"

Isabel shook her head. "Nay. I know only that the one killed and the one killing hated me. I could see it in their eyes. As the one lay on the ground after being stabbed, his hatred poured out at me, in his words and in his eyes." Her tears began to flow and she tilted her head down so their gazes would not meet. He felt her humiliation.

He held her quietly in his arms. She had been deeply hurt by these memories and by the words spoken against her by these men. He suspected strongly that one of these men was her husband, but he did not voice that to her for fear of frightening her even more. William waited a few minutes, listening to her breathing and to the storm raging outside, letting her regain her strength. Her words startled him, for he thought she'd fallen asleep.

"He pushed me back, slashing with the blade. I stumbled as much as I could, but then I began sinking into the mud beneath my feet. I could not move fast enough to avoid his blade and when he struck me in the side with a deep cut, I began to faint. I remember falling backward into the water and feeling it surround me. I began to welcome the blackness that overtook me."

She paused, taking and releasing several deep breaths. "He laughed then. I heard him clearly through the silence of the marsh. I tried not to scream. I wanted him to think me dead and I wanted to die. Then he said they should seek out his brother for more sport than I had been."

William tried to distract her from the horrifying truth that brother had killed brother. "How did you get out of the water?"

"I have no memory of that. I kept hearing someone call me, telling me to crawl, to keep moving. I followed that voice."

He thought she was talking about him in the first days after she'd been found, but he was wrong.

"I think I heard my sister calling to me. Through the darkness and the fear, I heard her voice speaking."

"Your sister?"

"Did I tell you she is my twin?"

He held her away and looked at her. “Your twin? You did not tell me this. When did you remember her?”

She shook her head. “I do not remember her except as a child, when we ran on that beach. But there is another memory of us holding hands and making a pledge. And I just know we shared the same birth.”

A twin sister. Did she know more?

“Do you remember her name? Do you remember calling out to her—on the beach or after this attack?”

“Nay, Royce. I do not.”

He asked her no more, for he could feel her exhaustion. It had grown dark inside the cottage now. Only bolts of lightning lit up the interior as they flashed outside. The wind battered against the walls and he was glad they had this refuge for the night. Or for however long the storm needed to release its fury.

The silence was companionable for a while, then he felt her begin to shake again. No, not shake. Cry. Her tears were warm where they touched his skin inside the blankets. He turned onto his back and drew her under his arm and next to him. Her cheek rested on his chest now and it was even worse. The sobs grew stronger and her grief deeper as she cried out in reaction to all the memories she now knew.

"He hated me, Royce. I could see it in his eyes," she said. "Even as he was bleeding to death, he hated me for my failure."

He said nothing. He was at a loss now, not on the solid ground of reason and strategy. She needed emotions and the support he did not think he could give. William held her and let her cry—'twas the only thing left to him.

"What could I have done that was so grievous that I deserved to die? What failure on my part caused a hatred so deep that he would kill me over it? Why…?" Her words drifted off into sobs again.

"Isabel, do not lash yourself over the words of a killer."

"Not just his words, Royce. Look at the elaborate planning that was needed to rid me from his life. Mayhap I should have died that night?"

"Never say that again, Isabel," he said, probably a bit harsher than he needed to, but it pained him to have her take the blame for this. "They did this deed. Let them take the blame for it."

"I should have died that night," she repeated,

her voice forlorn and hopeless. "Why did you have to save me?"

Her anguish tore at his very soul. These bastards had destroyed not only her life but her being. How many times had he done that? Destroyed innocent lives in pursuing his own goals? Too many. And their faces flashed before his eyes in a reminder that she could have been talking about him in his previous life.

But he knew that she was an innocent and that she did not deserve this. What could he say to make her see that? What words would soothe her and let her know that she did matter? What could he say?

The truth.

The one he tried to ignore even though Lady Margaret had hinted at it. The one he feared and wanted the most. The obvious reason she had not died that night or since.

"I saved you, Isabel, because you were sent to save me."

Chapter Sixteen

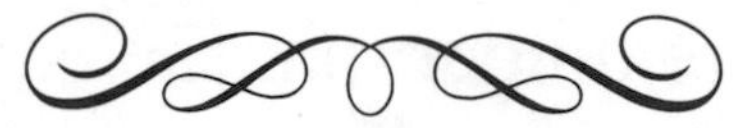

He waited for lightning to strike him. It did flash but safely stayed outside in the storm. William saw the disbelief in her eyes at his admission. He could hardly believe he'd said the words to her, but 'twas as if the weight of the world had been lifted from him. Was it true?

"How can you say that? You did not need to be saved."

Could he tell her the truth of his life? In spite of his love for her, he knew he could not. Not yet. But he could explain some of it.

"Isabel, I shut myself off from living when I came here three years ago. I know you suspected as much. I shut off my feelings, my wants, my plans, even my thoughts of having a future. I simply wanted to exist. Then you came and interfered with my well-thought plan."

He could not see her face during his admission and wondered what she must think. Unused to the risk, he stumbled a bit on his words as he spoke. If she rejected him now, he doubted he would ever have the courage to offer again. William turned onto his side.

"I interfered?" she asked in a whisper.

"Oh, aye, you interfered." He smiled, though she could not see it. "You showed a spirit and determination to live that impressed me. With nothing to go on, you have carved out a life here, gaining support from one and all with your kind ways."

She laughed softly. "I do not believe I was always kind to you. I disturbed you."

"You disturbed the darkness within me. You unearthed feelings I thought long dead—ones of honor and trust and even love." He reached up and stroked her cheek, wanting to repeat the kiss they'd shared in the chapel. But he did not dare loosen the last vestiges of control he still held.

Startled when she mimicked his touches with her hand on his cheek, he stayed still and endured it, for he feared 'twould end soon.

"And you do not believe you deserve honor or trust or even love, do you, Royce?"

"It is not a question of believing it or not, Isabel. It is just that I do not deserve or expect them now."

He swore that she snorted at that. How could he make her understand without going into his sordid past? He had lived like an animal, seeking its own gratification and not caring who paid for it. He did not deserve to have a life and dreams when he'd stolen those from too many to count.

"You take in a complete stranger and save her life. You guard the lady of the keep's secrets and protect her honor against any who would defame or embarrass her. You make a small boy far from home feel important and needed."

"How do you know these things?" He had spoken to no one about Margaret's history or Cadby's duties.

"I may not know who I am, but I can see who you are. I watched you in your work and in your dealings with the people who live here. Deep inside you lives an honorable man who you fight to keep hidden there."

"I am not an honorable man, Isabel. Think it not of me, for an honorable man would never be speaking of love to you when there can be nothing between us. An honorable man would have taken you back to the keep to protect your virtue from his basest desires." Anger and those desires swelled up inside him and he needed her to stop him. "An honorable man would never do this."

He took her mouth in a possessive kiss that told her everything about what he wanted from her. Even without specific memories, she knew as a woman about this kind of passion. The heat and power of it threatened to overwhelm her as he leaned over her and gathered her close. Like coiled springs within her, spirals of pleasure moved through her as he took and took and took of her mouth. She felt him harden against her hip and her body readied in response. Her breasts swelled and the core of her body tightened.

Isabel reached up, untangling her hands from the covers and pulled the layer of blankets from between them. He hissed as their skin touched from chest to hips to thighs. She wrapped her hands in his hair and kept his mouth on hers, letting him plunge his tongue inside it and taste hers.

She could taste and feel his need for her and it refreshed her spirit. In her other life, she was unneeded, unwanted, a burden. But here, Royce needed her and wanted her…and loved her. After a kiss that left them both gasping, he tried to move away.

"I cannot offer you more than this, Isabel. There is no future for us, in spite of your soft words and in spite of my deepest desires. Please, let me go while I can still stop this."

The pain and fear in his voice and in his soul screamed out to her. What could he have done that was so heinous that he did not deserve to live as others did? Had three years of deprivation and solitary existence not been penance enough for his sins?

"A dishonorable man would lie with pretty words to have what I am offering to you, Royce. I fear what is coming and I know that neither of us can offer more than this night." He had not moved away but did not come closer either. "Please. Give me tonight so I can face what I must in the coming days."

She lifted her head up until their lips met, but she did not kiss him. If he loved her, he would know that she needed this now. She needed to feel valued as a woman. She needed…him. He spoke against her mouth.

"This is wrong."

"This is right," she countered, her lips tingling under his, "if there is love."

"I do love you, Isabel."

Her heart soared at his declaration. She'd known since that day in the chapel, but he had not said the words out loud.

"Yet there will be naught but heartache from this."

"Then our love will save us from that. Love me, Royce."

With a growl, he moved over her and this time did not stop the kiss even when they were breathless from it. The heat between them rose and soon her skin was slick with sweat. She touched him where she could reach—his chest, his shoulders, his back. Sliding her hands down to his buttocks, she felt the strong muscles there and imagined how they would feel when he entered her.

When he rolled off her a bit, she thought he was leaving, but the touch of his fingers on her breasts eased her fears and stoked the fires of passion. The kiss ended, but she could not stop gasping as each touch ignited another spark within her until she wanted to scream from it. His mouth replaced his fingers on her nipples and she did scream, the feelings were so intense and still increasing.

Royce's lips drew on her until the tips of her breasts hardened. So ardent were his attentions there that when his hand traced a line down from her breast to her stomach, she did not notice it. Almost. She clutched at his chest and his shoulders and her legs trembled from the sensations. The core of her ached for his touch and her hips arched to meet his hand.

Finally, finally, he slipped his hand between her thighs and his fingers into the wet heat of her center. She did moan then as her legs fell open and let him do what he would there. His mouth followed his hand down her stomach and she felt the ripples of pleasure move with him. He crawled over her and knelt between her legs, lifting her legs over his shoulders and kissing and licking a path down the tender skin inside her thighs.

She wanted to keep quiet and make no sounds, but her body had other ideas. With the first touch of his mouth on the throbbing flesh there, she screamed again. When his fingers and tongue danced over her there and something grew tighter and tighter within her, she heard the moans being pulled from her. Her sounds seemed to spur him on, for each one was met by a brief pause and then more kissing and fondling.

Her peak was coming. Isabel felt him slide his fingers inside her and then he sucked hard on the tiny exposed bud of flesh where all of the pulsing and heat seemed to come from. Everything within her exploded, releasing waves and waves of pleasure that moved through her body and her soul and her heart. But he did not stop. He was relentless, bringing her to this again and again until she could scream no more.

He lifted her legs off him and then slid up her body; each touch of him against her ignited heat once more. Even though she thought she was done, he had other ideas. As he reached her mouth, he took her hand and put himself in it, wrapping her fingers around his erection. Now he moaned as he moved against her grip and she felt him grow harder and thicker in her hand. She tasted her essence on his lips and in his mouth.

Royce moved up until he could place himself at the opening of her core. Their hands guided his hardness to her. Then he stopped and lifted his mouth from hers.

"Tell me now, Isabel. Say it now and I will

stop." His words were a gruff whisper, filled with passion and promise. "Tell me no."

"Yes," she whispered back as she arched against him, bringing him inside her. "Yes!"

He released her hands and thrust into her with all the power those muscles had promised her. He filled her and pulled back, almost leaving her empty. Then he lifted her hips and plunged again and again, groaning loudly himself at each thrust.

She could not breathe. She could not think. She could only feel and she felt every one of his thrusts into the center of her. The throbbing and aching increased again and she knew he would bring her to the edge with him. She lifted as he moved, drawing him in as deeply as she could, feeling every inch of his hardness within her flesh. And then it happened.

She heard her scream burst forth as though she was not inside herself. His loud yell of completion poured from him as he released his seed within her. Even though he had stopped pulsing inside her, he remained there, filling her emptiness as no one else could. Completely spent, she did not resist when he slid her leg over his hip and turned onto his side, all without ever pulling from her.

The last thing she remembered were the words he whispered into her ear as they lay together.

"I do love you, Isabel. God forgive me, but I do."

The storm raging outside was of no comparison to the one raging within him. Guilt, anger, fear and still more desire surged in his heart and soul over claiming her as his own. Grief was there, too, at the knowledge that no matter her thoughts on this, there could be nothing between them.

He had taken what she had offered. He had marked her as his own with his mouth and his seed. He had lied to have her even as he told her part of the truth, for the whole of it would have scared her back into the storm rather than anywhere he was. So much for being an honorable man.

His thoughts wandered over what had happened between them and what was to come. She would regain her memory and return to her family and he would live out his life here without her. Convinced that nothing more could be, at least he would have incredible memories to savor when she was gone. Memories that could get him through times of weakness and wanting. Memories that would remind him to never overstep the life he knew he must live.

Isabel sighed in her sleep and he turned to her. He had slipped out of her wonderful body some time ago, but did not want to lose the touch of her on him. He shifted her to face away from him, straightened the blankets over them and fit himself behind her to sleep. She laid her head on his arm and he pulled her close with the other one, wrapping around her to keep her warm.

She slept like the dead, her breathing low and quiet. He should feel guilty over that as well. Emotionally and physically exhausted, she'd run to him for protection and he'd swived her without regard for her condition. Honorable? Ha!

An errant thought crossed his mind. What if her memory did not return and she wanted to stay with him? Could he have her and still keep his past secret?

The irony made him chuckle—she did not know her past and did everything in her power to remember it, while he knew his and did everything in his to forget.

But wait. He could tell her he had committed serious sins, acts against others, and that he had given up his life much as a pilgrim did to seek forgiveness. It was near to the truth. Of course, he knew deep within that forgiveness would never be his.

Or could it?

This was exactly what he had feared when the first crack had started in the walls he'd built around himself. She gave him hope. Her love made him think that the impossible was possible.

Why then was she there? If Lady Margaret was correct, then her appearance had a purpose and certainly it had to be one other than giving him hope…and sex? Was he expected to give her his protection? Offer her a life where she could be safe from the men who had plotted her death? Was that his role?

He needed to think on this when his head was clear and his body was not besieged by her nearness. When the storm had cleared and they returned to the keep, he would seek Orrick and Margaret's counsel before making any decisions.

William snuggled closer to her and kissed her lightly on the head. As she had said, they had this night before reality intruded and fate did its worst. He would take the night.

Chapter Seventeen

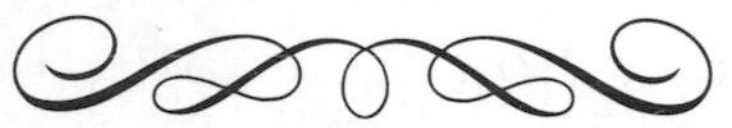

Two nights passed before the storm showed signs of weakening. Isabel slept through the first night and day and he found her awake and watching him when he came back to lie with her during the second night. William had packed up everything in the cottage, for until she was gone, he would live in the keep.

That had been one decision he'd made. She needed him and he would be there for her. He did not let himself believe that they had more than a few days to a few weeks, but he accepted that he needed to embrace all she offered during that time. When she was gone…when she was gone, there would be time enough to reclaim his solitary life and move back here.

He had not bothered to dress in the still-damp

clothes, so he slipped back under the blankets and gathered her in his arms.

"Good even to you, Isabel."

"Royce," she said his name on a sigh as she stretched her legs and rubbed against his. His body reacted immediately to her touch. Turning in his arms, she kissed his chest then his neck and then his chin. Unable to resist, he leaned his face to hers and let her continue. He kissed her back once and then moved away.

"You were exhausted," he said. "And you must be hungry. There is some bread and cheese and ale from the abbey."

She rubbed her cheek on his. "In a minute or two. I have not slept that well since…since I left your care."

He touched the place under her eyes where the dark smudges were. "Your lack of sleep has been showing." The light of the candle he'd left burning illuminated her face. "And I added to your exhaustion."

"Yes," she whispered to him, laying her hand on his cheek. "You certainly did."

He was trying to feel guilty about taking her with such passion and force, but the playful expression on her face and the satisfied glint in her eyes made that difficult.

"Isabel, I feel badly about misusing you. Do not make light of my behavior."

She sat up and her black hair surrounded her like a curtain. Tussled from being wet and then her sleeping on it, its length fell over her chest and down into her lap.

"I do not feel used, Royce. I feel loved. Well loved." She smiled at him. "But not abused or forced. You gave me what I needed last night," she paused, and he interrupted.

"The night before that."

"Truly? I have slept through a night and a day?"

"And nigh to another night as well."

"Very well," she said, waving off his words. "You seek to deflect me from what I would say, from what I would have you hear."

"I would rather no words, Isabel. Words cannot be taken back when everything changes," he said, pressing his fingers to her lips. "I know you were feeling unloved, unwanted and hurt by what you remembered. I wanted to banish those feelings from you and make certain you knew you were wanted and needed by me."

"There, you said them for me." She laughed at

his expression, for he had indeed. She slid back and tucked a blanket around her. Standing, she walked to the table and fetched the bundles of food and the skin of ale and brought them back to the pallet.

How could she ever think she was not wanted? Even in the basest sense of it, with her beauty and grace and fair form, what man could look at her and not desire her? With her hair serving as her only cover, the soft ripeness of her breasts and hips were evident. What man would want to kill her?

Her husband.

"You look as though you ate something sour."

He watched as she settled herself next to him on the pallet and she let the blanket fall to her waist. Her nipples peeked through the layer of hair and his mouth watered at the thought of kissing them again. He sat up and slid back against the wall, keeping the blanket over his legs and other now-obvious parts.

"Now you look hungry." Her words carried no accusation, just a description of what she most likely saw on his face. He reached over for the loaf of brown bread and tore off a piece. He stuffed it in his mouth, chewed it quickly and swallowed.

"I am hungry. I have been waiting for you to wake before I ate." The flash in her eyes told him she knew his real hunger.

She broke off a chunk of the hard yellow cheese and chewed it slowly. After washing it down with a mouthful of ale, she shook her head at him. "What were you thinking of when your face turned so… intense?"

"Your attacker."

Her eyes glazed over as he could tell she watched the attack again in her thoughts. There was no pain or fear now, only remembrance. "I think I knew him."

"I think the attack was planned by your husband and his brother."

She blinked several times and nodded her head. "Husband?" she asked in a whisper then she nodded. "I think you are correct, Royce."

He did not want to cause her more pain. "If you do not want to speak of it, we will not."

She gave him a tentative smile. "The memories do not frighten me any longer. I suppose that now that they are clear, they will not haunt me again."

"A noble couple attacked and killed and no outcry has rung throughout the kingdom. How can that be, Isabel?"

They were silent for a minute or two as they both thought on the question. It had bothered him since he realized that her husband had arranged to have her killed. Then, from her description of the attack, it would seem that his brother, selected to carry out the task, had turned on him as well.

"Do not dwell on that. For now, eat and rest until we can return you to the keep. Lady Margaret must be nigh to hysteria over the thought of you being out in this storm."

She gifted him with a smile, but she was different now. "Do storms like this come very often here?"

He shook his head. "Not very often, usually once or twice a year. They blow in from the sea, across this corner of land and then out into the firth and north to Scotland."

"How did you get here? I thought you were with Lord Orrick at the abbey?"

"I was. When the weather turned bad, he thought we should head back sooner rather than wait. I stopped here, wanting to gather up the rest of my belongings and bring them back to the keep."

"Your horse? Is it outside?" She looked toward the window.

"It got away when I followed the dog to you.

Do not fret. It will find its way back to the keep as it always does."

"And then Lady Margaret will truly worry—a riderless horse returning in a storm."

He nodded and smiled. Lady Margaret in that state of mind was not something he wanted to see. "I suspect, with the diminishing winds, that we will have an escort back shortly after dawn."

She glanced at him, the blankets and their garments still strewn over the benches and chair. Then she looked at herself. "I guess that clothing will be necessary, then?"

"I fear so. 'Twould not go well if we greeted my men as we are now."

She laughed, but again he sensed something was different, quieter, changed. She teased him, but there was less joy in her now.

"Would you hold me, Royce? Just hold me?"

He wrapped the remaining food and tossed it onto the table. Then he opened his arms to her and she moved into his embrace. Sometime later, she fell asleep and he moved them both down onto the pallet. But he was awake when the winds calmed and the rain stopped. William did not want to miss a moment of holding her close, for he feared this would be the last time.

* * *

Isabel closed her eyes and feigned sleep. Royce was right—she was exhausted from the last two days' experiences. And now she was heartsick as well as brainsick. Turning away from him, she lay on her side and tried to sort out her feelings.

Royce was also correct about the man in her memories being her husband. As soon as he had spoken the words, she knew. But why could she remember nothing else?

During the time Wenda had taken care of her, the woman had mentioned that she thought this was her mind's way of protecting her from things too terrifying to face. Was that it?

It all came back to the reason a husband would kill his wife. Was there some flaw in her so excessive he had to rid himself of her in this manner? Royce shifted closer to her in his sleep. His body was warm and hard and safe. She thought of his passion and her response, welcoming him into her body without hesitation.

Was that then her sin? Had she failed to be faithful to her vows? Had she given herself to men other than her husband and he needed to rid himself of a faithless wife? Her easy passion with Royce pointed to that. And she was definitely not a virgin when she lay with Royce last night. No, she had enjoyed that side of marriage, she was certain of it.

Was this her flaw?

She closed her eyes again and saw the attack as it had happened. Her husband, surprised by the attack on him, fell from his horse, bleeding profusely from the wound in his stomach. She tried to listen to his words more closely, but she had been dazed by the blow to her head.

"'Tis your fault, bitch. Your failure brought us to this."

She flinched not only at the words, but also the vehemence with which he flung them at her. Hatred for her burned in his eyes. She did not see the same when he glanced at the brother who had stabbed him. It was only for her—the cause of his troubles.

A throbbing pain started in the front of her head and spread to the back of it. She rubbed at her temples, trying to ease the tightness. Then Royce's hand covered hers and began to rub away the pain. Isabel relaxed at his touch and soon the growing tension was gone.

"Did I wake you?" she asked.

"I have been awake." He smoothed her hair

back from her face and kissed her neck. "I could not sleep knowing that with the dawn, this will end."

"How much longer, then?" It was quieter outside, but she could not tell if it was growing lighter or not. The candle on the table had gone out a while ago.

"Not long enough," he whispered as he moved his mouth over her ear, touching with the tip of his tongue. She shivered at the tickling, arousing sensation and moved back against him, feeling the proof that he was affected, too.

"Then hurry," she urged. Isabel needed to feel his desire again. Just once more before she faced the rest of her life without him.

For in the dark of the night, she had realized that she could never be with him again, never offer a future to him. Until she could understand her failings in her life and in her marriage, she could not risk ruining his life. This idyllic time set against the storm raging outside would be their one chance to share their love. She leaned back against him and waited.

This joining, with him behind her, was different than their first. Instead of raw passion, this one was made of softer touches, heated kisses and a quieter moment of completion. And when he drew from her at the end, she understood why. This was a farewell for them. His words of love were saying goodbye and she accepted what he had tried to tell her from the start, from the moment when they became aware of each other as man and woman.

He left with the excuse of getting the bucket of rainwater from outside so she could wash before dressing, but even with a reason, the parting was painful. She gathered her clothes and the new memories she would carry with her and prepared to return to the keep.

As predicted, his men arrived with horses not long after dawn. Edlyn was with them, but she had finished dressing and needed no help. Her gown and bliaut were stiff and uncomfortable, but Edlyn assured her that a hot bath and fresh clothing awaited her at the keep.

If any of them thought that something untoward had occurred, they gave no sign of it. Connor gave Royce a full accounting of all the damage wrought by the storm and of Lord Orrick's plans for repairs. The men were boisterous and anxious to get back so Royce helped her onto the horse brought for her and mounted his own. With his belongings in sacks tied to the horses' saddles, they left for Silloth Keep.

Isabel tried to pay attention to the route they took, but several times they changed direction because of downed trees and branches. When Royce caught her eye and nodded at one such broken tree, she knew it was where he had found her. She shivered as she noted the size of the branch that had fallen from above.

The rest of their journey took only minutes, for once they reached the larger paths of the village, they could move with more speed. Soon they approached the keep, rode through its gates and into the courtyard. By the time they dismounted, Lady Margaret was there.

"Royce, my lord awaits you at the stables. He asked that you join him there after breaking your fast." Royce handed off his horse to one of the boys and then turned to both of them.

"By your leave, I will go there now." At Lady Margaret's nod, he looked at Isabel with a closed expression that she not read. "Be well, Isabel."

They watched in silence as he walked away and then the lady clapped her hands. "Rosamunde, please go to the kitchens and tell them to bring food for Isabel to my solar. Jehane?

Is the bath ready? See to it now for Isabel stands here looking ready to collapse. And Edlyn, gather clean clothing for her."

The women named scattered as she called out their orders and soon it was only Isabel and Lady Margaret standing at the steps to the keep. The lady's astute eyes examined her several times before she spoke.

"Something is different, Isabel. Are you well?"

"I am well, my lady."

"Royce saw to your care?"

"Aye, my lady, he did." Isabel knew she was probing. She did not have the strength to face questioning now. "May we speak more after my bath?"

"And after some food as well. At least you look well rested."

Isabel almost laughed. The lady would find out what she wanted to know or would guess until the truth was admitted to her. Isabel just did not know which would come first.

Chapter Eighteen

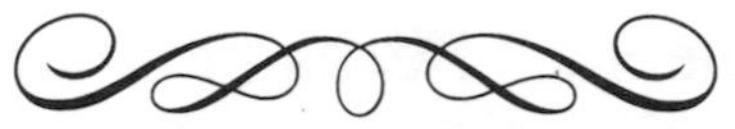

The interrogation did not happen as quickly as Isabel had suspected it would due to the large and widespread damage caused by the storm. As far as the abbey to the southeast and the salt lathes to the east and north, Orrick's lands had been pummeled by the ferocious storm. Isabel heard many of the old ones talking about not remembering a stronger one. Arguments ensued since this was not the longest-lasting squall to hit, but it was declared the most powerful.

One and all joined in as the keep and village buildings were put back into good condition. For six days, the repairs went on and the regular pace and schedule of their days was thrown off by what needed to be accomplished. Isabel did not believe that she participated much, except to trail behind Lady Margaret and carry out her instructions.

She did feel comfortable during her assignment in the keep's gardens, which had sustained some damage from fallen trees and broken branches. With the help of two sturdy servants, she was able to put it back in order and minimize the loss of many of the needed herbs and plants.

She saw little of Royce during that time. A glimpse of him here or there as he went about his duties was all she gained. Since even the meals were not served as usual, there was no chance to share one with him. She heard from Lady Rosamunde that Royce accompanied Sir Gautier to Abbeytown to assist the good brothers in some repairs.

At least the busy days kept Lady Margaret from pursuing answers for the many questions she had. Time and again, Isabel would spy the lady staring at her, as though searching for something about her person that was different. She did feel different, resigned, but it was not time to confide in Lady Margaret as to the cause of it.

And resigned she was. Isabel had decided to give her memory until the end of summer, another month, before she could impose no longer on these good people. Then if no more of her life before the attack was revealed to her, she would ask Lady Margaret to sponsor her to the convent of her sister. Mayhap there, in contemplation and prayer, her life would be given back and she could gain an understanding about her flaws and failings that had led her husband to plan her murder.

She fell into bed thoroughly tired but woke completely refreshed. The nightmares had ceased now that she remembered. There were other dreams, of Royce and of their time together. Sometimes she would awaken out of breath from the heat of them. Those she did not want to cease.

After about a sennight, normalcy was restored to Silloth Keep and it did not take Lady Margaret long to pounce. The summons to the solar came one night after the evening meal and Isabel knew it was time. The servants and other women were dismissed with a word and she waited for the questioning to begin.

"You are well, Isabel? The work this past week has not hurt you?" Margaret's stern gaze moved over her, looking for weaknesses. "You are sleeping?"

Nodding, Isabel answered dutifully. "I am well.

The work has done me no harm. I am sleeping well." Not as well as she did when in Royce's embrace, but well enough.

"Now that we have the preliminaries out of the way, let us proceed to the heart of the matter." Her directness startled Isabel at first, but then she thought she appreciated it. Subterfuge took too much strength and time.

"Ask what you will, my lady. You deserve the truth."

"Royce told me that more of your memory has returned. Can you speak of it to me?"

"I will tell you what I can. It does not frighten me the way it once did. Now that the whole of it has returned, it troubles me not."

Isabel recounted the tale of the attack and what she could remember of her attackers. Margaret paled at the descriptions, but asked a few questions to clarify the incident. When she finished, the lady rose and poured them each a cup of strong wine. After a few minutes, Margaret spoke again.

"He also told me something you did not say. About the words this man, probably your husband, spoke to you. He said they deeply hurt you?"

"My lady, I would rather not speak of them. It is too fresh."

"The very reason we must speak now. Do not give these accusations power over you by hiding from them. And, if they are as Royce led me to believe, do not give them substance they do not have."

"Is there anything he did not tell you?" A bit of sarcasm entered her voice.

"Actually, yes, there is. In spite of Orrick's questions, Royce has this exasperating habit of crossing his arms over his chest and glaring instead of answering, at least when he chooses not to answer."

Isabel smiled then. This was the Royce she'd met. So many of her questions went unanswered in those first few weeks. If they were about him, he would do exactly as Margaret had described.

"And then did he try to distract you?"

Lady Margaret smiled then. "Just so. Men can be so stubborn, Isabel. Sometimes they can be misinformed. But other times they are just plainly wrong. Tell me what your husband said and let us discern which is the case."

If the subject was not so serious, she would have laughed at Lady Margaret's assessment of men's behaviors. But even thinking of her husband's words brought pain to her heart.

"I was to blame for his plans."

"How so? What do you remember?"

Isabel wiped her hands on her gown and tried to calm the shaking that had begun to overtake her. "I could feel his hatred. His eyes were filled with it. And he did not direct it at the one who held the sword covered in his blood. He hated me." She shivered as she could once more see his face.

"The one who attacked him? The one who called himself 'brother'?"

"Aye, my lady. Although I am not clear on that. I cannot imagine a brother killing a brother."

"Then you have no knowledge of the Plantagenets. They have fought brother against brother, brothers against father and so many other combinations that it would make you scream. Believe me, Isabel, when enough is at stake, it is each for themselves."

"But my lady, what could be at stake with me?"

"'Tis always the same with women and men of noble birth—lands, power and heirs." Margaret reached out and took her hand. "Mayhap you stood in the way of an inheritance? Or you failed…?"

"Failed to produce an heir?" Isabel waited for an onslaught of feelings to guide her in this.

Surely, if that was the cause of her husband's hatred, she would remember it now?

"'Twould be an explanation, but it holds no memories for me. This is hopeless. And I confess, my lady, that I am not anxious to remember such a flaw in myself that could cause the hatred it did." Isabel stood and walked around the chamber. She could not sit still now.

"I do not mean to agitate you in this way, Isabel. Let us talk of something else since this is not fruitful. Tell me of your stay with Royce during the storm."

"Can we not speak of needle and thread instead?" Isabel stood near the loom holding the tapestry and pointed at it. "I would rather not speak of the time with Royce." She felt the tears burning her eyes and did not want them to fall. Blinking, she turned away from the lady's further scrutiny.

"Did he dishonor you, Isabel?"

She did cry then. Nothing within her could keep the tears from pouring out. "Nay, my lady, he did not."

Isabel never heard the lady's approach, but she felt Margaret's arm come around her shoulders to support her. "What happened there, Isabel? I will keep your confidence."

"He showed me what was possible and what could not be."

"'Twould seem you are a widow. More things are possible for widows than unmarried women."

"How do I know if these memories are true? Could these be just some images my mind has made up to fill in the gaps? Mayhap I am still married? This may not have been my husband at all, but a brother or someone else?"

She turned to face the lady. "I cannot make plans or accept his love without knowing my truths. And I do not know when or even if that will happen."

Lady Margaret reached up and wiped her tears with a piece of linen. "You show remarkable sense, child, in the face of all this uncertainty in your life. Waiting is probably the best choice at this time." She accepted the handkerchief and finished wiping her eyes.

"I had thought to give myself another month before making any decisions. If nothing changes, I may follow your suggestion and seek refuge at that convent you mentioned. Until then, may I continue to accept your generosity?"

"As I told you before, Isabel, once offered, Lord Orrick's hospitality is not withdrawn.

Royce has been here three years and there has not been talk of him leaving. Connor the Scot, Sir Richard, Sir Hugh and many others have sought the sanctuary that this place offers. Even I have been here a score of years and Orrick has not asked me to leave yet."

Isabel laughed at her words. A tinge of the truth lay there, along with a hint of the lady's own interesting history. She did not have the right to ask of it and would not chance insulting someone who had given her so much already.

"And Royce? What of him?"

"Royce faces his own choices. The difference is that his are of his own making."

"And mine are not?"

"Nay, Isabel, you were nearly killed and left for dead. That was not of your own choosing. So, do not worry over that."

"What do I do now, my lady?" She was tired of this struggle.

"Rest. Eat. Read. Pray. Work on another tapestry with me. Work in the gardens or in the village as you can. One thing we have not tried yet is music."

"Music?" Nothing came to mind about her musical abilities.

"I have a psaltery here that has been neglected in these last months. Mayhap you have the skills and talent to play it?"

"I know not." She shrugged. "I will try."

"'Tis what I wanted to hear. Be open to these things and I am confident we will find some familiar things for you. I am always here to talk with you, Isabel. No matter the time."

"You have my gratitude, my lady."

Margaret led her to the door and pulled it open. As Isabel walked out, the lady touched her on the sleeve.

"I have been praying over this, Isabel, and I am convinced that the Almighty has a plan for you. He brought you here and he will provide for you. Never doubt that."

Their first meeting was not as painful as he thought it might be. Asked by Lord Orrick to join him in the solar, he arrived a few minutes early and paused outside the door to listen to the music coming from within. The soft lilt of a pipe, the stronger sounds of the psaltery and the drumming on a tabor produced a tune worthy of dancing. Tapping his foot to the melody, a familiar one, William was surprised when the door opened.

Jehane invited him in and closed the door quietly behind him.

The music continued as he was waved over by Lord Orrick. He was not surprised to find Isabel in this women's domain, but the sight and sound of her plucking the psaltery was not what he expected. As he watched the small group play, he was once again amazed at her abilities. The song drew to a close and he added his applause to the others.

At that moment, Isabel looked up from the wooden instrument and caught his eyes. Here, in the midst of the others, she'd become the lady again—she wore a clean gown, her hair lay arranged and covered and not in the riotous curls he'd seen last, and her behavior was polite and appropriate.

He wanted the woman back. As if she'd read his mind, she gifted him with a smile that told him she was thinking of their time spent together. On his way back to the keep that day, he'd made up his mind not to sink back into the darkness and to enjoy whatever moments they shared in these days before she left. It was time to put his decision into practice, something harder than he thought it would be.

"Shall we try another, Isabel?" Rosamunde asked.

At Isabel's nod, Rosamunde lifted the flute to her lips and began another tune. She slowly played the first notes and then a few more. As he observed them, Isabel closed her eyes and listened. First her head began to move up and down in time with Rosamunde's tune, then her fingers caught the strings, matching the melody. A few notes later, Lady Margaret added a beat to it and the three played as one.

'Twas good to see her enjoy herself. Accepting a cup of ale from one of the servants, William sat on a bench and let the music flow over him. If he let his thoughts go, he could imagine many nights like this one. Isabel and him being part of this household, sharing a life, sharing a love.

He caught hold of his thoughts before they became too wild and out of control. In doing so, he did not realize he'd been shaking his head, until Lady Margaret gave him a pointed look.

"You did not like our selection, Royce?"

"Your pardon, my lady," he said with a bow. "I was woolgathering while I listened. I am most impressed by the talents you and your ladies displayed here tonight. Will there be more?" He raised his cup in salute to each of them in turn, ending with Isabel.

"Shall we try one more?" Lady Margaret asked. "Isabel. Why do you not begin? Just play whatever tune comes to mind and we will follow you this time."

She took in a deep breath and released it, trying to relax. He could see the trembling in her hands and admired the courage within her. Of course, as had been with him, Lady Margaret and Lord Orrick's support, whether vocal or silent, made the difference. Isabel rested her fingers on the strings for a moment and then moved them to some melody she either remembered or felt. The other two women nodded and joined her in the now-familiar song.

He could like this. After three years of denying himself these comforts of a normal life, his hunger for them grew. Disturbed by how much he could desire those things he had given up, William made his way to the far side of the room and gazed into the brazier that kept the chamber warm.

Any contemplation of making an offer to Isabel needed the support of Orrick. If he wanted to take this step, it would require that Orrick know the truth and be willing to keep up the charade. He would speak to the lord and gain his acceptance and then approach Isabel. He was so caught up in his thoughts that he did not hear her draw near.

"Your look is as dark as your tunic, Royce. Was my playing not as good as you said?"

He spun to face her. "Do not think it, Isabel. I must admit that your abilities surprised me again. What made you try to play the psaltery?"

"The question should be 'who made me' and the answer is obvious." She smiled and lifted her cup to her mouth. "'Twas one of her suggestions and you can see it had merit."

"Do you remember anything when you play?" He moved to her side as he asked. "Do any images or sounds come to you?"

"As I must always answer, nay."

Her face showed a deep sadness and he was not pleased that he had caused it. William tried to stop, but he could not resist reaching out to stroke her cheek. "'Twill come, Isabel. When the time is right, you will remember."

When he thought she would turn into his palm, she stepped back. A frown deepened on her brow and her eyes narrowed. "I have made one decision."

"And that is?"

"If nothing changes, if I remember nothing more, when summer is ended, I will move to the convent where Lady Margaret's sister is."

"Move to the convent?" Louder than he'd planned, his comment drew some undesired attention from the others in the room. He cleared his throat and began anew. "Is that wise?"

"Wiser than staying here with no clear past or future."

"Isabel," he said, reaching out and grasping her hand. With her back to the room, no one could see his touch. "Make no commitment to this for now. Please."

"I have made none. Yet."

William now felt not only the walls inside him, but also the underpinnings of his world of these past few years, crumbling into dust. All the detachment he'd worked toward, all the distance he'd placed between himself and others, all the indifference he'd cultivated toward life in general was disintegrating beneath him. Could he survive if he reached out to her now? Could he survive if he did not?

"Give this some time. Give us—" he entwined their fingers and stroked her palm with his thumb "—more time?"

Isabel's body tensed and shivered in response to his touch and he was glad for her reaction. She had not closed her heart to him yet. There was still time. Still time for…what?

"I would speak to Orrick and then we must talk more. Give me a few days?"

"Isabel?" Lady Margaret called from across the room. It invaded the private moment they were sharing, but William knew they could go no further here, now. He needed to undertake some arrangements before he could make any offers or promises to her.

"Coming, my lady," Isabel answered as she release his hand. "Lady Margaret has urged me to keep an open mind about my future. And since you have asked the same, I will do so."

She walked away and William found it difficult to breathe, the heart he had thought dead long ago pounded in his chest until he believed it would burst. And in spite of the strangeness and discomfort, he liked the feeling.

Chapter Nineteen

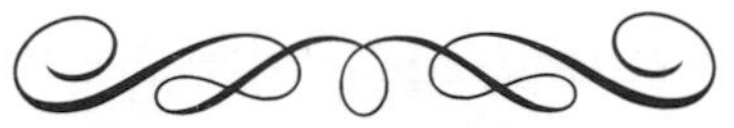

It happened as she was walking through the village, returning from an errand for Lady Rosamunde to Wenda's cottage. Isabel noticed a smaller lane leading off in a direction she'd not seen before. The sun shone down brightly and she had no desire to rush back to the keep, so she decided to follow that path and see who lived on it.

Only a few small thatched-roofed crofts lay beside it and Isabel was turning back when the voices came out of the nearest.

"You stupid cow! 'Tis your failing, after all." An older woman berated someone. "If you were a better wife, this would not happen."

Isabel could not stop herself and in a moment she stood outside the cottage from where the voices came. Closing her eyes and hoping she'd be forgiven for eavesdropping, she listened.

"But, Mother, I try to be a good wife to your son. Truly," answered a younger woman.

"A good wife? A good wife? See how you behave to me? No wife of my son should be arguing this and not to me."

"But..." A slap ended the younger woman's words.

"You are too haughty. You do not obey. You resist your husband's attempts to correct you. You are not a good wife to my son."

There was a pause, however this time the younger woman did not answer back. She was learning.

Isabel could not breathe. She remembered the endless berating, the relentless breaking down of her will, her resolve and even her self. More words broke into her reverie.

"If you would comply, if you would not look at him with such challenge in your eyes, if you were not such a failure then mayhap God would not be punishing him and us like this. You must put yourself under my son's dominion if you want to take this sin from you."

Isabel lost her balance and reeled back. Stumbling away, she could not see or hear but for the words and sights coming from inside her. This old woman had spoken the same words as…as…her husband's mother.

"You come here with such pride and such condescension in your eyes. Think you are so much better than he? Than us?"

"No, my lady. I do not." She could not help raising her eyes and meeting his mother's. The stinging slap did not surprise her this time.

"You treat him with disrespect. You treated his family with disrespect. 'Tis another of your failings before God and before us."

"I do not—" Her words were cut off by another blow. She could feel the tear in her lip where the lady's ring cut it and the warmth of the blood as it began to flow.

"Do not speak to me with such arrogance. You are nothing but what my son makes you. You have nothing but what he gives you. Listen to my counsel and learn that quickly." She was tempted by anger alone to reply, but the woman's eyes had taken on a dangerous glare. "He has urged me to teach you the ways of a good wife. It begins now."

"I am a good wife," she argued, unable to keep the words in.

Her mother-by-marriage delivered another strike that was belied by her short stature. "First, you will seek the forgiveness of God, then you will seek it from my son. Some solitary time of contemplation will aid you in seeing the errors of your sinful ways."

Servants caught her arms and dragged her from the solar, down corridors and steps until she was far below in the belly of the castle. No one helped her as she struggled and called out. The servants would not; even her own maid had been sent back to her family. She was alone.

Soon she found herself in a small, cold, wet cell. Her husband's mother stood outside the door and glared at her. With her nod, the door was pulled shut and she heard the bar drop into place on the outside. Glancing around this cruel chamber, she saw no candles, no bedding but for matted straw in the corner and a bucket that could only be for…

"Pray. Think about your sins. Ask God to grant you his forgiveness so that you come to my son with a clean heart and a willingness to submit to him in all ways."

"My lady. Please do not do this. I am a good wife."

As the light and people disappeared from the hall, she sank to her knees, unable to fight the tears, the weakness inside her any longer. Curling over, she whispered in her pain.

"I am a good wife."

Stunned by these memories, Isabel sank to her knees on the ground. She could not control the rolling of her stomach or the dizziness it brought. The heaving went on for a few minutes before it calmed and she waited for its end. She tugged off her veil and barbette and let the breezes cool her overwarm face and neck.

Her legs trembled so she did not attempt to stand. Sitting up, she dragged herself to the nearest tree and leaned against it. Royce had urged her to think on these memories while they were still new in her mind, so she closed her eyes and listened again to the scene she'd relived. Not only were the words still fresh, but so was the pain they caused.

Once more it all came back to her weakness, her failure as a wife. These memories showed her that her sin was known by many more than just the man she thought was her husband. His family knew of whatever dishonor she'd caused and joined in his fury at her over it. It was her fault.

Now it was the feelings that flooded back on her. The pain and the weakening. She'd been kept without food or even water for days in the cell before being returned to her chambers. But more than the thirst or hunger, the thing that had scared her the most was that she'd given in and begun to believe their accusations.

It had not happened at the time of this memory, for Isabel could feel that this was early in their process of intimidation. No, it had been later. After believing herself stronger than them and their methods of tearing her down, at some time many months or even years later, she had accepted their accusations as truth and accepted that she was not worthy of her husband's respect and esteem. That she had failed and could not be forgiven for her lacking. That she deserved their treatment of her because of her sin.

She did not know how much time had passed, but when she spied the small leather pouch she had fetched from Wenda for Lady Rosamunde, Isabel knew she must return to the keep or she would be missed. Regaining her feet, she took several deep breaths trying to release some of the tension that filled her. Looking around, she saw the beginning of the path that would lead through the center of the village. Picking up her veil and barbette straps and the herbs procured from Wenda, she headed in that direction.

Still overwhelmed by the memories, Isabel thought on Wenda's words about why she could not remember. Was she hiding from the truth with this loss of memory? Thinking back on all the memories she had regained, she seemed to be looking at two different women—the happy one who lived among a loving family and the beleaguered one who lived with a controlling and manipulative husband and his family.

Who was she? Which of these women? And which one did she go back to when the rest of her life was recovered? Walking back toward the keep, she did not need to fret over that question, for it was the easiest of all she'd asked herself to answer. She would choose the first self. And, living here, with the support of Orrick and Margaret and the love of Royce would be the closest she could come to reclaiming that type of life if her memory did not return.

Isabel reached the center of the village and the well that was its lifeblood. Many women gathered around it, filling buckets and jars with water for their chores and their needs. Without her veil on to cover her scar, Isabel drew one of her braids over her shoulder and forward.

"Are you well, my lady?" one woman asked at her approach.

"I am overly hot and came to seek a drink of cool water on my way back to the keep."

The group closest all nodded in understanding since the sun glared down on them now. A younger woman leaned over the edge of the well and pulled up the bucket within it. Taking a beaten metal cup from a ledge in the stone, she filled it with water and offered it to Isabel. She drank it down, letting its chill soothe her burning throat.

"You look ill, my lady. Have ye no maid with you?" One of the women motioned to a young girl from nearby, took her hand and led her to Isabel. "Would ye like her to walk back to the keep with ye? She be a good girl and knows the way, she does."

Isabel was about to accept the aid when his voice called out to her.

"I will take you back, Isabel."

She shaded her eyes from the glare of the sun and looked up to see Royce sitting on his horse, watching her at the well. How long he'd been there or how much he'd seen she knew not, but his presence was the comfort it always was to her. He reached out his hand and beckoned her.

"My thanks for your kind offer—" Isabel tried to remember the woman's name from their previous meetings "—Maude. But I will avail myself of…"

She could not think of what to call him to the common folk. At the knowing glances and speculative winks, she simply stopped trying to explain and walked to him. Royce leaned down and lifted her to a place in front of him on the horse. Seated in his lap, she felt his arms surround her as he took control of the reins.

"Come, Isabel. The cool ocean and the beach call to me."

She did not object to this change in plans and, with his invitation, lost all thoughts of urging a return to the keep. He pushed his horse to a fast walk and directed it to the path leading to the beach. Isabel permitted herself the guilty pleasure of leaning against his chest and feeling the security of his arms about her.

The sand was still packed down from the receding tide when they dismounted, and it was easy to walk upon it on their way to the water's edge. They walked wordlessly to an outcropping of rocks and he pointed out the driest one for her to sit on. It was already absorbing the warmth of the sun and was pleasant to sit on with the ocean breezes rustling past them.

He wore his chain mail, its hood resting on his shoulders. Tugging off his leather gloves, he tucked them under his belt and reached for her hand. The anticipation of the touch of his mouth on her wrist was exquisite and Isabel felt shivers move through her as he turned her hand and kissed her there. His gaze caught hers as he did and she stared back, imagining the touch of his mouth in all those other places, the ones that tingled now as she watched him.

Royce ended his intimate touch and placed her hand between both of his. "I would have you with me, Isabel."

She swallowed several times, trying to ease the tightening in her throat. Before she could speak, he did once more.

"I would have you with me always. If you would have me." His voice was gruff, the way it had been when he spoke of anything between them. Was he offering her marriage?

"And I would be with you, Royce, but…" Her

words trailed off as she considered his offer. "I cannot promise myself to you while my past hangs over my head." He looked ready to argue, but she continued with another deep concern of hers. "And what of your past? You remember your life before Silloth, sometimes too well, I think. Would you share that past with me even as you ask me to share your future?"

His face grew serious and his eyes darkened at her request. "Isabel, I seek to forget my past as you seek to remember yours. Can you not accept what I am now?" That admission cost him much, she could see that now. The pain and fear in his eyes told her more than his words, but the glimmer of hope there tore her heart apart.

What could she say? The cowardly part inside her wanted to scream acceptance of him and his offer. Having glimpsed the pain of her life in the memories today, she wanted nothing so much as to leave behind the pale, terrified woman she had become under her husband's hand and return to the happy, alive one she knew she had been before her marriage. And the one she knew she could be with Royce.

"Do you offer marriage?"

"I am free to marry, Isabel. There is no impediment preventing me from taking those vows. Can you believe me on this?"

This was new to her. She had seen him angry or patient, hungry or satisfied, even imperious or cooperative. She had heard him ask questions, make requests and even issue orders. But she had never heard him beg for anything. He was risking so much of himself, so much of his heart for her. She did believe him. There were many things in his past he refused to tell her, but she would wager her soul that he did not lie to her now.

"Do you swear on your honor as a knight?" She guessed about this, but she wanted some sign of his commitment, some piece of his past. She was on dangerous ground as she tested him in this way.

"I cannot. I wish that I could, but there was no honor in the knight I once was." The bleak look in his eyes caused her to look away. He stood and took a few steps from her. He faced the ocean with his eyes closed now and the urge to run to him was great.

She slid from the rock and walked to him. Knowing that she was taking a great step, she reached up from behind him and encircled his waist with her arms. "Can you promise me on the man you are now?"

He turned and gathered her closer. "What man is that?" His face was blank now, as though he had pulled all of his strengths and weaknesses inside to avoid the coming threat. She reached up and stroked his cheek as he had done to hers many times.

"The man who Orrick and Margaret trust. The man who saves strangers and stray dogs and boys. The one who I love."

He kissed her with a fierce determination and one that spoke of promises and possession. But she could not relinquish control yet. "You have not asked for my promise yet?" He released her and waited on her words. "You may not like it when you hear it."

"Do you love me?" he asked.

"Aye, that I do, Royce. But I can only promise to consider your offer. I cannot promise more than that until I know more."

"Do you know of an impediment between us? Is not the man you know to be your husband dead, leaving you free to marry again?"

"Yes," she whispered, "he is dead." She knew that for certain.

"Is there something else that stands between us?" When she thought to tell him about what she'd remembered earlier, he shushed her. "And I will hear nothing of these shortcomings you fear. Tell me of something with substance and not the ravings of a man cowardly enough to kill his wife in the dark of night."

Isabel looked into his eyes and saw the love he had for her beaming at her. "There is nothing but my fears."

Royce leaned down and she readied herself for his kiss. He stopped just before his lips touched hers and spoke. "I will give you the time you need to accept those fears and me. I will not press you for a decision until the summer's end."

Disappointment filled her. She wanted to feel his need for her. She needed his strength and determination, for she knew now that he'd made the decision to seek a new life, she could draw on that in her own weak times. He leaned his head back and roared out his laughter at her expression.

"Do not worry, Isabel. I plan to woo you during this time to make certain I receive the answer I want."

Woo her? That sounded promising.

"How will you woo me, Royce? What do you plan?" She smiled and for the first time allowed herself to feel some hope of a new life.

"As in any good battle plan, I will not give away my strategy, lady," he said as he finally touched his lips to hers, reminding her of their time in his cottage. "But I will say that I will woo you ardently." He wrapped her braids around his hands and pulled her face closer. "Ardently."

His mouth possessed hers, then. Tasting and touching, lips and tongues met and met again. Just as his hands released her hair and began to slide down over her breasts a sharp whistling caught his attention and took it from her. She turned and followed his gaze up until she saw a guard on the tower waving at them.

"'Tis Connor telling me that we are seen."

"Seen? From there?" She shaded her eyes and tried to tell if it was truly his man Connor on the roof of the keep. "How do you know it is him?"

"Our signal." He stepped away and whistled in a different way in answer. The man at the top waved again and then continued walking along the battlements.

She thought that the moment between them was over even as he wrapped her in his embrace again. "I suppose that your ardent wooing is over?" Her body now thrummed with a new need for him.

"If it is ardent wooing you want," he said, kissing her lightly, "'tis ardent wooing you will get." He scooped her up into his arms and carried her away from the water. "There is a place farther up near the cliff that is suitable."

"Suitable for what?" The tips of her breasts tightened at his words.

"Wooing," he said as he dipped his head to enter the small alcove in the cliff.

He stood her before him and unhooked his belt. Leaning over to shrug off his mail, he pulled his hauberk and tunic off as well. Standing before her in only his hose and boots, she tried not to stare too much at the proof of his intentions. He followed her focus down and then smiled at her with the wicked smile she'd seen only once or twice before. The one that made her hungry for what he promised.

"Ardently," he said as he took her in his arms.

It was not too much later that Isabel decided she could like ardent wooing.

Chapter Twenty

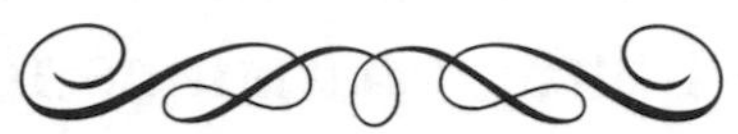

Once allowed to run free, he discovered that his love and his need for her was almost unmanageable. They had been reprimanded by the lady of the keep for their behavior, but when she burst out laughing at their explanation for Isabel's wet, sandy and disheveled condition upon their return one afternoon, the message was lost. He did restrain himself more in front of others, but on those occasions when he arranged to get Isabel alone and in some place conducive to his aim, he wooed her ardently.

Nevertheless, deep inside him lived a kernel of fear that this happy ending would never be his. Mayhap it was caused by his guilt or his fear over his past catching up with him. Mayhap it was simply nervousness over the chance to marry the woman he loved. Whatever the cause, it was there, and no amount of praying it would go away or ordering it to cease helped to make it disappear.

August's heat gave way to September's cooling and the keep and those living there finished the harvests of the farmlands under Orrick's control and continued the preparations for the coming winter. Wood was cut and stored, thatched roofs were repaired or replaced, animals to be slaughtered and salted were chosen and fatted.

William spent his days carrying out the duties entrusted to him by Orrick and spent his evenings with Isabel. Occasionally he managed to sneak into her chambers to await her return. A few times, he lured her out to the cottage in the forest. Most times he simply enjoyed whatever moments they shared.

If she remembered anything more of her life, she never said so. He would see her eyes glaze over as though she was watching her thoughts, but she denied any new knowledge whenever he asked her about it. After years of punishing himself for the sins he'd committed, William allowed himself to start anew. When Lord Orrick summoned him that early September morn, he had no inkling that his world was about to crash down around him.

"My lord, you called me?" William entered the solar after knocking, as was his habit. Orrick and Margaret were both present and neither one looked pleased with meeting him.

"This came from Brother Ralph. Since it concerns you, we thought you should handle it."

William took the parchment from Orrick and unrolled it. He dreaded the news it would bring and, as he read each line, his worst fears were made real. There was a woman waiting at the abbey to ask about her missing sister. He closed his eyes and cursed the Almighty for this cruel trick.

"William, have you told her who you are yet?"

He whirled around at hearing his true name spoken. Lady Margaret stood next to him, watching him closely. How could she have known? For how long had she, had they, known?

"I am Royce."

"William de Severin, we met once. Many years ago, when you served as page to Henri FitzEmpress. Some of the other boys teased you and chased you into an alley."

He could not believe his ears. The incident had happened so many years before and so many important things superseded it that he had quite forgotten it. A lady, one of King Henry's many mistresses, had saved him from serious injury with her appearance. A boy at the time, he had never paid attention to who it was.

Lady Margaret walked over and sat next to her husband again. William looked from one to the other. They knew. They knew him and they knew what he had done.

"I did not know you at first. You had changed so much since then. But I noticed the birthmark on your hand and remembered seeing it on that bloodied boy in the alley at Chinon."

"Why?" Why had they never let on that they knew who he was?

"Quite simply, because you saved my lord Orrick's life."

William was stunned. Unable to focus his thoughts or to speak all the questions within him, he sat down hard on a bench near them. Holding his head in his hands, he felt as though he were standing in a quagmire with nothing firm to hold on to. Taking a deep breath, he realized he must face the man whose trust he had betrayed.

"My lord," he said, standing once more before Orrick, "I have repaid your support with betrayal and lies. I cannot remain here, I know, but you should know how much the sanctuary provided has meant to me."

Orrick rose and took him by the shoulders. If the lord saw fit to beat him where they stood, William would not fight back. 'Twas the least of the punishments he deserved.

"I have not asked you to leave. There is much to do before winter and I would have the service you swore to me. I am not willing to release you."

"You and my lord can sort out what service you owe and what oaths were sworn at another time. At this moment, the important thing is whether or not this woman awaiting some answer of Orrick of Silloth is truly looking for Isabel or someone else." Margaret pushed the men apart and picked up the scroll that he had dropped. "I ask you again, William. Have you told her who you are?"

Still overwhelmed to find out that they had known him, William could not answer. He could not tell Isabel about his past, his sins and his weaknesses. She would think him the monster he was if she discovered the lives he had ruined in his arrogant quest for wealth and power.

"I cannot, lady. If you know me, then you know she would revile me more than I already hate myself."

"Tell her, William. If you love her, tell her and let her decide. Trust her and the love you share enough to give her the truth."

"You cannot know the extent of my wickedness if you think that she will continue to love me when she hears of my sins."

William watched as Margaret and Orrick exchanged a long and meaningful glance. Then they looked at him. "She could," the lady said as she clasped Orrick's hand in hers. "Seek her out before you leave to speak with this woman."

William nodded, but the words of agreement stuck in his throat. He feared losing Isabel more than anything now that he'd had the chance to begin anew. His defenses were gone and, if he needed to barricade himself from those outside and go back to living the existence that she had banished, he could not.

He bowed and left the solar. For once he would disregard the advice of both lord and lady and first determine the identity of the woman waiting at the abbey. For all he knew, this woman could have been part of the plot to kill Isabel and he would be placing her in danger if he revealed anything about her.

The ride to Abbeytown would give him time enough to try to pull his concentration and the shattering pieces of his life back together. By the time he arrived there he would surely have figured out a way to survive the terrible reckoning he could feel approaching.

Brother Ralph greeted him warmly and showed him to the prior's chambers. He would say nothing of his letter or of the woman as they walked through the courtyard and into the building that housed the prior, the clerks and the other lay brothers who assisted in the running of the abbey. Soon he was asked to wait and then left alone. Steeling himself for whatever came, he tried to calm down and regain his composure.

The door was opened in a few minutes and Brother Ralph escorted in a lady with her two attendants. He stood and bowed to her as they were introduced.

"Lady Alianor of Hexham, this is—" Before Ralph could finish, the lady interrupted.

"Lord Orrick? My thanks for coming to meet with me."

Brother Ralph stammered and stuttered in that way that many monks had when confronted with a woman of great vigor. Queen Eleanor had that effect as well.

"Actually, my lady, I am Royce of Silloth, Lord Orrick's man in this matter. How may I be of assistance to you?"

Brother Ralph excused himself as quickly as possible and the door slammed behind him. Rather than being insulted, the lady laughed and sought a chair a few paces away. "I seem to have that effect on some men. Although my husband urges me to temper my behavior, he has learned to live with it." Soft laughter came from her two companions who stood a respectful distance away.

"Your husband, my lady?" William had paid no attention to the political alliances and intrigues since leaving John's court and could not recollect who she might be related or married to.

"I have the honor of being wife to Guy, the Earl of Hexham, sir." He recognized the name. A powerful man from a powerful and well-connected family.

"What help can I offer the Countess of Hexham?"

She paused and looked at the two women with her. Without a word, they curtsied before her and started to leave the room. One opened the door and nodded to her. "Still there?"

"What is it, my lady?"

"A man following us. I thought he was sent by my husband, but we know him not."

"A thief, perchance?" William walked to the door and peered out over the woman's head. "Where?"

He looked in the direction where the woman nodded and caught only a glimpse of the man in question. Too well dressed for a thief, he thought.

"No matter. My lord husband has sent along enough guards to protect the entire kingdom from an invading army."

She waved the women off and then sat back down. As soon as they were alone, she caught his glance and held it. His heart almost stopped as he realized that she looked at him with Isabel's eyes. The same shape and color, the resemblance was unmistakable. Not willing to give up information yet, he bowed his head and waited for her to speak.

"Pray, be seated, Sir Royce. Your journey was a swift one and there is wine or ale if you need refreshment."

"I have made this ride countless times, my lady. I am well." He did sit so that she could not see his legs shake.

"I am here on a private matter and have been told that I can trust Orrick as a man of discretion. Does this go for his man, also?"

"It does, my lady. I will keep in confidence, except to him, anything you share with me." And most likely keep it from him, as well, William thought. "If this is a private matter, is your husband aware of your visit here?" He needed to find out how many were involved in this.

"I would not be here without his support. He knows every detail of my undertaking." She smiled at his insolence in asking such a question.

"And your undertaking is…?"

"I seek my sister."

"She is missing?" he asked, holding his breath for the answer he knew was coming.

"Actually she is dead, sir." She was watching him, assessing his reaction to her strange words. He frowned and laughed.

"Is this some kind of a sham, my lady? Why do you seek your sister if she is dead? Should you not look in the place she is buried if you wish to offer prayers for her soul?" He could feel the sweat beading on his lip and trickling down his back. Could this really be Isabel's sister? Had she been involved in the attack?

"Pray forgive me, Sir Royce. I should begin at the beginning so that you understand about my search." She stood and he began to rise until she waved him back into his seat. "My sister is the eldest daughter of Charles, Duke of Richmond. I am his second daughter, but Anne and I are separated by only minutes."

"Twins?" he whispered. He tried to keep his expression one of polite interest, but had no idea if he was succeeding or not.

"Yes, twins, although not identical. She is dark in coloring and I am fair, however we share the same shade of eyes."

'Twas at that moment he realized that he finally knew her name—*Anne.* But would she ever be anyone other than Isabel to him?

"As befits the daughters of a duke, we were betrothed to the sons of great families to cement alliances and to smooth over some old disagreements. Anne was married to the nephew of the Duke of Lancaster and I, as you already know, to Hexham's heir. My husband has recently ascended to this title and inheritance with the unexpected death of his father."

"My condolences on his passing," he said politely. "And your sister passed away, also?"

She turned and stared at him. She seemed to be deciding how much and how to say what was on her mind. "She did not pass away as you say, sir. She was murdered, plain and simple."

He shifted on his chair at her accusations. "And your proof of this accusation?"

She looked at him and he noticed the tears in her eyes. Lady Alianor sat down and wiped her eyes before continuing. "I have no proof, sir, other than in here." She touched her chest over her heart. "I would know if she were dead. I would know."

He ached to reach out to her, but he dared not. In her pain, he could hear the echo of Isabel's words and her grief. "Where is she buried? Did you help prepare her for burial?"

"Oh, nay. Her husband's family took care of that before we were even given the news."

"Her husband was so grief stricken, then? He had the burial quickly?" William probed this sore spot.

"The only good thing that cur of a husband did was die with her."

"I apologize, my lady. I am confused. Her husband is dead, too?"

She was talking about Isabel.

Merde.

"I ask your pardon, Sir Royce. I am making a muddle of this. My father was told that both Anne and her husband Edward were attacked by brigands on their way back from a pilgrimage to the cathedral in Carlisle. Only his body could be recovered from the attack and was buried quickly because of its condition."

"It seems very clear to me, my lady, that your sister and her husband are dead. Yet, you do not believe this?"

"Anne and I shared many things as children. One of the things I treasure the most is the special bond between us that tells me when something is wrong with her and the same with her."

"I have heard of such things. And this *bond* tells you what?" He asked in spite of knowing exactly what she already knew—her sister was alive.

"Sir Royce, I would know if my sister were dead. I would have felt her death. And I feel only her distress. She cannot be dead." She twisted her hands in her lap.

He waited for her to calm before speaking. In his mind he could hear Isabel, *Anne,* telling him of hearing her sister's voice guiding her out of the marshes the night of the attack and urging her to go on. He wanted to scoff at the outrageous notion that two people could be connected in this way, but there seemed to be something between them.

"What, other than these feelings, makes you think that something other than the reason given you caused her death?"

"I was distraught when I received the news. I have not seen my sister since just after our marriages were held five years ago."

"So long?" With the families mentioned spread out over England, it would not be unusual for visits to be limited. But with two sisters as close as these were, not seeing her in that long would have been alarming.

"Her marriage was to repair a breach in trust between Lancaster and my father. They are not friends, but with Anne's marriage, they are not enemies. My father and Edward's father and uncle would have been pleased to never lay eyes on each other again. Anne," she said sadly, "was caught between them."

William stood and walked to where the prior had set out wine and ale. He poured two cups and handed one to Lady Alianor. She sat and sipped it slowly. He waited again as she collected her thoughts. He fought within himself against the urge to ease her pain by telling her the truth—that Anne was alive.

"What was there that made you suspicious about her death? And, I did not ask you, when did this happen?"

"This would have taken place in early June. We were told that Edward and Anne had traveled to the cathedral to pray for a child. Although I have been blessed twice with sons, Anne has not been so blessed." She held out a hand to him. "Sir? Are you well?"

He did not feel well at all for the bile churned in his gut at her words. This was the basis of Isabel's husband's hatred and the reason for his plan to kill her. She had failed to give him the heirs required of such marriages. William swallowed and took a mouthful of ale to keep from throwing up.

Isabel's tearful plea the night she followed him in the storm repeated in his thoughts. *What failure on my part caused a hatred so deep that he would kill me over it?* Trapped in an unfruitful marriage with no way out was a good enough reason, it would seem.

"Do not worry over me, my lady. I have been

suffering a sour stomach for a few days." Probably the guilt stirring his insides.

"I journeyed to the cathedral myself as a penance for my part in this. While there, I spoke to some of the monks who told me that Edward's party did not head south toward Lancaster as we'd been told, but that they traveled instead in this direction."

He did not forget the first part of her statement, but focused on the second. "What was their destination? Where do—where did they reside?"

"Edward received a keep in Allonby. They were retiring there to pray for God's mercy and to make all attempts to fulfill the terms of their marriage contract. That is not far from Silloth?"

"About two days' travel down the coast from Lord Orrick's lands."

William was torn now. Edward of Allonby had held so little trust in God's answer that he took matters into his own hands to rid himself of a barren wife. Depending on the terms of the property settlement on their betrothal and marriage, he could have inherited a sizable amount of lands and wealth either with the birth of an heir or on her death. 'Twould seem he tried for both methods.

He was certain now that Alianor had nothing to

do with Isabel's attack and that to keep them apart was wrong. He also knew that he was not suitable for the daughter of a duke, not even when he held all of his family lands and titles and certainly not now as the penniless knight in this corner of England. As surely as he breathed, he would lose her as soon as she was claimed by Alianor. Whether her memory returned or not, their plans for a life together, their love, had no place and no chance.

He needed time to consider what to do. Lady Alianor did not have any proof of Isabel's existence, other than feelings. If her father or her husband had truly believed in her intuition, there would have been armed parties of soldiers searching the land for Isabel.

Could he give her up now that he held the secret of her existence and her identity? Even when he was at his best, it would be a struggle to relinquish this woman. If Lady Alianor did not find her and was finally convinced that her feelings were incorrect, she would leave and never return, accepting that her sister was truly dead. And he would have her with him.

His long-unused conscience flared to life, gnawing at him with questions. How long would she stay with him if she discovered his past? How long until her memory returned and she realized that she was entitled to wealth and lands of her own, wealth and lands he could not offer her? Would she hate him then as much as she loved him now?

His head ached as much as his gut. He glanced at the countess and thought of what to say. How could he bring this interview to a close and get back to Isabel? William remembered one of the things that Lady Alianor had said.

"If I might ask, my lady, you said you did penance for your part in this. How do you bear the blame for your sister's death?" She glared at his words and he rephrased them. "If your sister is dead."

"This is the most difficult part, Sir Royce."

"If you would rather not speak of it, my lady, I would understand since this entire situation contains issues of such a personal and private nature."

She reached out and touched his hand. With a halfhearted smile, she said, "No, I will tell you the whole of it. Since I am asking your assistance, you should know the sordid story."

When put like that, mayhap he did not want to hear the rest?

"You see, I was supposed to marry Edward and not Guy. But when he accompanied his uncle and father to Richmond for the negotiations, he frightened me with his…intensity. Anne knew how I felt about him and went to our father and convinced him she was infatuated with Edward. Since which of us were named in the marriage settlements did not matter, she took my place."

Her tears fell silently this time and he could say nothing. Alianor must have known about Anne's treatment at the hands of her disappointed husband and his family. She knew that her fears had spurred Anne into stepping forward to protect her. And now the reason behind the unhappy marriage was clear—Isabel, Anne, was barren.

William needed to get out of that room, for the ground beneath him felt as though it was shifting and he feared that the walls around him would crash down soon. He needed to put as much distance between Alianor and himself as was possible, for she was causing his conscience to think about doing the right thing in this matter and he could not let that happen.

Not yet.

Not yet.

Somehow he obtained her promise to wait a few days while he brought this news to Lord Orrick. He agreed to come back to the abbey and bring her any news of any untoward occurrence that had happened in the area in the early part of June. He gained himself just about a week to come to terms with the knowledge he had acquired and to decide what to do.

In leaving, he almost knocked over the two women who waited for her outside the chamber. The bells of the abbey called the monks there to the hour of sext and William faced staying at the abbey overnight since dusk was at hand. As he walked through the courtyard, he decided not to ask for a room for the night there. He needed a drink. Actually, he needed many of them to drown out the questions and voices seething inside of him.

Connor hailed him from the gate and William smiled as finally something went his way. Since his friend always carried a skin of *uisge beatha,* he could count on a supply of mind-numbing whiskey on hand. As Connor directed him to their campsite, William could count the short time that his conscience had to bother him. He never made it past the third swig of the potent brew.

Chapter Twenty-One

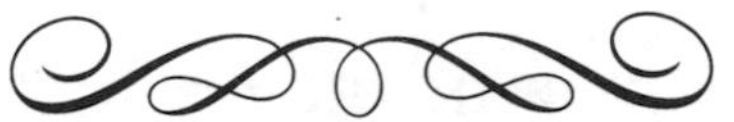

Isabel walked back from a short visit to the chapel and wondered if Royce would return before nightfall. He'd gone off, at the behest of Lord Orrick, and neither the lord nor his lady would say why or when to expect his return. Her time in prayer and contemplation had given her the answer she sought and now she wanted to share it with him…if he would only get back.

As if conjured by her thoughts of him, he walked up to her and took her hand. His eyes had a strange glint in them and he looked as though he had ridden hard and long to get back here. Quietly he tugged her to follow him and he led her to where his horse stood, saddled and ready outside the keep's gate.

"Royce, we are expected at supper." She began

to pull away, but his grip tightened. She looked at him to see why he did so.

"Isabel," he said, stumbling over her name. "Come with me now?"

She had never seen him in his cups, but she thought this might be the day after such an occasion. He looked rough to her, raw in some indefinable way. And never had she felt such need coming from him.

"Of course, I will."

He mounted first and then reached out to her. Without hesitation, she placed her foot on his and let him lift her before him on the horse. Their destination was never in question and in a few minutes, he brought the horse to stop outside his cottage. The first kiss began as soon as his feet touched the ground and continued as he backed her into the croft.

He peeled off her layers of clothing and when she could no longer breathe and wore nothing but her shift and stockings, he pulled away, intent on undressing himself. When he unbelted the chain mail and pulled it over his head, odors pungent enough to make her eyes water escaped from his road-weary tunic.

"I am offensive," he said so seriously that she laughed.

"You are that. If you kept some of the soap here, you could wash in the stream."

"We could wash in the stream," he repeated as he pulled open the small cupboard and found the pottery jar of soap. Over the past few weeks, more supplies and linens had been brought back here as their use of it as a private place increased.

She thought to object to walking outside in such a state of undress, but the light of the day was fading and they were far enough away from the village that no one should be nearby. Still, in only her shift, she felt naked before him. When he tugged off the last of his clothes, she did not know whether to object or admire. She admired.

Something was different about him. Mayhap it was the result of overimbibing? Men were known to wear the effects of too much wine or ale for days afterward. It was just not like him to behave so. They arrived at the edge of the stream and he continued to the place where she had washed her hair that day weeks and weeks ago.

"See the way this pool formed here?" she asked. "Just deep enough for bathing if the water is warm enough."

"I made it for just that purpose. By damming up part of the stream there—" he pointed to a pile of rocks and branches a few yards away "—it allows the water to collect, and then it flows out there when it reaches that level."

She had not noticed before that this was anything but formed by nature. She smiled at him. "What a wonderful plan! But I never saw you use it as such while I was here."

"I used it late at night when you were asleep. We were trying not to notice each other in those days and nights."

That had been exactly the situation between them. Isabel was certainly glad that was over. Royce walked into the pool and first sat then lay in the water and let it pour over and around him. After he was completely wet, he extended his hand for the soap she held in hers. Stepping into the water and closer to him, the coldness of the water surprised her.

"How can you stand this? It's so cold." She tried to give him the jar but he would not take it, forcing her to step closer. Finally she stood over him as he sat in the water.

"Would you wash me?"

His request was not the teasing she thought it

was and so she scooped out some soap and began to lather his hair. Leaning over she spread it down onto his shoulders and back. She tried to move away but he grabbed her legs and held her close.

"Your shift will get wet if you do not remove it."

"It will not," she said, taking another measure of soap, "if you are careful."

"Isabel," he said in the husky voice that foretold of pleasure, "I am not going to be careful and it will get wet. Take it off now or I will not carry the blame when you return to the keep in a wet shift."

There was barely a moment to spare, for she had no sooner lifted the shift over her head than he pulled her to him. Not knowing what to expect in this setting, she was surprised to feel his mouth on her thighs. Looking down to where he sat, she was puzzled.

"Here, step over me this way."

When she did as he directed, she stood above him with her legs spread over his lap. Exposed and aching, she moaned her pleasure as his seeking hands found the throbbing place between her legs. She reached out to find some balance and rested her hands on his shoulders.

He held her thighs apart and replaced his hands with his mouth and she bit her tongue trying not to let out the screams she wanted to make. Her knees weakened and she thought she would fall on him in the water. Royce guided her down until the heated core of her was on his hardness. In one swift movement, he filled her.

Joining in this way was new to her and she could feel his fullness stretching her inside until she moaned. With his hands free, he wreaked havoc on her body, touching her breasts and rubbing against the sensitive bud that seemed to be the center of all she felt at that moment. The tension, the excitement, the arousal gathered within her and she began to melt from inside out as her peak approached.

Royce had other ideas, for even as the first contractions pulsed inside her, he stopped and remained still. Not quite close enough to the edge to fall over it, she gasped as everything in her called out for release. When she tried to move on him, he grasped her hips and prevented her from doing it.

"Royce?"

"I want to make this last. Let me play you awhile."

She was not sure how this would work, but she

knew from that mischievous smile that he would insure her pleasure. Isabel gave herself up to him and he drew out the moment of completion for what seemed like hours by starting and stopping again and again.

When he finally let her reach her peak, she did scream it out into the night and her sounds echoed through the forest around them. And it was such a powerful ending that it went on and on, pulsing and racing through her in endless waves, until she collapsed in his arms.

When she regained her senses, she was in his arms in a shameful embrace being carried back to the croft. Draped over him like a shirt with her legs wrapped around his waist, she finally noticed that he was still hard…and still inside her! He walked them into the croft and knelt down with her and then laid her back onto the pallet.

"Isabel, I love you."

He said the words with a certain desperation that frightened her initially, but once he began thrusting into her already aroused softness, she accepted. His gaze never left hers this time and when she felt him harden even more, she knew his release was about to happen. He repeated her name over and over as he claimed her and as he marked her with each touch. His seed erupted against her womb and she watched his face as it finally lost the tension.

His body relaxed against hers and he remained within her for a long while. Lifting his weight off her, he rolled them to their sides and gathered her close. They were wet, but she had no desire to move from his side even to reach for a drying cloth.

"Royce?"

"Hmm?"

"If I give you my answer to your offer, will you woo me less ardently?"

He did not reply right away. She thought that mayhap he had fallen asleep and not heard her after all.

"Only if you want me to," he answered. "But I doubt I could."

She rested against him, enjoying the warmth and the quiet before actually giving him her acceptance. Isabel was certain he already knew what it would be, however she wanted to say the words to him.

"I would have you always, Royce, as my husband. For now and for always, come what may."

* * *

Her words killed him.

Given all he'd discovered, they ripped his heart and soul apart. He said nothing back since there were no words in his power to say at that moment. Overwhelmed by the emotions within him, he remained silent and simply held her, wanting to never let her go.

They both dozed off for a few minutes, but they could not remain there through the night. Lady Margaret, who had so many other reasons for hating him, would not forgive another violation in her courtly rules, and taking Isabel from the yard so boldly and keeping her away overnight would be a definite breach.

The fog induced by more than three swigs of Connor's potent whiskey hung over him still and he was grateful for it in some ways. It kept the voices out of his head. It kept the guilt and anger and other feelings at bay. The only thing he could think about was her. When he saw her walking in the courtyard, his only thought was to bury himself in her and to lose the pain of what was coming.

And she had accepted it. Him. She made no demands, expressed no preferences and suffered no hesitation. Isabel took him into her body, her soul, her heart with love. If anyone could heal him, it would be her.

It was not to be.

He took her love and possessed her body and soul even as he planned his betrayal of her and all they shared. She had brought him back from the edge of darkness and given life to his soul and he would repay her with deceit. Part of him screamed out even as he considered what to do. She did not deserve this from him.

She shifted in his arms and he kissed her neck, inhaling her scent and savoring it. He would keep it in his memory for the rest of his life, knowing that nothing, no one, could replace her.

He just wanted another week with her. If he was lucky, it would take that long for her sister to become suspicious of his late return and follow him here. Once Alianor arrived, 'twould not matter if Isabel…*Anne* remembered her life or not, her sister would never leave her behind.

And then he would move back into the darkness from where he'd come and never return. Regardless of Orrick's offer, William could not stay once Isabel left. He could not think about what he would do, but it would not be here.

The night arrived and its soft sounds surrounded the cottage. 'Twas time to take her back and face Orrick and Margaret with another lie. And more would follow until he left. They did not deserve it either, but soon he would be gone and they could relegate him to their memories as a mistake made in their lives.

Thoughts began to swirl in his mind, but he pushed them away. He would have his days with Isabel and then he would think, then he would make the decisions about who and what and where. For now, he would do the thing he had resisted for so long.

He would feel.

And so, with the determination of a man facing death and knowing when it would come, he forced the doubts and fears out of his mind. He would take this time with her and enjoy it to the fullest. William did not know the details of her marriage and did not need to in order to understand how unhappy it would have been for her. Her barrenness would have been held against her every passing day and in more ways than he could think of.

He would give her some small measure of happiness here until the truth came out. He would pleasure her until she screamed. He would love her with everything within his being and not want anything in return—no lands, no titles, no wealth. Only her love. Even for this short while.

Chapter Twenty-Two

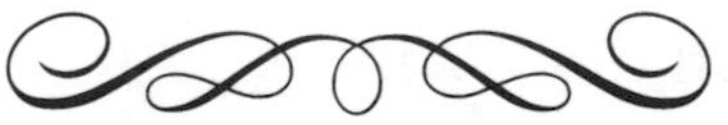

"Ah, the joys of being in love."

Isabel blinked, clearing her thoughts, and turned to Lady Rosamunde. "Your pardon, my lady. I did not hear your words."

Rosamunde laughed and Isabel looked at her. "You are wearing that dreamy expression again, Isabel. I hope you've asked Lady Margaret to send for a priest soon."

"Not yet," she answered. After she told Royce she would accept his offer of marriage, no more discussion of it happened. His attentions turned even more ardent, if that was possible, and she had been living in a whirlwind of passion and love for four days.

"At least after you marry, we can lock you in your chambers to get all of this fire out of you. Gautier and I," the lady's voice drifted off as she spoke of her husband, "were not seen for a sennight after ours."

She sighed and Isabel smiled. This seemed to be a place of happily married couples, a thing not always seen in noble and arranged marriages.

"Come then, Isabel. Let us be about our duties."

They had been enjoying a brief rest at the village well on their way back to the keep. Royce was away for the day, sent by Orrick to the southern boundaries of his lands to investigate reports of brigands. Isabel stood and stretched out all the sore and overused muscles of her body. And she gloried in every single one that reminded her of the ways Royce had loved her.

After meeting and learning the Royce who had saved her life, she had no idea of the passion that lived within him. She guessed that he'd been keeping all of it inside and denying himself the simple joys of living for the three years he'd been here. Now he seemed to be trying to release all of it on her.

Not that she was complaining. She would take it all.

"What I really need, Lady Rosamunde, is a nap."

That made Rosamunde laugh, but Isabel was serious. Mayhap with Royce gone for the day, she would get some rest. To recover from and to prepare for his ardent wooing.

As they reached the gate, Isabel realized she'd left her handkerchief back at the well. She told Rosamunde that she would return shortly and went back to get it. It was where she had left it and, after tucking it back in her sleeve, Isabel headed to the keep. The small entourage leaving through the gates surprised her for she knew of no visitors.

She dismissed her concern until she heard the laughter of one of the ladies in the party. The woman turned to one of her companions, said something and laughed again. In a moment they were on the north road and too far for her to see again.

What was Alianor doing here, so far from her home in Hexham?

She began to shake uncontrollably and tears filled her eyes to overflow. The tremors grew stronger until she could not breathe.

Alianor…her sister…

She…was…Anne.

Anne.

Daughter of Charles and Marie.

Sister of Alianor and Guillaume and the late Robert.

Wife of Edward.

Of Allonby.

Her life came back to her in a momentary flash. Childhood, womanhood, marriage, the attack. All of it. Her family. Anne blinked as images froze for a second and then were replaced by another. Everything she'd told Royce and the others was completed by the rest of her life.

Everything.

Edward was dead. She saw his face as he landed next to her on the ground. He glanced over at Culbert, his half brother who held the bloodied sword.

Culbert gained much with Edward's death—his wife already carried their heir in her belly. Stupid, stupid Edward! To put his trust in such a man was the stupidest thing he'd ever done.

Her father would seek vengeance for her "death" and regain the lands he'd given to Edward's family as part of her settlement. There would be war after all between Richmond and Lancaster.

Her husband was dead. She needed to tell Royce that she was free to marry. They could… she was…

Barren.

The word sliced through her. Taunts and insults and punishments and prayers jumbled together. One babe lost then nothing. She was empty of life.

Empty.

Anne gasped for breath and stumbled away from the keep. She needed to gather her thoughts and tell Royce everything. He would guide her in this. Glancing around, she knew where she had to go. He would find her there and know what to do. He would help her follow her sister and reclaim her life.

He would know.

William knew in his soul that something was wrong as soon as he entered the keep. A chill ran through him and he knew that it was over. Seeking out Orrick, he found him with Margaret in the solar. From their grim expressions, he'd been found out.

"You had a visitor today, Royce." Orrick put emphasis on his adopted name, letting him know how angry the lord was.

"A visitor, my lord? Who?" Why he carried on this charade he did not know. He rubbed his face and prepared for the worst.

"The lady Alianor of Hexham came looking for news of her sister. It seems that you spoke with her at length and promised to seek out news and return to her at the abbey." Orrick stood and walked over to him. "But you know all of that, do you not?"

"I do. Orrick…" At his fierce glance, William began anew. "My lord, I would explain."

"You have not told Isabel anything, have you?" Lady Margaret broke in. "Not your past and not her own?"

"Her name is Anne, daughter of Charles of Richmond and wife of the late Edward of Allonby, Lancaster's nephew."

His words gave them pause and they exchanged several looks before saying anything.

"Does she know? Have you told her?" Lady Margaret asked.

"No, my lady. I've said nothing of meeting with Alianor. She knows not. I just wanted more time…" he said as a way of explaining his behavior. "I knew her sister would come to claim her and that she will leave. I just wanted to hold her for a few more days. I wanted to be Royce and Isabel, who had a chance for happiness and not William and Anne who have none."

He turned to leave. He must find her and give her her life back. And lose her forever. "Where is she?"

"Lady Rosamunde said she complained of being tired and needing some rest and then she saw her no more. She is not in her chamber so…" Her words drifted off. They all knew where she had gone.

William left the keep and retrieved a horse from the stables. He felt his heart dying within him as he thought of the coming hours. What had he learned from this? That the Fates conspired against him? That he had no right to happiness or a life of his own after sinning as he had? That some cruel deity had given him a taste of what he was missing and then taken it from him?

Soon he stood before the cottage. No light shone within; no sounds came from it. But he felt her presence there. Opening the door, he stepped inside. He could see her sitting on the chair, on her chair. She said nothing and he could find no words to begin.

"I've been waiting for you, Royce. There is much to tell you."

"Why do you sit in the dark? Let me light a candle." He went to the cupboard, drew out a candle and lit it with the flint. Setting it in a holder on the table, William turned to face her. Her head was uncovered, her hair loose and hanging in disarray over her shoulders. The worst were her tear-swollen eyes. "Isabel," he whispered for the last time.

"My name is Anne," she said. "Anne of Allonby." Waiting for his reaction, she smiled and continued. "My father is the duke of Richmond and my sister, my twin sister, Alianor is a countess." Before he could force any words out, she cried out, "My memory is returned to me, Royce! I can have my life back."

She stood and ran to him and threw her arms around him. His hands itched to touch her, his arms ached to embrace her, but he would not. At his lack of response, she drew back and frowned.

"Did you not hear me? I can remember everything. Everything!" She began to chatter in her excitement and he waited. "My sister was here today. I saw her leaving the village and all of my memories flooded back over me. We are twins except that we are not identical—she is light and I am dark. She had two sons."

Then she stopped and looked at him. She flinched as the truth seeped into her. "Royce? You knew? You knew who I was?"

"Isabel, I…"

"Anne. My name is Anne." Tears flowed again and her lip trembled as she accused him of his first sin. "How long have you known?"

He did take her by the arms now and tried to pull her close. She resisted him for the first time. "I only learned it last week, Isabel…Anne. Your sister came seeking you and I heard her story, your story. I wanted to tell you, but…"

"But?"

She looked at him with a glimmer of hope in her eyes. He would give her none for there was none to give in this.

"I did not want this to end." He let his gaze pass over the room so that she thought he meant the sexual part of what they shared.

She gasped and stumbled away. "You knew and you kept it from me so that you could continue to seek your pleasures with me? Like a common whore?" She sobbed out to him in pain. "Why? We could be together. My father—"

"It is over, Anne. There can be nothing more for us."

"But Royce, it does not have to end here. You could return with me."

"I cannot return with you."

"You can. My father will let me marry you. You

were a knight. I am sure you are from a good family. Once he knows who you are…once you tell me who you really are…we can make arrangements."

He shook his head. "I cannot tell you of my past, Anne. And I cannot go back with you."

"Royce, we can marry and—" She stopped and looked on him with anger. "You never intended marriage? This was all a pretense?"

"I did intend marriage." His voice sounded wooden and rigid even to him. But he forced the feelings deep inside him and would not let them out. He would not do this again. He could not survive having hope and seeing it killed this way. And at such a cost to him and to her.

"When? When did you stop?" Anne's sobs turned to a gasp. "When you met my sister? She told you, did she not? The reason my husband wanted me dead. I am barren."

He felt the agony of her despair as she once more accepted the guilt placed on her by a husband who wanted her dead. He saw her buckle under the weight of her failure as a woman to conceive and carry a child, an heir, for her husband. He watched her personality shrink from the lively and vigorous Isabel back to the taunted and unwanted Anne. And he did nothing.

Tell her! Tell her you would take her without children. Trust her with your truths. Her love is strong enough.

The words vibrated inside his head and he wanted to tell her. Her anger, he could bear. It would help her to get away from him. But the revulsion and horror and hatred she would feel would be unbearable. No, this way was better.

"You asked me once if I knew in my heart of any impediments to our marriage," she whispered. "Now I know there is one."

"Come," he said, reaching out to take his hand. "Lord Orrick will make arrangements for you to meet up with your sister. She said she will be waiting in Thursby for another day before returning to Hexham."

She backed away from him, not allowing his touch. 'Twas just as well. "And you? What will you do now?"

"I will submit myself to Orrick's justice for betraying his trust."

Lying became easier when it was practiced and that one slid smoothly out of his mouth. 'Twould be gentler to let her think his word to his lord meant more than his word to her. It would separate them faster.

Anne held herself from him but followed him outside. He knew she would not let him hold her in front of him on the horse, so he mounted and pulled her up to ride pillion behind him. As they headed toward Silloth Keep, she touched him as little as possible, only enough to keep her on the horse.

He escorted her to the solar and she walked silently at his side into the chamber. One more duty and it would be over.

"Lord Orrick. Lady Margaret. May I present to you the lady Anne of Allonby, daughter of Charles, the Duke of Richmond?"

He did not look back. He closed the door to the solar and walked out into the night. Back into the darkness he deserved.

Chapter Twenty-Three

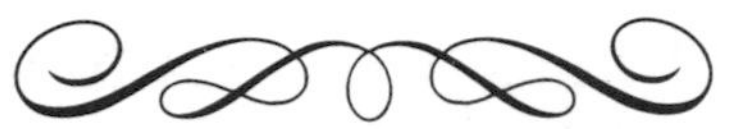

Her words came to him on the second day he could remember after Isabel, she would always be Isabel to him, left. He was washing off the filth he'd collected as he'd drunk and vomited and drunk some more seeking a way out of his pain. After finishing up Connor's brew, the pain had stopped and the haze caused by the liquor continued to keep it at bay.

Unfortunately, Orrick sought him at that time and demanded he return to his duties. Connor was the enforcer of Orrick's will and William found himself dragged to the kitchens, stripped to his skin, and dumped into a steaming vat of water. Then his head was dunked under the water and held there until he fought back. Once Connor was convinced William was awake, he turned him over to the servants for cleaning.

He submitted mostly because he lacked the strength to fight back. And because he did not care about what he wore or did not, what he ate or did not, whether he slept or did not. None of this mattered any longer.

His face and neck were scraped of the beard he'd worn and his skin burned from it. Splashing water on it to cool the burn, he heard Alianor's words in his mind.

My lord husband has sent along enough guards to protect the entire kingdom from an invading army.

But they could not protect her from a lone assassin.

He jumped from the tub and grabbed the drying cloth as he did. Alianor was being followed and, if Anne joined her, they were both in danger. William raced through the kitchens, up to his chambers and quickly dressed. He must find Orrick and leave immediately. It could already be too late.

Anne's appearance and return from the dead sent Alianor into a faint. Her ladies fluttered around them, bringing a cool cloth and a cup of ale and anything else they thought might revive her. Anne waited and then shooed them all out of the room so that her reunion could be a private one. But not before urging them to keep her identity and her presence there a secret.

That suggestion came from Lady Margaret, who grasped the danger that could still exist if her existence was revealed without an appropriate level of security. After meeting Alianor in Thursby, the plan was to continue on to the convent of Saint Mary Magdalene and to wait there while Alianor summoned her husband. With the protection of the earl, her survival could be announced and then the guilty person could be charged.

But, first, she had to see her sister. Alianor had been placed on a pallet and Anne sat next to her waiting. Her hands shook as she readied herself to see the one person closer to her than anyone else. What would she say?

Nigh to five years had passed since she'd seen or spoken to Alianor. Their weddings began the separation and then Edward had completed it in more ways than just not permitting visits. As her problems conceiving and bearing a child for him became known, he made certain she knew of her sister's success. And that he had desired her sister over her and only agreed to marry her for the land that was returned by her father.

After hearing it over and over from him and from his mother as well, Anne knew that part of her began to hate her sister. Oh, she'd fought it at first, even losing control and telling Edward how much Alianor feared him and that she had taken her place. She'd placed another powerful weapon in their hands and they'd used it against her relentlessly.

She, a mere woman, had dared to intervene in the dealings of men? She had interfered with God's plans and those of her betters and her barren condition was God's punishment for her haughty arrogance. She must be punished for and cleansed of her insubordination before God would grant her a child.

She shook her head, ridding herself of those thoughts. Anne may have accepted that during their marriage, after her resistance and her will was beaten down, but she knew now it did not have to be that way between husbands and wives. Alianor's presence here, even that her husband permitted her to travel without him across England on her belief alone, was proof that love and trust could co-exist in marriage.

A gasp told her that Alianor was awake.

They stared at each other for moments before the tears erupted and then Anne was clasped so tightly by Alianor that she thought she might pass out. It went on for several minutes, the crying and hugging, the murmured words of lost sisters and praise that she was alive. Finally, when all their tears had been cried, they were able to talk. Alianor would not let go of her hand.

A few hours passed as they caught each up on what had happened and Alianor filled in even more gaps in her knowledge, especially of happenings since Anne's disappearance and accepted death. Anne marveled at her strength of spirit and fierce determination to seek revenge on her behalf for all the wrongs done to her. The pain and suffering she'd suffered at Edward's hands had served a purpose—they had protected and saved Alianor from becoming the unspirited wife of a controlling husband. She knew in her heart that Alianor had become the person she was now because she had married Guy instead.

When the talk came around to the most recent months of her life, Anne found it difficult to reveal what was so painful to her. In spite of promising herself that she would not say his name, her sister had wheedled it out of her and then held her as she cried out her sorrow.

Day became night and still they talked. Plans were made and a messenger was sent to Hexham, requesting Guy meet them at the convent outside Carlisle. No reason was given, but with a blush, Alianor assured her that none was necessary. No one outside her ladies was told anything but that Lady "Isabel" was traveling back with them, continuing the masquerade until Guy's counsel and protection was attained.

Since the next day would be a difficult and full traveling day, they retired early. Alianor insisted that they share the chamber and Anne did, feeling stronger just with her support and presence. The day dawned sunny and clear, which Anne took as a good sign.

They were making good time toward the convent when the commotion began in the rear of their party. Hexham's men-at-arms encircled the women of the group and took a defensive position as Alianor's commander investigated the disturbance. He returned some time later and escorted a small group and two dead bodies to Alianor. Anne watched as Royce, Connor and two other of Orrick's men came into view.

Unable to look at him without pain, Anne focused her eyes and ears on Alianor.

"My lady," her commander began. "These men are from—"

"Lord Orrick of Silloth. Who are these men? Yours, Sir Royce?" Alianor demanded. Anne recognized the anger in her tone and feared it was on her behalf.

Royce moved forward and bowed from his horse. "Nay, my lady. We found them following you, preparing an attack from behind."

Alianor's brows rose as she considered this. "How did you know of them?"

"Your words, my lady, when last we spoke. You mentioned that your husband had sent along enough guards to fend off an invading army. I realized that a lone assassin can be more effective at hitting a target and hiding in the forest."

"'Twould seem you were correct and you have my thanks. And, Lady Isabel's as well, I am certain."

Why had she done that? Anne wanted to fade into the trees and not be seen at all. And especially not by him. All she could do was nod and not meet his gaze.

"Isabel, are you familiar with either of these men?" At Alianor's wave, a guard turned the dead men over so she could see their faces. Anne gasped as she recognized one of the men from the night of her attack. "Marie? Is this not the man we noticed at the abbey?" Her lady nodded and she looked at Anne. "'Twould seem that discretion is still not a trait of mine. My purpose has been discovered and I have jeopardized you once more."

"My lady," the commander said. "I think we should get to the convent as soon as possible without any more stops. Once there, you will be safe until your husband arrives."

Alianor called the guard to her and whispered some additional comments to him. The commander rode back, issuing orders in a low voice so that his words did not carry outside the group. At his word, Anne and Alianor, still surrounded by other guards, began to move forward.

"What did you tell him?"

"I invited Sir Royce and the others to join us at the convent. He deserves at least a good meal for saving our lives."

"Alianor! How could you?"

"He came to save your life, Anne. Not mine.

And from the looks he gave you he has something to say to you."

"He said all there was to say and did not speak words I wanted to hear. You may eat with him if you like, but I will seek solace in prayer tonight."

They rode for some time before Alianor spoke again.

"You know this will mean war."

"War?" she asked. "Why?"

"Father arranged your marriage to close the breach between him and Lancaster at the king's order. And Father returned that bloody piece of land that Robert lost his life defending as part of the settlement."

"Aye, I know those things."

"Since your death, that land remains with Lancaster."

"Why was it not returned when I was reported dead?"

"Their agreement called for it to remain in Lancaster's hands unless your marriage ended in an annulment. On the birth of an heir or on your death, they retain it."

Anne was stunned. She knew that Edward's father had refused to allow him to seek an annulment and now she knew why. She guessed that

Edward had given up hope after five years and one miscarriage and tried the easier method—her death. Of course it would have to happen in such a way that he could not be blamed or the land would be lost. An attack by brigands while traveling was a good way, especially if there was a family member there to identify the remains and bury them quickly.

"And now?" Anne was almost afraid to ask.

"When your survival is revealed and you identify your attacker, Father will go to war."

"And many will die." The whole reason for her marriage, the reason she had not gone to her father when Edward had turned abusive, would be overturned and many in her family and in their allies' families would die. Because she was alive.

"So be it. Those mangy curs deserve to die after what they did to you." Anne wanted to smile at her sister's bloodthirstiness, but the subject of war was too serious. "Worry not," she continued with a dark look in her eyes, "they will pay."

Anne could see Alianor standing on the beach once more, brandishing her sword of driftwood and scaring off the imaginary Viking soldiers as they attacked. She may be the older one, but

Alianor had always been the stronger one, the bolder one in their play.

She rode in silence the rest of the way, never daring to look back to see where he was, but always wanting to. They arrived at the convent and were shown to quarters reserved for higher-ranking guests in the lay wing. Anne discovered that Orrick's men had stayed back an hour to search for any others who might be following the party.

True to her word, Anne asked to be shown to the chapel when dinner was announced to Alianor. Her sister took her aside, none too happy at her decision.

"I did not know you to be a coward, Anne."

"You have not known me for five years, sister. I have changed much in that time." Sometimes, she'd discovered, 'twas easier to be a coward and live to tell. "Besides, your words today made me think about the effect of my 'resurrection' on our family. I want to think on it."

"You fear war?"

"I fear losing Guillaume to them. I fear causing so many deaths when my death will keep the peace."

"And I am unwilling to lose you again, Anne." Alianor looked at her. "But, go and think and pray on these events. I want you to be at peace with this before we do anything more."

Anne walked into the chapel and knelt near the altar. She prayed for guidance, she prayed for options and she prayed for peace. Lady Margaret's words and suggestions came back to her. Mayhap she should enter the convent? Alianor would know where she was, could even visit her from time to time, but war would be averted. And, if she chose one like this one, she could live as a lay sister and not take vows.

Is that what she wanted? To live with these other sisters and work in service to them?

No. She wanted one thing, one person, and, damn her weak heart, even knowing that he did not want her, she still loved him. She really needed to talk to someone. She needed the counsel of someone she trusted. She would seek out Alianor and come to a decision by morning. Too many people were already aware of her identity. The sound of footsteps approaching drew her attention. Thinking that Alianor had come to berate her for missing dinner, she stood and turned to her.

It was him.

Royce stood just a few paces away. She lowered

her eyes, not daring to meet his gaze. She needed to leave before she said something stupid. Or did something even worse. Anne had begun to walk away when he reached out and touched her sleeve.

"I am here to beg forgiveness."

She purposely misunderstood him. "If you ask Sister Genevieve, she can arrange for one of the priests to hear your confession. Now, excuse me." Gathering her gown, she stepped around him.

"I have begged God's forgiveness so many times that he ignores me now. Nay, Isabel… Anne, I have come to ask for yours."

His voice sent chills rippling down her spine. She must go. Now.

"I am so happy over being reunited with my sister, Royce, that I will forgive you any transgressions you may have committed against me. Now, I bid you good evening."

One…two…three…just two more steps and she would be out of the chapel. She held her breath and took the first one. Staring at the floor and clenching her fists to keep from crying, Anne prepared to take the final one. Royce stepped in front of her and stopped her from leaving.

Chapter Twenty-Four

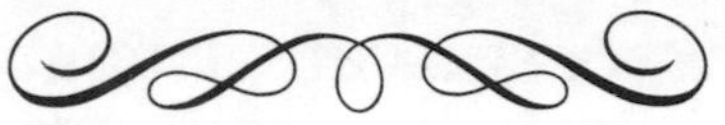

"In the months I have known you, you have never been a coward." Did he know his words echoed her sister's?

"You are the second person to call me that today and I have to say I like it no better now than the first time." She stepped back away from him but did not try to leave.

"I have no right to say that to you, since I am the one who behaved cowardly when last we spoke."

"Royce, I do not have the strength to face you again. It will do no good and it…" She stopped the words before they came out. *Will break my heart.*

"Anne, just hear me out. You need say nothing if you do not wish."

She looked around and spotted a bench against

one wall. Walking to it, she sat down and prepared herself as best she could.

"When I spoke with your sister and discovered who you were, I was terrified. I kept it to myself to keep you with me."

"You told me that already. Like a…"

"Nay! There you have it wrong. When I knew you would leave, I wanted you to leave without regrets. Unfortunately, I did not display the same planning abilities that you do when you set your mind to something." He walked in front of her, but she refused to meet his eyes.

"I said some very stupid things to you and I would have you know the truth." He crouched down in front of her, making it difficult to look past him. "I made you believe that the blame lay with you and it did not. I treated you no better than Edward did and I ask your pardon for that."

She blinked faster, trying to rid her eyes of the tears, but it did not help. She glanced at him and then away. Her heart would not survive this. Her soul would not.

"Before you waste any more tears on me, you must understand why I cannot offer you marriage now. I would rather you hate me than yourself."

"I already know, I am b-b…" She choked on

the word that had been used as a weapon against her so many times.

"Nay, Isabel…Anne." He shook his head at using the wrong name. "I fear you will always be Isabel to me." He frowned at her and then continued, "Much as I will always be Royce to you."

"Your name is Royce. We chose Isabel when I could not remember mine." He was not making sense.

"My name is William de Severin. Royce was a family name I was given growing up since my father was also William."

"William? Why did you change your name?" She could not help but ask.

"If you ask anyone at court, they will tell you that William de Severin died on the field of honor three years ago, settling a dispute with the Earl of Harbridge. The earl cut his throat and gained the countess and her lands and titles and wealth. I got this." He lifted his hand to his throat, now without a beard, and pointed to the jagged line on one side of it. "Luckily the earl is as skilled as he is merciful or I would have truly died that day."

"I do not understand. Why did the earl fight you?"

"I think I should begin a bit earlier in the tale.

May I sit?" He pointed to the bench next to her. Not waiting for her answer, he sat down.

"When King Richard was held for ransom, I fell in with John, whom I had known as a boy in Anjou and Poitiers. I was intent on finding excitement and wealth and a rich wife to support my tastes. I was arrogant then and did not see the evil in him. I thought only of the spectacles and the tournaments and traveling across the Plantagenet empire. I became his champion and his enforcer as well."

"Prince John? You support the prince?"

"I did. If he was challenged, I fought in his name. If his will was not followed, I made it happen. I did things in his name that brought darkness to my soul and that God will never forgive."

She shivered at the ominous tone of his voice. This was a different man than the one she knew.

"He strung me along like a puppet, offering me what he knew I wanted, each reward larger and larger until he knew I would not resist. And I played his games." He rubbed his face and held his head in his hands. "Then the prize I'd waited for was put in front of me. He must have realized I was tiring of being his man and so he tempted me with Emalie."

Her stomach churned at his tale. She did not know him, but she knew men like him, toadies to royalty, hangers-on who sought the castoffs of royal favor.

"Emalie?" She was afraid to ask and, when he began speaking in a bleak voice, she feared what was coming.

"Gaspar Montgomerie owned much land and held the ancient title of Earl of Harbridge. His daughter Emalie would inherit everything, to be passed on to whomever she married. John decided I should be that man." He smiled grimly, but he did not look up. "Gaspar had other ideas and sought support from Eleanor and Richard. Before it could arrive, he was killed."

She could not believe what he had said. "You killed him?" Her hands shook now. She clenched them together to try to control them. She could not believe it of him. Certainly he had killed men in fighting and in defense, but in cold blood?

"As good as. I did not put the poison in his cup, but I did not stop it, either." He leaned back against the wall and looked at her now. "This is why I could not tell you of my past. I see the hate growing in your eyes already and my tale is but half-done."

Anne swallowed several times to clear her throat and asked him to continue. As sordid as this was, she wanted to know his role in it. Something just did not sound right with this to her.

"Gaspar died and Emalie was alone. John presented me to her as the man her father wanted her to marry. He even presented her with betrothal papers outlining our settlements signed by her father. She knew they were false and she resisted."

She was getting sick. Anne was glad she'd had no dinner, for it would never stay in her stomach as this story went on. Already she felt the urge to heave. "And you cooperated with him? You were the prince's accomplice in this?"

"By this time, I can say that I'd had enough. John did what he did best, something he'd demonstrated with countless others before me—he sought out my weakness and used it against me."

She feared the answer but asked anyway. "Who was yours?"

"Clever girl! You saw what I did not. He knew that the allure of gold and lands were losing their power with me, so to keep me playing his tune, he took my sister into his custody."

"Custody? Your sister?"

"Aye, Catherine. A lovely girl of fifteen. I was her guardian after my father's death. She was an innocent, much like others John and I had debauched together. He held her and never let me see her. When I would hesitate, he would remind me of her innocence, her beauty, his control."

"Did he…?" She could not say the words.

"He promised her safekeeping to me so long as I followed his plan to claim Harbridge. With the betrothal papers, all we needed was a consummation to make it a marriage that could not be denied. I consummated the agreement with Emalie."

She gasped, then. He had raped this woman to gain control over her lands and titles. For John, he had taken this woman by force. She shook her head, still not believing that the Royce she knew was this man William he described.

"I loved Emalie. At least I thought I did. I tried to convince her to accept me, but she was as stubborn as her father had been. And smarter." He smiled and she could hear the admiration in his voice for this woman. "She did not behave as most noblewomen would. You know, Anne, you remind me of her in that." He caught her gaze and then looked away. "When John went to her and proclaimed her dishonored, she denied it. He almost spit! He had expected her to meekly submit and to control her wealth and her person and she laughed at him."

"That does not sound like a good thing to do."

"Nay, 'twas not. She had also sent to Eleanor and Richard asking for help. Once the old queen arrived and intervened, providing a husband for Emalie of her choosing, John stood to lose everything he had arranged. His last gambit was for me to go to the bishop in Lincoln and claim the prior betrothal and to claim," he paused, "the child she carried as mine."

"She was pregnant?" Her breath hitched and she broke away from his eyes. "Was it your babe?"

He looked as though he was about to say something else when he spoke. "Yes, the babe was mine."

She stood now and paced in front of him. "How could you do such a thing? You raped her? You made her pregnant. And you still continued to act with John?"

"He had Catherine," Royce forced out from between clenched teeth. "What else could I do? I thought the worst was over, I would be good to Emalie as her husband, I could make this unholy alliance work and still save Catherine from his evil."

"There is more to this sordid tale. Tell me the rest so we might end this." She was repulsed by the evil he had done.

"We had everything arranged. John had paid the bishop handsomely to decide in our behalf. But Emalie's husband was a surprise. He would neither be bought nor acquiesce. He challenged me to combat to decide the fate of the countess and her child."

"Did you kill him?"

"I should have since I was the better fighter. And since John increased my need to win by telling me of Catherine and how he would keep her if I died. He told me such sickening details of things she had already seen that I knew I must win. She could not endure such horrors because of my weaknesses."

He stopped and she could feel his pain welling up. As much as she wanted to hate him, she could not. Once caught by John's evil, there was no easy way out from it. His sister must have suffered so much while his prisoner.

"She still lives? Your sister?" Anne remembered that he had mentioned her once.

He took in a breath and let it out, his voice was shaking as he spoke now. "Aye. John underestimated Christian of Langiers. John did not plan on him accepting a dishonored bride and he did not expect him to fight with all means at his disposal. And he did not expect him to win."

"And he won? How?"

"He was a man of honor. He learned of Catherine and sent his men for her. They freed her from John before we fought. During the fight, he told me that only through my death could she and Emalie be safe. At first I did not want to believe that something as simple as my death could free them both, but he swore for their safety. Then as the battle went on, he told me again that he had Catherine, that she was safe from John."

"Could you believe him?"

"I had to take that chance. As I said, Emalie's husband, the earl, had shown himself to be honorable to her, accepting her pregnancy even though he knew she did not carry his child. When the opportunity presented itself, I gave him the opening he needed to kill me. I knew my death would at least protect my sister."

"But you did not die."

"Nay. He knocked me to the ground and I felt the slash of the sword as it went in. I waited for the twisting of the blade that would have finished me." He touched the scar as he spoke. "His words told me I was dead. There was so much blood from injuries to both of us that he was able to make it look as though he had killed me."

Royce, or William, took another deep breath. She saw the sweat on his brow and that his hands shook as he relived the battle and his death. She sat back down at his side and waited for him to explain what brought him to Silloth.

"I was told later that John stalked off the field furious at this lost opportunity. The earl's man arranged for me and Catherine to be placed at a nearby convent to be cared for. When I had healed enough, I left."

"And Catherine? Was she safe?"

"The earl had saved her body, but not her mind." His voice and breath caught and he sobbed out his answer. "Her mind dwells someplace else. The sisters there said she had seen such horrors that her mind fled from them. She lives, but she…"

She had remained detached, resisted the sorrow of his story until that moment. His anguish and torment over his sister's punishment in his stead and for the terrible acts he'd committed poured out of him and she held him in her arms, letting him gain some measure of comfort after all this time. Anne had never seen a man cry and this tore her apart.

"Because of me," he cried out. "Because I was weak and I was evil. Because of my actions and mistakes, she will suffer always. I should have died that day," he gasped. "It would have been less painful than living with the knowledge of what I did to her and to so many others."

Several minutes passed and they sat without speaking. She cried silently with him for all the sins he had committed and for all that he had lost as a result. Surely God in his mercy had forgiven him? Finally he quieted and sat back against the wall. Dragging his sleeve over his face, he took another deep breath and regained control over himself.

"So, for three years I have not seen her. I left Harbridge and even England for a short while, fighting wherever I could find someone to pay me. I would send back whatever I could through a monk or a traveler visiting the Gilbertine convents across England. I tried to die so many times that I've lost count of them, but it would seem that my punishment is to live with the knowledge of what I have done."

"And then you found Silloth?" He had found a true sanctuary there, as she had.

"I was drifting at that time. I avoided any place I had visited with John or in my younger days. I came upon an unfair fight between some outlaws and a nobleman, although Orrick was holding his own for a while. When they took advantage of his injury, I stepped in. I did not see their third companion and ended up in worse shape than Orrick."

"The scar on your back is from that fight?" She remembered seeing it when he undressed the first time, after they fell into the stream, and could almost feel it now under her fingertips. It ran the length of his back.

"Aye. Margaret had sent out a search party looking for him and they brought both of us to her. She stitched me back together and offered me a place in their household for saving Orrick."

"Sanctuary," she whispered. And a place where he could do penance for his sins. Three years of penance, giving up all comforts and simply existing.

"They asked no questions of me or about my past, which suited me well. I told them I could promise them nothing, but an honest effort for a place at their board. They agreed and you know the rest."

He stood and took her by the arms, lifting her onto her feet before him. "I do not expect forgiveness from you, Anne, but the fault lies within me. I did not protect Catherine in life, but with me dead, Emalie's husband, the earl, continues as he pledged. She is cared for and hidden from John and his vindictive actions. So long as he thinks me dead, she is worthless to him. If William de Severin lives, she becomes his target once more."

"So William must remain dead and buried?" She understood now why he could not return with her. He nodded. "And Royce of Silloth?"

"Must live out his life without attracting any untoward attention. He stays in that little corner of England where royalty never treads. And when I found out for certain who you were, I knew it was over. The love you brought me, the love I did not deserve, could not be. You are the daughter of a duke and I cannot offer you anything unless I take my place as the son of an ancient and noble family from Anjou. And I cannot take that place without endangering Catherine."

She never thought she would welcome his kiss again, but when he touched his lips to hers, she drank him in, accepting his love for one final time. Her heart knew this was their true farewell and that they would never have this again. Anne felt the tears rolling down her cheeks and knew 'twas over.

She reached up to touch his cheek, but he turned and kissed the inside of her wrist as he had so many times before. Then, before she broke down completely, she had to ask him one more thing.

"This was not about my barrenness?"

"It was never about you, Isabel. 'Twas never a failure in you. 'Twas always about mine. And falling in love with you was a weakness on my part since I knew from the start that no good woman would have me once she knew about my past."

She nodded. "Goodbye then, Royce."

"Goodbye, Isabel."

Chapter Twenty-Five

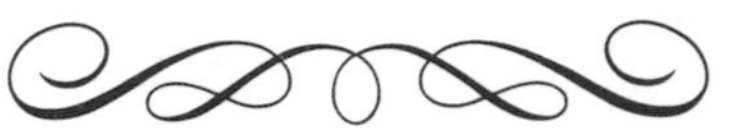

Anne heard some movements in her room before she entered, but thought that her sister was simply restless in her sleep. She closed the door quietly and undressed for sleep. Finding some water in a jug, a basin and a cloth, she poured the cool water over the cloth and held it to her eyes and nose. Swollen from crying, she waited for some relief. A noise from the bed got her attention.

Alianor lay under the covers and was faking sleep. Anne smiled at memories of this game from when they were children. She walked over quietly and dribbled some water on her, awaiting a reaction. Her sister sat up, admitting detection and defeat. 'Twas then that Anne noticed Alianor's eyes and nose were swollen and red, too. When she would not meet her gaze, she knew the truth.

"You listened? To all of it?" Tugging down the blanket she held revealed that she was still dressed.

"Of course," she said, sliding back to make room for her. "You would never tell me."

"It was private. You should not have eavesdropped."

"He loves you." When she turned away to replace the cloth, Alianor grabbed her hand. "He loves you, Anne. Do you love him?"

She nodded because she could not say the words.

"What do you plan to do now?"

"I think I should stay here."

"Here? As in here at this convent?" She nodded again and her sister burst out laughing.

"You, a nun? I think not! You could not obey mindlessly whatever they tell you to do."

"I am old and wiser now. I have learned…" She could think of nothing to say.

"Older and wiser, my arse! You will be thrown out within two months of settling in." Alianor pulled her into a hug. "Do not do this. Think, think about what your life would be like here."

"It would be peaceful. It would be challenging. And people would not die because of me."

"Ah. Father's war has you worried, then?"

Anne smacked her on the leg. "Alianor, you are so irreverent. You should not speak of war so lightly. People will die if I come back with you."

"But most of them will be the worthless Lancastrians. 'Twould be a service to the world to rid England of a few more of them."

"Alianor!"

"'Tis true! But back to your problems. Other than losing a few…you know, why can you not take your place with us?"

"There is nothing for me. Father could not arrange another marriage since I am barren. 'Tis an impediment to a true marriage. Should I sit at home with mother and embroider the rest of my life?"

"And here? You would do what?"

"Anything that needs doing. Sew, clean, cook. Care for the sick."

Alianor flinched with each word. "It will not work."

"I have no choice. I cannot return with you."

"Anne, I cannot lose you. Not now."

Anne gathered her sister close and embraced her. "Fear not—I will always be there for you."

Anne slid back and removed her headpiece.

Loosening her braids, she knew her sister still had something to say.

"He meets with Sister Genevieve before prime tomorrow. Something about a package to pick up and some supplies for Lady Margaret."

"And you think what? That I should go to him and beg him to keep me?" Anne slid off the bed and threw the cloth at the basin, splashing water everywhere. "He is not ready to love."

Alianor rubbed her forehead and grunted. "Not ready to love? Did you hear anything he said tonight?"

"He kept the truth from me. Not only about you, but also about himself. He did not trust me with his past." That was the worst part for her. He said he loved her, but he did not trust in it.

"It takes some time for men to speak of their love and to learn to put their trust in a woman. It took Guy months and some drastic action on my part before he could admit to loving me."

"Alianor, what did you do?"

Her sister sat with an angelic expression as she outlined her attack on Guy's heart. "First, I threw out his leman." At her gasp, she explained further. "Ours was an arranged marriage, Anne. I did not expect love from him immediately, but I did expect him to give up his mistress or, at the least, not flaunt her to me."

"But, Alianor, 'tis a husband's right."

Anne received a hand in the face, waving off her words. "Mother already gave me that lecture and I did not like it then or now. I had fallen a bit in love with him and did not want to share him. So, after I rid the castle of Madeleine, I took him prisoner in our chambers until he admitted he loved me."

"Are you certain he did not say the words just to escape you?" She could not believe her sister's actions. But, thinking back on her as a child, mayhap this was not so surprising.

Alianor thought about her question before answering and a strange look came into her eyes. She shook her head. "Nay. He did not just say the words to escape me. He gave himself to me that day."

The poignancy of her answer touched Anne.

She wanted that. That confidence in the love someone held for her. 'Twas not meant to be hers, she feared.

"You accuse him of not trusting you with his past," she said. "Can you trust him with your future?"

Anne could not answer. She walked to the other

cot and lay down. Pulling the covers up to her shoulders, she thought about all that had been said and thought and felt. Surely the answer was in there somewhere?

William took the packages from Sister Genevieve and promised her safe delivery to Lady Margaret. He ran into Isabel, damn it, *Anne,* as he left the prioress's room. She looked well rested and content. Good. Hopefully his words had given her some measure of release from the unnecessary guilt she carried.

"My lady," he said, moving aside. "I did not see you there."

"I have been waiting for you, Royce."

He looked toward the gate and saw the traveling party of the Countess of Hexham leaving. Isabel, *Anne,* stood before him. "Are you not returning with your sister?"

"Nay," she answered, shaking her head.

"Are you staying here at the convent, then?" He could not picture her being happy here, but it was not his place to judge her plans.

"Oh, nay. Lady Margaret and Sister Genevieve pointed out that I would not be happy here." She leaned in and whispered, "They said

I had too much of my sister in me to ever hope to take orders."

He thought he must have had too much of Connor's brew again, for nothing was as he thought it would be. Isabel, damn it, *Anne,* was cheerful and pleasant to him.

"Then where will you go?"

"Silloth. Margaret and Orrick have offered me a place at their board."

He reeled back at her words. She was coming to Silloth? He shook his head. How could he live there and live without her? This was more than he could deal with. He would have to leave. How could he watch her and not be able to love her?

"They have suggested that I consider marriage to Hugh or to Richard, but I know that no good man will have me since I cannot give him children. All I have to do is find a man who is not good."

With so many disjointed thoughts going through his mind, it took him some moments to figure out her teasing way of asking him to marry her. Could it be true? Could they do this?

"You trusted me with your past last night and my love for you is still here, Royce. Can I trust you with my future?"

"Isabel, damn it, *Anne,*" he said.

"Isabel is fine. It is my name now."

"Is this truly what you want to do? Please, tease me not for I could not bear to lose you again."

She stepped closer and answered him. "In all seriousness, I cannot openly return to my family. The war which cost my eldest brother his life will be revived to gain vengeance in my name and I stand to lose too many. So my death gives them a chance at life, much as yours did for your sister. I can trust her people to keep my secret."

He nodded, understanding her choice as she had his.

"And returning to Silloth?"

"Margaret and Orrick did make that offer to me, a place there with or without you. However, Margaret and Alianor both suggested ways to be certain that I would return there as your wife."

"Will you be my wife? Be mine always, come what may?"

"I will, Royce. Come what may."

Epilogue

Silloth-on-Solway, England
October, 1198

He dragged her off the horse and kissed her breathless. Until, that was, his men began to cheer and whistle at his actions. He tugged her hand and took her away from the building site. She went with him to the edge of the stream and behind some trees.

"I have missed you, wife," he said, in the possessive growl that made her blood run hot.

"I have missed you, husband." She returned his kiss and resisted the urge to undress him further. He was working in only his breeches and boots with his chest bare and his hair pulled back revealing the strong chin she loved to kiss.

"If you continue to look at me with that hunger

in your eyes, I will never get this house built in time for winter." He kissed her once more and then took her hand. "Come, walk with me."

Anne told him of her journey with Lady Margaret and of the package she'd retrieved for him. She took it out of the saddlebag and handed it to him. He looked at her and she waved him off for a few private moments of reading about his sister Catherine's progress. William had shown her the other letters on their return to Silloth and he shared each new one with her as they arrived. To receive this one so closely to the last one could mean something good or bad.

His expression was one of disbelief when he returned to her side. "Have you read this yet?"

"No. I would never read it before you."

"The reverend mother's news is incredible. 'Twould seem that the Earl of Harbridge's younger brother is to inherit his lands in Poitou and he has chosen Catherine as his bride."

"Pardon?" She could not believe these developments. Well, since the news she had for him was of the unbelievable kind, mayhap she should not be so quick to judge.

"The letter says that in spite of many obstacles and the initial objections of the earl, Geoffrey and

Catherine marry in three weeks, on their r from Poitou.

"Married," he said with a smile. "Mayhap t Fates have decided to be kind to the de Severin after all?"

"I am pleased with my de Severin," she whispered.

He folded up the parchment and handed it to her carefully.

"There is more news, Royce."

"More news? Share it with me."

How did she say this to him? "I spoke to Wenda today about my tiredness and lack of appetite."

"For food," he added with a seductive smile that had caused this.

"For food. 'Twould seem that your ardent wooing has had some results."

"I am tiring you out with too much of it?"

"Nay. Aye," she said, smiling at him. "It appears that I am not barren after all." She waited for it to make sense to him.

His roar drew the other workers to them, even as he took her in his arms and spun her around. She laughed and laughed until he stopped and held her close.

"I told you it was no fault of yours."

u are correct as usual, husband." William ed her over and over and then she heard n whisper.

"Come what may."

* * * * *

HISTORICAL ROMANC

LARGE PRINT

AN IMPROPER COMPANION

Anne Herries

Daniel, Earl of Cavendish, finds the frivolity of the *ton* du after serving in the Peninsula War. Boredom disappears when he is drawn into the mystery surrounding the abduction of gently bred girls. His investigation endangers his mother's companion, Miss Elizabeth Travers. Tainted by scandal, her cool response commands Daniel's respect – while her beauty demands so much more…

THE VISCOUNT

Lyn Stone

The young man who appears late at night at Viscount Duquesne's door is not all he seems. Dressed as a boy to escape the hellhole in which she has been imprisoned, Lady Lily Bradshaw must throw herself on the mercy of a ruthless rake. Viscount Duquesne soon finds himself captivated by this bold lady – and he can't resist her audacious request for a helping hand…in marriage!

THE VAGABOND DUCHESS

Claire Thornton

He had promised to return – but Jack Bow was dead. And Temperance Challinor's life was changed for ever. She must protect her unborn child – by pretending to be Jack's widow. A foolproof plan. Until she arrives at Jack's home…and the counterfeit widow of a vagabond becomes the real wife of a very much alive *duke*!

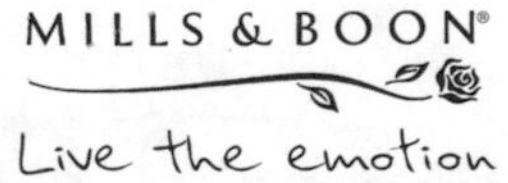

HIST0407 LP

LARGE PRINT

NOT QUITE A LADY

Louise Allen

Miss Lily France has launched herself upon the Marriage Mart in style! The wealthy and beautiful heiress is determined to honour her much-loved father's last wish – and trade her vulgar new money for marriage to a man with an ancient and respected title. Then she meets untitled, irresistible and very unsuitable Jack Lovell – but he is the one man she cannot buy!

THE DEFIANT DEBUTANTE

Helen Dickson

Eligible, attractive, Alex Montgomery, Earl of Arlington, is adored by society ladies and a string of mistresses warm his bed. He's yet to meet a woman who could refuse him… Then he is introduced to the strikingly unconventional Miss Angelina Hamilton, and Alex makes up his mind to tame this headstrong girl! But Miss Hamilton has plans of her own – and they don't include marriage to a rake!

A NOBLE CAPTIVE

Michelle Styles

Strong, proud and honourable – soldier Marcus Livius Tullio embodied the values of Rome. Captured and brought to the Temple of Kybele, he was drawn towards the woman who gave him refuge. Fierce, beautiful and determined – pagan priestess Helena despised all that Rome stood for. She knew she must not be tempted by this handsome soldier, because to succumb to her desires would be to betray all her people…

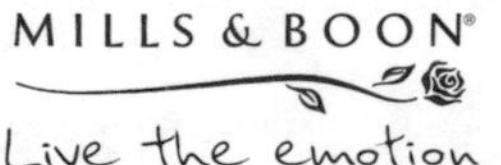

HIST0507 LP